bonds of earth

G N CHEVALIER

Dreamspinner Press

Published by
Dreamspinner Press
382 NE 191st Street #88329
Miami, FL 33179-3899, USA
http://www.dreamspinnerpress.com/

Bonds of Earth
Copyright © 2012 by G N Chevalier

Cover Art by Justin James   dare.empire@gmail.com
Cover Design by Mara McKennen

ISBN: 978-1-61372-327-2

Printed in the United States of America
First Edition
January 2012

eBook edition available
eBook ISBN: 978-1-61372-328-9

To Jim

acknowledgments

DESPITE the popular image of the lonely writer toiling in the musty garret, no creative endeavor is ever accomplished alone. I owe a great debt of gratitude to many people, including the wonderful writers and friends who took the time to read, encourage, and offer suggestions that made *Bonds of Earth* a better novel: Sara Booth, Karen Byerly, Carla Coupe, C.A. Detmers, Dorinda Hartmann, Morgan Howard, Mary Lou Klecha, Rose Light, Michelle Monroe, Tracey Nickerson, and Brenda Yawn. Jane Henderson Roy, good friend and proofreader extraordinaire, was a tremendous help in moving this project forward. Liz Wade and Carla Coupe provided timely and supportive advice when I dearly needed it.

Megan McGinnis's input was invaluable in making *Bonds of Earth* what it is today. Holly Giostra deserves a large share of the credit for the fact that you are now holding this book in your hands. Jennifer Dowell took the beautiful, evocative photograph for me that now graces the cover. Elizabeth North, Ariel Tachna, Lynn West, Gin Eastwick, Mara McKennen, and the rest of the team at Dreamspinner Press made the publishing process a wonderful, collaborative, stress-free experience.

Finally, I'd like to express my gratitude to four people who cannot be properly thanked in mere words: my parents Helen and Marcel, who valued the creator in me from an early age; Viola, my biggest fan and dearest supporter; and Jim, who always believed.

Thank you all so much.

April 1919

THE early spring evening still held a reminder of the winter's chill, but as soon as Michael opened the door of the Saint Alexander's Baths, it might as well have been high noon in the middle of summer. The sultry heat and humidity washed over him, drawing him inside and tugging him down the wide steps to the place that, for all its chipped paint and flickering Mazda lamps, had become his second home, his refuge.

By the time he reached Millie's office, he had shed his jacket and collar and was working on the buttons of his vest. He was not looking forward to this conversation, but there was nothing else to be done. He had no choice.

"Darling! You're early!" The sweet scent of Millie's perfume momentarily drowned out the stronger odors of the bathhouse as she hugged him to her ample bosom. When she released him, she peered into his eyes, that sapphire-blue gaze seeing right through him, as it always had. "What's the matter?"

Michael motioned her to her overstuffed chaise; she shot him another glance but did as he wished, and he sat in the chair opposite. "I wanted to let you know I have an interview tomorrow for a position. I'm probably going to get the job; my uncle's all but fixed it."

Millie pursed her rouged lips. "Refresh my memory, dear. You have so many relatives."

"Padraig, my mother's eldest brother. He's a gardener—works for the City most of the time, though he also does some work for the types with mansions near the Park."

"You're going to work as… a *gardener*?" Millie's sour expression made it clear what she thought of that idea. Reaching out, she gripped Michael's broad hands in her finer ones. "Your poor, talented hands—you'll ruin them!" she exclaimed in horror.

Michael squeezed her fingers before drawing away. "I'll be fine. As Uncle Paddy says, it's a good opportunity for a working man." He forced a twisted smile that wasn't intended to convince her of the statement.

Millie made a derisive noise. "Yes, well, you know what I think of *that*." She sighed. "I suppose it's not the end of the world. At least you should still have a bit of time to work here, especially in the winter."

Michael shook his head, the rage he'd been feeling since hearing from his meddling bastard of an uncle threatening to stop his throat. "If this comes through, I'll be leaving New York. One of the old blueblood biddies needs someone to tend her Hudson River estate. If I'm lucky, I'll manage to visit Manhattan once a month, if that."

Millie stared at him, her carefully plucked eyebrows climbing. "But why? Why leave the city? Everything is here."

For a moment, Michael considered telling her. For all her flash, she was a kind-hearted soul, and she'd been a good friend to him over the years. All the more reason, though, not to burden her with his troubles. He knew full well she'd survived more than he ever had, and while she would be outraged on his behalf, it would do neither of them any good. Instead, he shrugged and murmured, "Time for a change, that's all."

Millie shook her head, then leaned forward slightly. "Have you given any more thought to what we talked about last week?"

Michael settled further into the chair. "You know I haven't."

Millie scowled, the deep lines revealing her age in a way that Michael was sure would horrify her. "If you'd just stop being such a—" she began hotly.

Cutting her off with a sharp gesture of his hand, he said, "I'm not going to take your money, Millie. I already owe you too much. And even if I could, I don't want the things you think I want. That discussion is finished."

"Consider it a loan," she persisted. "You can pay me interest if it offends your virtue. And you owe me nothing. You've long since paid me back for everything I put toward your education. You know that."

Michael stood, suddenly eager for the conversation to be over. "I'm sorry. And please don't think I'm not grateful you gave me my old job after I came back from the war. I didn't know what I was going to do, and you made it possible for me to—"

Millie waved away his words, and he smiled in spite of his mood. "Well, you've got no one to blame but yourself. I was a rough, ungrateful Mick ruffian before you taught me manners."

Rising to her feet, Millie took his face gently between her palms. "You were never a ruffian, my darling," she said softly. "And I wish you'd think about what I'm offering you. When you left six years ago, you had such *dreams*."

Christ, Millie, he wanted to say, *you have no idea. For you, it's been a few short years. For me, it feels like a fucking century. And every time I dream now, it's a nightmare.*

"This is a good position," he said, parroting his uncle's speech. "A good opportunity."

"Well," Millie said, releasing him with a final pat, "perhaps the country air will clear your head."

Michael leaned down and brushed his lips against hers softly. "From your mouth to God's ear." *Too bad the old bastard is deaf*, he added silently.

Sighing, Millie hooked an arm around his neck and pressed into his embrace for a moment before releasing him. He tried not to notice that her eyes were bright when she pulled away. "Get to work, you loafer," she whispered. "Your customers are waiting."

Michael touched her cheek with his fingertips, the faintest hint of beard greeting them even through the heavy layer of paint. *At least you still have your disguise, Henry m'dear*, he thought, allowing himself a moment of fierce sentimentality. "Mustn't disappoint the customers," he murmured, planting one final kiss on her forehead before plunging back into the tropical atmosphere of the bath, filled with the seductive scents of sweat and lust.

Michael was almost disappointed when his shift progressed much the same way it always had: the same customers, the same faces, nothing out of the ordinary. The pressure from the bulls had let off in the last month, so there wasn't even the excitement of a possible raid to break the monotony. The Greenwich Village baths like Millie's attracted a mixed crowd, bohemians and fairies and rough Ninth Ward Italian boys who weren't allowed to touch the nice girls their mothers wanted them to marry. They all liked Michael because he'd forgotten more about massage than most of the city's rubbers knew, and because he had long since trained his voice to be nearly as soothing as his hands. It didn't hurt that he was over six feet besides, with a longshoreman's build, hair the color of a raven's wing, and blue-gray eyes that more than one customer had called "hypnotic." Michael didn't give a tinker's damn what they called his eyes or any other part of him; a hollow shell would serve them as easily as he did, and they'd still come away satisfied. Most nights, a hollow shell was all they got.

Geoffrey, one of his regulars, arrived not long before closing. He was a middle-aged fellow, soft hands and a soft manner, the sort you usually saw at the Everard rather than up in the Village baths. A businessman, Michael guessed, or perhaps a lawyer, someone inclined to seek out a bathhouse where he would not be recognized. His face wasn't remarkable, but his eyes were dark, almost black, like a Gypsy's. He was always polite. Michael liked the way he said his name, though he liked the way he tipped even better. The skin of Geoffrey's shoulders was pale as milk, and his arms and chest were slim but not without muscle. He preferred for Michael to start with his neck and work his way down his front first, starting with *effleurage* and graduating to frictions and *petrissage* of his arms. His father had suffered from debilitating arthritis, he told Michael, and he was terrified that the same would happen to him.

"I have to believe that your treatments will be a help to me," Geoffrey would say, as Michael gently stroked his fingers.

"Can't hurt," Michael would reply.

After that, Michael would move on to his lower extremities, kneading from the feet to the calves to the thighs, hands moving constantly, checking for signs of weakness or fibrosis automatically, although after four months he knew Geoffrey's body almost as well as his own, was familiar with the span and stretch of every muscle and tendon. By the time he reached the hips, Geoffrey was usually restless and showing the first signs of arousal. He was an odd one; most men who came to the Saint Alex were hard the minute they walked in the door. But then most of the clientele of the Saint Alex kept the animal inside them close to the surface, while men like Geoffrey spent their whole lives hiding theirs from the light of day. Regardless of where each of them spent their days, darkness was the safest place for desires whose indulgence could bring arrest and imprisonment.

This was usually the time when Michael asked him to turn over, but tonight he felt a strange need, a desire to make a connection, and so he said, "You probably won't see me next week."

Geoffrey's eyes opened, dark gaze startled and confused. "I'll be leaving the city soon," Michael explained. "I don't imagine I'll be back here."

"Oh," Geoffrey said softly. "I'm very sorry to hear that."

"You're just worried about your arthritis," Michael remonstrated.

"No!" Geoffrey exclaimed, pushing himself up off the table, his expression earnest. "I don't—I haven't only been coming here for that."

Michael looked pointedly down at the towel that was barely covering Geoffrey's groin. Geoffrey's face flushed. "Not only for that, either. I—"

"What's your real name?" Michael demanded, suddenly in earnest for no reason he could explain, to himself or anyone. "I know damned well it's not Geoffrey." The other man's face grew fearful. Michael cursed himself silently but pressed on nevertheless. "You can tell me. I'll share it with no one."

Geoffrey shut his eyes and took several deep breaths, as one preparing for a dive into freezing water. Finally, he whispered, "Joseph. It's Joseph."

"Well, Joseph," Michael said, leaning forward and bestowing a gentle kiss on his brow, "how's about you turn over for us now, hm?"

Joseph nodded and sank back onto the table as though the admission had exhausted him, robbed the resistance from his bones. He lay limp and unresponsive at first, but Michael had the sweetest hands of any rubber in the baths, and within minutes Joseph was trembling and moaning and grinding his hips into the table. His pleasure sounds drew a crowd, and by the time Michael began to press inside him there were a dozen hands on Joseph's pale back, striping it with every shade of olive and tan and brown.

Joseph gave him five dollars before he left, and Michael kissed him for it, lingering in the soft, pliant depths of Joseph's mouth as though they were lovers loath to part from one another. When Joseph drew back, he searched Michael's face for a moment before turning and walking away, soon disappearing in the fog that surrounded them all.

MARGARET looked up from the money Michael had pressed into her hand, her face revealing her confusion and hurt. "You've only just come back, and now you're going away again?"

Michael stroked Donald's cheek where the baby lay warm and cozy in his bassinette, a sturdy drawer pulled from the dresser. His nephew looked exactly like Margaret had at that age: both strong and fragile, a contradiction that lived inside her still. He reluctantly lifted his head to meet her gaze. The fragility was harder to find now, but she was no less dear to him for that.

"It's a good opportunity," he repeated, hoping that the speech he'd used on Millie would work on her as well. He didn't have the patience to come up with new arguments, particularly when the reason for his exile was staring him in the face.

No, he thought sharply, *it's not her fault. It's Paddy's. Don't forget that.*

Reaching out, he took her hands in his. "You know I've been at loose ends since coming home," he said, trying a smile he knew didn't reach his eyes. "God knows you've probably grown sick of my black moods." She opened her mouth to speak, but he shook his head to forestall her. "Perhaps this will give me a chance to break out of my rut."

She looked up at him sadly, squeezing his hands as she spoke. "I wish you could tell me what happened over there," she murmured.

"No, you don't," he replied gently. "If you had seen a tenth of what I've seen, m'darling, you'd pray every night to have God take the memory of it from you."

Margaret's face crumpled as she took his face in her hands. "If telling me about it would help you, I'd gladly bear it, Michael. I'd—"

Gut knotting, Michael hugged her to him tightly so that he wouldn't have to see her face. "Don't cry. I'm not worth crying over."

"You're worth more than all the gold in the world," Margaret murmured against his shoulder, repeating words he'd said to her since the day she was born. "We never used to keep secrets from one another. You used to tell me everything."

"Not everything," Michael said, trying to keep his voice light and failing miserably. "I want you to love me, don't I?"

Margaret tipped her head back and stared at him. He filled the silence before she could ask the question, because in his agitated state, he might finally tell her the truth, Paddy and the police and God be damned. But he also knew that if he spoke now, he would lose the last thing that still mattered to him, and so he only smiled and said, "Cheer up, now. I'm only going up the Hudson, not across the Atlantic. I'll be back to visit before you know it."

Margaret lived only a block from the place in which she'd been born, in a tenement less ramshackle than most thanks to Michael's weekly supplements. When they were children, Michael would sneak her out on summer Sunday mornings before his aunt woke them for Mass and spirit her off to Central Park. They'd spend the day lost among the tall trees far from the beaten paths, imagining themselves intrepid explorers in uncharted territory, and return sunburnt and tired and exhilarated. Paddy would cane Michael for it, but he'd never lay a hand on Margaret, perhaps because he knew Michael would kill him in his sleep if he ever touched her. *Someday,* he would tell her, *someday we'll be gone from this place.*

But in the end, she had never escaped this handful of overcrowded streets of filth and feuding humanity, and even though she was barely twenty-one, he doubted she ever would. And Michael had fled across an ocean only to learn that the world was steeped in such filth as made the Bowery seem the most pristine wilderness imaginable.

"Uncle Michael!" Michael turned to see Edith, her short sturdy legs stumbling as she raced to reach him. Striding toward her, he caught her just before she would have fallen and swung her up into his arms.

He tickled her, and she giggled happily. "Anna took me to the park!" she exclaimed, flinging an arm out to indicate the skinny olive-skinned girl standing in the doorway. She nodded to him, then began talking quietly with Margaret.

"Well, that was very kind of Anna," Michael said softly, "but we must keep our voices down. Your brother's sleeping."

A tiny line appeared between her brows. "I don't like him," she confessed in a whisper. "When he came, Papa went away."

Michael squeezed the child a little tighter. Paul, Margaret's husband, had left three months ago for Philadelphia, claiming to be following a lead on a steelmaking job. Margaret hadn't heard from him since. "Your Papa has left to find work," he said, as soothingly as he could. "He'll send for you before you know it."

Edith's frown didn't abate, as though she could tell he didn't believe a word he was telling her. "You mustn't blame your brother," Michael added. "He needs you to love him and take care of him."

"The way you took care of Mommy?" the child asked.

Michael stroked the fine blonde hair back from her forehead. "Oh, I know you can do better, m'dearie," he murmured. "Much, much better."

"REMEMBER your promise," Paddy warned as he stopped the truck in front of the tall wrought-iron gates.

"I don't need to be bloody reminded," Michael spat back. "You've made it damned clear what my choices are."

"Watch your language," hissed Paddy, peering nervously out the windows of the truck. "I hope you don't talk like that in there."

Michael sighed, suddenly wanting it all to be over with. "I'll get the job, Uncle."

"See that you do," Paddy sniffed. "When I think about your poor mother looking down on you from above, knowing what you've done—"

"Uncle—"

"She sees you, don't think she doesn't—"

Michael reached for the door handle. "I suspect heaven's not that much different from this world as they'd like us to believe. Ma's likely too busy washing rich men's socks to be looking down and watching me fuck—"

The word was barely out of his mouth when his uncle clapped him soundly across the face with his open hand. Michael wouldn't give him the satisfaction of flinching, even though it hurt like the devil. After all, he was used to it by now.

"Shift yourself," Paddy said lowly. "Or I'll call for a constable. And then I'll tell Margaret just what kind of a pervert you are."

Without another word, Michael reached for the door handle and let himself out of the cab. The street was busy but not clogged; in this part of the city, the sidewalks were wide, and there was fresh macadam on the roads. There were well-dressed clerks hurrying to and fro, and the occasional young woman wearing a shirtwaist and heavy skirts. Many women had given up—or been forced to give up—their office positions as soon as the war ended. He knew Annie Sewell from the floor above him had had to go back to her first job working in the kitchen of one of these fine houses. A year ago she'd been eagerly talking about her new "career" as a clerk and how her boss didn't try to take liberties with her the way the old master had.

He gave his name to the stiff who answered the door and waited in the library for the lady of the house to appear. He'd kill for a cheroot right now, but he'd sworn off the things because he didn't want all the teeth to rot out of his head by the time he turned thirty. With what this position was likely to pay, it wasn't a sound idea for him to take up the habit again. The fewer vices he indulged, the more of his wages he'd be able to save, even after sending Margaret whatever he could.

What he was saving them for, well, that he couldn't say exactly. That would require planning, and Michael had worked hard to avoid making plans for some time now.

"Mr. McCreeley?"

Michael turned to face the well-dressed woman with silver-blonde hair who had spoken to him. "McCready, mum. Michael McCready."

"Yes," she said, looking him up and down with a delicately wrinkled nose. He didn't offer his hand, merely bowed slightly at the waist and nodded. She hesitated for a moment, perhaps trying to decide which of her chairs she'd risk sullying. Finally she picked one and waved him to it.

"Your uncle does you a great service. He says you are an excellent gardener—surely a great credit from such a fine one as Mr. Sullivan."

Michael smiled. She couldn't know how funny he found that statement and would just take it as pleasure at the compliment. "Yes, mum. He's taught me all I know."

"I understand you worked with him before you went overseas?"

"Yes, mum." That much was at least partly true. He'd sweated for Paddy since he'd gone to live with him at the age of twelve, because if he hadn't pulled his weight, Paddy wouldn't have fed him. As it was, there'd been more than a few nights when Paddy had drunk so much of his paycheck that there wasn't enough food for Michael, Margaret, and Paddy's six children besides. When the settlement house do-gooders had quit dragging him back three years later, he'd escaped to work for himself.

She asked him more questions, and he answered them easily, embellishing in places and omitting in others, telling her the things she would want to hear. While she droned on about the requirements of the position, he let his mind return to his last job interview, nearly two years ago now.

Doctor Randolph Parrish of the American Convalescent Hospital in Somerset sits behind his huge oaken desk, one finger tapping the side of his nose as he studies the report. Short and rotund, he has the appearance and mannerisms of a jocular Christmas elf and the steel-gray gaze of a Viking warrior. Michael finds himself drawn to the contradiction.

"You want to join my staff, then, do you?" Parrish says, raising his eyes to contemplate Michael.

"Yes, sir." Michael does not say that he has requested this transfer because he's only a few short steps from madness. Parrish deals with shell-shock victims every day; he can recognize the signs of a man who is heartily sick of the trenches.

"Your record as an ambulance driver is commendable," Parrish says, "and you have completed a year of medical school?"

"Yes, sir. In Dublin, before the war."

"Where did you study massage?"

Michael launches into the carefully prepared speech. "I'm mostly self-taught, sir, though I did study the Ling methods, as well as some of the more modern techniques."

"Hm." Parrish nods thoughtfully. "Do you have any experience with electromechanotherapy?"

"No, but I did use hydropathy in my work. I've read Doctor Baruch's writings and attended one of his lectures at Columbia." Michael doesn't add that he'd snuck into the medical building and stood at the back of the hall while the real students looked askance at him and his threadbare suit.

Parrish flips through the papers in his hands. "I don't recall seeing references from your massage work."

"I spent over three years working at one of the finer men's clubs in Manhattan," Michael replies smoothly. "Unfortunately, the letter of reference my employer sent never reached me overseas." A brief flash of anger accompanies this statement, but he tamps it down swiftly. The truth is that the word of the man who transformed Michael from ignorant tough to idealistic young medical student would be worthless to a man like Parrish. It is equally true that no amount of anger will change this fact. Worse, his physical therapy experience is all in the baths, and although he spent long nights applying the techniques he learned in long days of self-study, he knows that the merest whisper of

his years at the Saint Alex will lose him more than this position. A self-confessed invert is doomed to prison at best and a mental institution at worst, where the alienist's latest "cure" will be only too joyfully inflicted upon him.

"Will you be going back to medical school afterward?"

The question takes Michael by surprise, and suddenly he is trapped by that sharp gray gaze. It seems as though Parrish can read every one of his secrets as easily as the headlines of the morning's Times. "I don't know," he says, surprising himself with an uncharacteristic display of honesty.

Parrish leans back in his chair, folding his hands over his ample belly. "The men on this ward have need of an experienced masseur. More than that, however, they have need of a man who is committed to their recovery, more so in most cases than they are. You must be prepared to never let them see your disgust, your fear, your despair, and I guarantee you, you will feel those things every day. Privately, you may be as uncertain as you wish, but you must never show them a moment's hesitation. Do you understand?"

Michael wants to tell him no, wants to walk out of the room right now and resign from the Red Cross—he's a civilian, there is no force holding him here—but this is his last chance. He can see the hundreds, thousands of dead rise up before him, and he wants so desperately to help something to live, wants to make one last attempt to revive the dream he can barely remember before it leaves him forever.

"Yes," he says. "Yes, I understand, sir."

"Well, then, God help you," Parrish says wearily, rising to his feet and offering Michael his pudgy hand, "the position is yours."

"The position pays well—thirty dollars a week," Mrs. Anderson said, the mention of money bringing Michael back to the present. He nodded at the woman politely. Millie paid him forty, and he often made that much again in tips. But at least here he'd have no expenses for food and lodging.

"That's very generous, mum." It was, truthfully, more than he'd been expecting; the bluebloods loved their charities, but they were notorious for paying their help next to nothing.

"Well," she said with some asperity, rising to her feet, "you look like you've a good strong back, and you have a pleasant manner. With Mr. Sullivan vouching for you, I'm willing to offer you the position. I'm off to Philadelphia at the end of the week, and I can't be bothered with interviewing twenty men who are probably equipped with few qualifications and even fewer references."

"I'm honored to accept, mum. When shall I start?"

"As soon as possible. Can you be ready to leave Thursday?"

Two days. "I believe so. Yes, mum."

"Good. I'll have a ticket waiting for you at the station for the five o'clock train. Thomas will meet you in Stuyvesant." She waved a hand at Michael's unspoken question. "Thomas Abbott. He and his wife are the caretakers, but he's advancing in years and isn't able to tend the garden any longer."

"Are they the only residents, mum?" Many of the estates on the Hudson were little more than summer homes or places to deposit the maiden great-aunt or the mad relative. He wasn't looking forward to sharing a house with the family embarrassment.

"No. My nephew—my brother's only son—has been living there for several months now." She made another sour face. "He's recently returned from the war as well."

Michael nodded. No doubt he'd served his country as an ass-licking aide-de-camp or rear-echelon paper-chaser. "And I suppose I will be reporting to him?"

"You will be reporting to Thomas," the woman informed him, ice in her words, "and Thomas will report to me. You will have no need to bother my nephew."

"Yes, mum," Michael said woodenly. Wonderful. The man was either mentally incompetent, a drunkard, or a completely useless bastard—or perhaps all three. Well, Michael had certainly put up with worse.

"If you have no more questions, I believe our business is concluded most happily for both of us. Thank you for your time, Mister

McCreeley."

Michael did not even consider correcting her again. "Thank you, mum. I will do everything in my power to give you satisfaction."

"I'm sure you will," she said distantly, already having dismissed him in her mind.

Taking his cue, Michael bowed slightly and let himself out. Once back on the street, he took a deep breath of the Manhattan spring air, which even in this fine neighborhood had the slight tang of the city's ever-present layer of filth in it.

"I'll miss you, you ugly old bitch," Michael murmured, startling a young woman bustling past him on the sidewalk. Nodding at her, he tipped his hat and headed off in the opposite direction, toward the streetcar.

STUYVESANT was exactly what Michael had been expecting, which was to say not very much at all. There was one main street that housed a greengrocer's, a milliner's, and a general store, a couple of side streets with tall oaks lining the dirt roads, and exactly three motorcars, one of which had been assigned to pick him up from the station.

Thomas Abbott may have been an excellent cart driver back in the day, but he obviously had little understanding of how motorcars worked. Michael thought about offering to take the wheel but doubted it would be well received. The old man had taken one long, disdainful look at Michael upon first meeting him, then gruffly introduced himself. His hands were as long and bony as the rest of him, and he had the air of someone who was used to looking down his hooked nose at the rest of the world in the way that some household servants had. Michael wasn't yet sure if he hated Irishmen or merely strangers in general.

"It's not a very big town," Michael observed as the shops soon gave way to farmers' fields and the wide lawns of fine homes.

"It suits us," Abbott said shortly. "But don't worry, you won't be seeing much of it."

Michael bit back the reply that this would not exactly be a hardship; no point in aggravating the old coot. "Lots of work to be done around the place, is there?" he asked instead.

Abbott cut his eyes at him. "Madam wants the gardens restored to the way they once were. Can't imagine why." As soon as the words were spoken, he pressed his lips together as though he'd revealed an intimate family secret to the milkman.

Michael said nothing to this, because there was nothing to say. The reason for the job didn't much matter to him; he had it now and had to make the best of it, like it or not. And for all that he'd hated working with Paddy, he had to admit he'd enjoyed working in the dirt as a child, making things grow with his own hands. He'd bought a couple of books on garden design and maintenance before leaving the city. They sat in the bottom of his pack, ready to be taken out and studied when he had a few spare moments. He hadn't done this kind of work in over a decade, and then it had been under Paddy's direction, but there was no chance he was going to present himself as an ignorant Mick to anyone.

He made no more attempts to engage Abbott in conversation, and Abbott seemed content with this arrangement, so they passed the rest of the bumpy, gut-churning journey in silence. Even when the old bastard nearly drove them off the road, Michael held his tongue. He had to admit it would be the supreme irony if he met his fate here in this peaceful place, among the tall, stately trees and the birds bursting into song above them. For one who now associated death with blasted, barren landscapes and battered bodies that were more carcass than man, it seemed impossible to believe that anyone ever died here.

Eventually Abbott wrestled the car up a long, winding drive that led them to a sprawling two-and-a-half-story monstrosity surrounded by trees and gently sloped grounds. Michael took in the state of the landscape as they drove past. Beds that looked as though they hadn't been tended in several years ringed the house, and an assortment of ornamental shrubbery on the front lawn was beginning to grow wild, odd limbs poking up from the otherwise round or oval shapes. Michael gasped as the sight revived a memory that slammed into him without warning, stealing his breath.

The merciless September rain beats down on them as he and Eddie carry the dead man to the pile of bodies outside the Casualty Clearing Station. Peeling back the tarp someone has thrown over it to keep off the worst of the weather, Michael reveals a pale white arm poking out from the otherwise neat mound.

Laying down the stretcher, he grasps the hand and tries to tuck it back in amongst the bodies, but it won't stay. Rigor has set in, and it keeps popping out again. It's almost comical, a routine for a vaudeville performer in hell.

"What's so fucking funny?" Eddie's exasperated voice cuts through his thoughts, and Michael realizes he's been laughing like a madman.

"Nothing," Michael gasps, still trying to catch his breath.

"Then help me lift him, will you?" Eddie orders, hefting the feet of their latest charge. "This rain is making him weigh a goddamned ton."

Michael bends down, hooking his hands under the armpits of the body, and they swing him up onto the pile, then cover the remains as best they can with the tarp. When he looks back as they walk away, the arm is still visible, its pale hand waving goodbye.

The car jerked to a stop in front of a wide triple-bayed garage that had doubtless been a stable not so long ago. Abbott shut off the engine, then closed his eyes briefly as though sending up a silent prayer of thanks.

"Well, get your things and let's get you settled," he muttered, though his tone was slightly less cold than it had been at the start.

Abbott's wife proved to be more welcoming than her husband, insisting on sitting them both down for the noon meal before any more was done. Mary—for so she insisted he call her—was plump, with strong features and capable hands, her silver hair perfectly tied back into a complicated bun. She made, Michael swiftly decided, the best dumplings for stew he had ever eaten, and he told her so. Smiling, she accepted his compliment graciously, then turned back to the stove.

As soon as he was finished eating, Abbott rose from the table and took the tray his wife had prepared mere moments before—clearly, she had timed it to be ready upon the conclusion of his meal—then walked out of the kitchen with it. Michael admired the precision of it the way one might admire an intricate watch mechanism. It was obvious they were used to one another's company, their silences only contributing to the feeling of harmony between them. There had been no such cooperation to be found at his uncle's home. His Aunt Kathleen had borne the burden of raising the children, preparing the meals, and ensuring that Padraig didn't piss away all of his weekly earnings in the tavern before she could lay her hands on a portion of it. By the time he and Margaret had come to live with them, she'd had no smiles left in her.

When Abbott returned, he took Michael up two flights of stairs to his room—a surprisingly large space in the attic above the kitchen. The clapboard was painted the color of freshly churned butter, the bed was covered in a bright cotton quilt, and the washstand was adorned with fresh towels, a china bowl, and pitcher. Michael set down his pack, feeling out of place in the overly cheerful room.

"This isn't a hotel," Abbott muttered. "You're expected to keep it clean."

Michael smiled, the gruff words oddly comforting. "Of course," he replied easily.

Abbott watched him carefully for a moment before snorting. "Come along, then. I'll show you the rest."

After a brief tour of the property, Abbott left Michael at the groundskeeper's shed near the back corner of the grounds, where the grass yielded to untended forest. "Dinner's at six on the dot," Abbott informed him. "Leave your muddy boots outside on the porch, and don't be late." Before Michael could trust himself to offer a suitably deferential reply, the old man was already headed back across the lawn toward the house. Shaking his head, Michael schooled himself to calm and dove into his work.

He spent the rest of the afternoon cleaning the shed. After sweeping out the structure from top to bottom, he dedicated some time to sharpening and oiling rusted tools before turning his attention to the small planting greenhouse attached to the southern wall. What soil remained in the dozens of clay pots was gray and dry; he dumped the earth into the nearest bed and scrubbed the pots clean. The first of next week, he'd find a way back into town. Doubtless the general store would have seeds available, or at least a catalogue. When he was done, he placed the pots back on their shelves in neat rows, surprised when a mild wave of satisfaction rose in him.

Before dinner, he made a more thorough survey of the grounds at the back and sides of the house. The more he saw, the more the pleasant feeling of accomplishment he'd cultivated tidying up the shed faded. The beds were even more overgrown with weeds than he'd imagined, although the next couple of weeks would tell for certain how many of the original plants had been choked out. Even now a few spindly tulips were showing themselves, and here and there the pale shoots of peonies fought to push through the dead leaves. He would need to work carefully to coax whatever remained back to health, but all was obviously not lost.

Dinner was lighter fare, a plowman's plate of breads, cheeses, cold ham, and homemade pickles that Michael devoured eagerly. Their only other company was a thin, red-haired girl of seven or eight who stared at Michael silently for the entire meal. She was introduced to him as the Abbotts' granddaughter, Sarah, but no more of her history was forthcoming. Knowing well the value of silences, Michael respected hers, though his head was filled with questions. Although they looked nothing alike, she reminded him of Margaret at that age, just after their mother had died. His sister had borne that same hollow-eyed look, that same ethereal quality, as though she had been suspended between the worlds of the living and the dead. It had taken all of Michael's strength to bring her back to earth, but he had done it. He wondered if some tragedy had led this girl down the same path.

Michael noticed that the lunchtime ritual was repeated once more, with Abbott taking a similar tray up the steps and down the hall. After the door had closed behind the old man, Michael remarked, "I'd have thought the master of the house would dine on caviar and roast duck, not brown bread and cheese."

Mary took Michael's plate from the table before he could stand to do it himself. "He eats the same as the rest of us," she said, her voice carrying an edge that surprised him. When he offered to help with the dishes, he was gently but firmly rebuffed. At a loss, he bade them good night and climbed the stairs while Sarah stared after him silently.

Used to working until the wee hours, Michael lay in bed for some time, restless and disoriented. He finally rose and quietly made his way down to the kitchen, where he shrugged on his coat and slipped outside.

The night was warmer than he'd expected, and he soon shed the coat once more. Guided by the bright moonlight, he found himself among the shrubs in the front garden, wandering from plant to plant. Touching the branches with gentle fingertips, he felt for the hard, round buds, then broke off an end and sucked at the wound he'd made, tasting fresh, new sap.

As he turned back toward the house, he felt an odd prickling sensation crawl across his skin and raised his head instinctively. The front of the house was dark, but he caught a brief flash of movement in one of the second-floor windows. Michael looked up and fired off a smart salute before continuing on his way, the tip of the branch still clamped between his teeth.

WHEN Michael awoke the next morning at dawn, Mary was already downstairs cooking thick bacon and what looked like a dozen eggs in a cast iron skillet. She was being helped by Sarah, who flitted back and forth between table and stove and icebox like a restless moth skirting a campfire.

On her next run, he reached out and plucked the heavy coffeepot from her hands. She gazed up at him, her round eyes startled and faintly angry. He merely stared back at her steadily, holding her gaze until she turned back to the stove.

Half an hour later, he was on his knees in the first bed carefully pulling up weeds when he looked up and saw her standing at the opposite edge. He opened his mouth to speak, then closed it again when she too dropped to her knees and began copying him. He watched her for a couple of minutes, but she picked out the weeds easily, pulling up the whole plant with the roots and avoiding the perennials. They worked together without saying a word to one another until Abbott called for her.

She stood up and brushed the loose dirt from her skirts. "I can help you after school," she said in a high yet strong voice.

"I'd like that," Michael said carefully. "Thank you."

She nodded, apparently satisfied with his answer, then ran off toward her grandfather, who was waiting for her beside the motorcar. Michael stared after her, feeling humbled by her simple and inexplicable display of trust, as though a wild animal had just emerged from the forest and taken a crust of bread from his open hand.

BY SATURDAY at sunset, Michael had weeded and mulched the flowerbeds surrounding the back and sides of the house and prepared a new vegetable and herb garden near the kitchen. On Monday, he would see if he could drive into town—by himself, he hoped—and place orders for seed and fertilizer. Mary had told him Hudson, a few miles to the south, had a feed and grain store with a wide range of flower and vegetable seeds available, and that she would telephone ahead to let them know he could charge whatever he wished to the household account.

Saturday night found him lying in his bed yearning for the distractions of the city. Millie had given him every other Saturday off, and he'd spent it as he wished, usually in the bed of someone warm, willing, and well heeled. The week before last he'd had a beautiful young man who'd claimed to be a playwright. He had a huge flat in the Forties, a bar stocked with very fine cognac, and a mouth that was made for cocksucking. They'd agreed to meet again tonight, and damn it all, Michael had completely forgotten to get in touch with him before leaving.

He felt a small twinge of regret, because it wasn't likely he'd have another such opportunity at any point in the near future. In addition to every Sunday, his current job afforded him one weekend a month completely to himself, but by the time he took the train back into the city and found a likely prospect, it would almost be time to head back again. No doubt he'd go when he got the chance, but it almost seemed more trouble than it was worth and a taunting reminder of all that he was giving up. He didn't want to be another yokel visitor to New York on the lookout for a fast fuck; he wanted to walk its streets and know that he belonged there.

His first time comes when he's fifteen. He's been slipping away to the fairy dives for nearly a year, avoiding the roving gangs of Irish, Polish, and Italian boys that troll the streets of the Bowery at night and sneaking in through the kitchens to watch the drag shows, the parades of color and life and laughter. The waiters recognize a young up-and-comer and allow him to mooch off the half-empty plates before they're cleaned, looking the other way when he downs the warm dregs of a beer glass.

He falls helplessly in lust with one of the waiters, a tall, strapping Polack with the palest blue eyes he's ever seen. It takes him months of careful observation and study—not to mention the time to grow into his skin—to feel confident enough to approach him. Sebastian is reluctant at first, but Michael convinces him with his hands and his mouth and his eager, responsive body that he knows exactly what he wants.

When Sebastian shoves him roughly against the brick wall out back of the music hall and pushes inside him, Michael knows there's no way he can go back home to Paddy's beatings and that cramped tenement stinking of cabbage. For better or for worse, this is his life now.

Frustration shoved his hand under the sheets, and within moments his fingers were wrapped around his hardening erection. Breathing shallowly through his nose, he closed his eyes and thought of the playwright's soft skin under his hands, the taut thighs and tight ass, the sharp little incisors that bit the inside of Michael's wrist as Michael fucked him.

While memory was a poor substitute for reality, it did have certain advantages. For example, he could conveniently forget the annoying grunts the young man had made while Michael had plowed into him; they'd been entirely too porcine for his taste and had been less than arousing. In his fantasies, though, only soft sighs and breathy moans emerged from that pale throat, and in no time at all he was close to coming from only a few firm strokes.

He was careful to keep his movements slow and steady, never jostling himself so far as to excite the creaky bedsprings, not with the

Abbotts sleeping almost directly below him. But when he rolled up and over the first cresting wave, he nearly gave the game away, for without his consent his body jerked and stiffened, toes clenching in the sheets as he spilled into his handkerchief, and the bed rocked and squealed in protest.

"Fuck," Michael whispered, the sudden tension in his muscles swiftly draining the dregs of his pleasure. Concentrating on his body, he gradually relaxed each part of himself bit by bit until he lay still and boneless, then wiped himself with the handkerchief and set it aside. That was one piece of laundry Mary wouldn't be seeing.

It was not much different from his situation at fifteen, living in his first rooming house and muffling his moans with his fist so as not to wake the landlady, imagining how it would feel to have a rough, strong hand wrapped around his cock. It had taken him eleven years to come full circle, and now he was right back at the starting place, hiding his desires in the dark like a frightened boy.

Just as sleep finally claimed him, beckoning to him with clawed white hands from beneath a rain-soaked tarpaulin, he thought, *Not quite like the beginning after all.*

SUNDAY was entirely his, but as Michael had no use for prayer and even less for leisure, he decided to start on his study of the gardening books. By late morning, when he heard the motorcar putter up the driveway, he had already finished one, its margins filled with his scribbled ideas and plans.

Setting the book aside, he descended the stairs for dinner. Sarah was no more talkative than she had been the first day, but he fancied that she did seem a little more at ease around him. He was growing curious as to the cause of her silence; it seemed to run deeper than simple reticence around strangers and more shallowly than a fixed component of her character. Something told him she had once smiled a great deal more than she did now.

Although they had never exchanged words in the presence of others, Michael risked asking her a question as they helped her grandmother dry the dishes and her grandfather sat smoking his pipe at the table. "I thought I'd survey the woods this afternoon," he said. "I wanted to find some seedling trees we can replant in the gardens. Would you like to go with me?"

She looked up at him, seemingly startled, and Michael cursed himself for making her uneasy again. When the silence stretched, Mary saved the situation. "Sarah has a lesson with Mister John," she said calmly. "She spends every Sunday afternoon in his company."

It took Michael a moment to process this. "John—?"

Abbott withdrew the pipe from his mouth. "*Mister* John Seward," he said. "Son of Doctor George Seward, who built this house."

Ah, so that was the fabled nephew. Smiling sardonically, Michael nodded and said, "I've heard of him, yes. Didn't know his name, though. Do you suppose he'll ever drop by to say hello?"

To his surprise, Abbott's expression betrayed a hint of sadness before resolving itself into anger. "He's above concerning himself with your comings and goings," the old man snapped. "Just do your job." Laying down his pipe, he rose from his seat and took his granddaughter by the hand.

Before he could lead her away, she looked up at Michael again and said tentatively, "I should be finished by three o'clock."

Michael couldn't help the genuine smile that tugged at his lips. "I'll wait for you," he promised.

Although she did not smile in return, the faint rosiness that sprang to her cheeks told him his answer pleased her. When Abbott and Sarah had left, he turned back to the dishes to find Mary gazing at him with something akin to fondness. He shot her a questioning glance, and she shook her head.

"You can't know, of course, dear," she said softly, handing him a cup, "but it's been a very long time since I've seen her ask for anything. It's only…." She trailed off, and Michael was horrorstruck to realize her eyes were bright with unshed tears. "I'm glad you're with us," she said after a minute, turning back to him and patting his hand before passing him a plate.

Her words stunned Michael into silence. Taking the dish from her, he dried it with care, gliding the towel slowly over the smooth surface.

WHEN four o'clock came and went, Michael's curiosity—which until now he'd imagined long dead—rose up in him and sent him off into the main wing of the house in search of Sarah. Michael was concerned that the master of the house was keeping her indoors against her will, doubtless boring her with some stuffy lecture on social graces.

He was soon drawn to the sound of chamber music wafting from a phonograph and followed its summons down a long hall to an open doorway. Cautiously, he stopped outside the room and peered around the frame.

Sarah was inside, along with a dark-haired stranger who had to be the nephew, their backs to the door. The little girl was standing, the man sitting, both of them with easels and canvas in front of them. Beyond those, a wall of wide, tall windows opened on the backyard.

The fact that the lord of the manor was teaching the caretaker's granddaughter to paint was astonishing enough, but when Michael looked more closely, the paintings themselves surprised him even more. Both of them were dark, tangled messes, the girl's composition dominated by angry streaks of red slashing through a black and brown background. It looked like nothing so much as the mouth of hell, and the idea that this small thing might be well enough acquainted with the place to paint it so accurately chilled him to his bones. What had she seen, what had she survived that would cause her brain to conjure up this nightmare vision?

The record hissed to an end. Sarah walked over to lift the needle and shut off the machine.

"How are you progressing?" the man asked, turning to her. Michael watched Sarah walk back to the painting, a thoughtful expression on her small face.

"I don't know," she said slowly. "Would you mind looking at it?"

"Not at all."

"Would you like me to bring it to you?" Michael watched her small hands grip the sides of the heavy canvas. He was shocked, for that was already more than he'd yet heard her say at one time.

"No, I'll come to you," said the nephew, and Michael received his second shock of the day when the man reached down beside his chair and picked up the cane that lay on the floor. He used it as a support as he levered himself to his feet, then walked over to Sarah's easel.

Maximus gait, thought Michael automatically, watching the way Seward thrust his trunk backward as his heel struck the ground in an effort to compensate for the weakness of his hip extensors. There was a slight limp favoring his left foot as well, and his right shoulder was markedly depressed, though whether that was the result of an injury to the spine or shoulder itself he couldn't be sure.

Not a rear-echelon paper-chaser, then, he thought, watching the body's motions with a clinical detachment he knew wouldn't last. And sure enough, as the other man bent over the little girl's painting, murmuring appreciatively about the finer points of her technique, he felt the familiar nausea and churning emotion well up in his gut.

He can still see them all, see them lined up, one after another after another, arms and legs missing, bones shattered, burned, gassed, bodies shredded and sewn back together again like a patchwork quilt with missing pieces. They are his to fix, his to make whole again, but most of them are more eager to die than to heal, and they will always be more successful in the first ambition than in the second. For a few excruciating moments, he is back on that ward, desperately trying to keep from screaming his frustration and horror at all the beautiful, broken young bodies—

Michael shut his eyes against the memory, and when he opened them again, he found Sarah and her companion staring at him.

"Oh, hello," Sarah said, darting her eyes at her teacher. "It's past three, isn't it?"

"Yes," Michael said stupidly. "I was...."

He stopped, dumbstruck. He couldn't admit that he had been worried about her in front of the man who had been charged with her care for the afternoon.

"Do you always go wandering uninvited through people's homes?" Seward snapped.

Michael's gaze rose and met green eyes filled with anger. Now that he was getting a good look at him, it occurred to Michael that Seward looked slightly younger than his own twenty-six years, though his features were prematurely aged by pain. His face bore the patrician characteristics of one of the Anglo-Saxon sons of privilege, with a long nose and high, proud cheekbones, yet Michael could not summon the usual contempt he felt for such men. Tamping down the first retort that came to mind, he said instead, "I apologize... sir. I was looking for Sarah."

"Well, now that you've found her, you can go back to the servants' wing."

Michael glanced down and noticed the cane was quivering under his weight. Christ, the man could barely stand for more than a couple of minutes at a time. Had his doctors made no effort to restore his strength during his convalescence?

"Well?"

The sharp word snapped Michael out of his reverie. He looked up and realized his error when he saw that anger had been transformed into rage by what to Seward must have looked like a gardener's impudent assessment of his frailties.

That's all you are now, Michael reminded himself harshly. *See that you don't forget it.*

Holding up his hands in a placating gesture, he said, "Once again, my apologies. I won't trouble you any longer." And with a nod to both of them, he turned on his heel and walked away.

He was halfway back to the kitchen when he heard the pounding of small footsteps behind him. Turning around, he was nearly bowled over by Sarah, who came to a skidding stop before him. Her tiny, elflike face was upturned and fearful, as though expecting a blow.

"I didn't think I would be so long. I'm sorry."

Michael shook his head and smiled. "It's all right," he assured her. "We'll look over the woods when you have time. Tomorrow or Tuesday, after school."

Her eyes grew round. "You'll wait for me?"

Michael smiled down at her. "Of course I will. Go on back now; you mustn't keep the master waiting."

Sarah frowned slightly, then shook her head as though dispelling a troubling thought and ran back the way she had come.

As Michael walked with leaden steps back toward his new life, he might have wished that his own troubling thoughts could be dismissed as easily, if he hadn't known it was utterly futile.

THE following week moved at a swift pace as Michael began serious work on the gardens. On Monday he was driven into Hudson by Abbott—the old bastard still didn't trust him with the car—and returned with a dozen varieties of seeds and the promise of a delivery of soil and fertilizer by midweek. By Friday, he had mulched and prepared all the beds and planted hundreds of seeds in the clay pots he'd found in the greenhouse. He'd also limed the lawn, and as soon as the danger of frost passed, he'd sow new seed in the bare patches where the moss had died off.

The monotony of his tasks was alleviated by his first letter from Margaret, painstakingly printed on the same cheap paper she had used to write to him in Europe for nearly six years. He let it slide between his fingertips, the rough surface familiar against his skin, before unfolding it carefully.

20 April 1919

Dearest Michael—

I received your letter of 15 April and I am very glad you are likeing your work. Will you be planting any foxglove? If you can find the pink kind I think the little girl you mentioned will like that very much. Lilly of the valley is very beutifull too. Does she really remind you of me? I wish I had some

*photographs of us both when we were young, that
would be a wonderful thing to show Edith and
Donald.*

*You asked if I had herd from Paul and I have not
but I am sure he will write me anyday now. He told
me it might be some time before he got in at the
steelworks and he did not want to get my hopes up
by writing to soon. I did here from Colm tho—he
says he is getting married and wants me to come to
the wedding. It is suposed to be in August and he
says Jimmy and Tim should be back then too.
Father's ship will still be in the Orient then but
Colm says he does not care about that. I wish they
would get along but you know Father never paid
much attention to them either, even when Mamma
was still alive. I know you will say you cannot come
but I hope you will.*

Michael sighed. It boggled him that Margaret still thought of
them as a family after all this time. She was his closest relation, the
only one, in fact, with whom he still maintained ties. When their
mother had died, the two of them had gone to live with Paddy, their
older brothers already off roaming the world like their father, working
as deckhands and stokers on the merchant ships. He hadn't seen his
brothers or his father in over a decade, though Margaret had kept in
touch with all of them. They might as well have been strangers to him.

*I cannot stop thinking about what you said the last
time we saw one another and it saddens me to know
you feel there is something you cannot tell me. I
have always told you everything that was in my
heart and I thought you had done the same. I hope
you know that I will always love you and want your
happyness above all.*

*Edith wanted me to put a kiss in the envelope for
you. I told her to kiss the paper, and she did, right
here—*

And here is one from me—

I will write you again next Sunday; God keep you safe.

Love,

Your Margaret

Saturday found him in the forest, digging up the youngling trees he and Sarah had found and marked earlier in the week. She'd done a fine job of selecting suitable specimens for the garden and had helped him draw up a new plan incorporating them into the back and side yards. As he dragged them out of the woods on the garden cart, he watched Sarah dig the new holes to receive them.

He could tell that Abbott disapproved of his granddaughter's association with him, but Mary obviously held the opposite viewpoint and openly encouraged Sarah to spend time with him outdoors when her chores were done. Sarah, he learned, was actually nearly twelve and so quite small for her age. He hadn't seen fit to tell Mary about the painting the girl had made, at first not wanting to alarm her and then not wanting to be viewed as a meddler. Besides, any demons that inhabited the child were probably well known to her grandparents and doubtless were linked to the absence of her mother and father.

As he'd worked in the garden through the week, he could sometimes feel that same prickle of awareness he'd sensed that first night among the trees. He did not look up toward the house directly, though sometimes he'd sneak a peek out of the corner of his eye, seeking the cause of that feeling. He suspected its origin was a pair of angry green eyes, but he couldn't be sure. Perhaps Abbott had taken to watching him to try to catch him goldbricking.

The old man was the only person who seemed to have regular contact with Seward. He disappeared into the bowels of the house three times a day to bring him his meals and once more later on in the evening, presumably to help him with his nightly routine. Although Michael endeavored not to dwell on it, he found his thoughts straying while he worked to the injuries and debilities he'd cataloged from that brief viewing of Seward, to the evidence of yet another unholy crime wrought by an unholy war. His unchallenged mind sought stimulation and found it in the contemplation of an exercise and massage regimen that would treat the pain and recover flexibility and strength. It would be a simple thing to set up a rudimentary gymnasium in one of the unused rooms—

And that was where Michael would usually catch himself and force his thoughts back into acceptable channels, ones more suited to a gardener. He would shift his concentration to his garden plan, to the schedule for watering, to anything, nothing.

The cart hit a tree branch and nearly toppled, and it took all of Michael's strength to keep it upright. Cursing softly under his breath, he backed it up and maneuvered it around the obstacle, then pushed it up the slight slope until he had reached the lawn. As he approached, Sarah looked up at him, her face streaked with dirt, her skirts muddied, her hands filthy.

Then he caught the flash of small, white teeth through the mess, and suddenly his mood lightened; it was the first time he'd seen her produce anything remotely resembling a smile. He brought the cart close and bowed to her. "Which of these poor offerings strikes my lady's fancy?"

The grubby child rose with the grace of royalty and pointed imperiously. "We must have the white birch," she intoned.

"Very well, Your Highness," he said, picking up the sapling by the canvas sack he'd tied around the root ball and carrying it over to the hole she'd prepared. As he set it in place, he happened to look up and caught the billowing of a curtain at a second-floor window.

I fear the King does not approve, he thought, turning his attention back to his work and to the princess with the tiara of stray leaves clinging to her hair.

MICHAEL knew something was wrong when Abbott returned from delivering Sunday's lunch. His expression was even more pinched and thunderous than usual, and his manner was agitated. Michael's first thought was that some mishap had befallen Seward, and he asked after him without thinking.

"Mister John's health is none of your business," Abbott snapped. At that moment, Sarah raced downstairs in a loose-fitting outfit with a cotton overdress.

"I'm ready, Grandpa," she said.

Abbott turned to her, expression softening only marginally, and shook his head. "He won't be able to see you today, child," he said.

Sarah's face did not fall at that; it went absolutely blank, as though, having experienced so many disappointments, she could no longer summon a response to them. "But you said he was feeling fine yesterday," she said in a small, flat voice.

"He was." Abbott looked away. "He's simply not up for a lesson today."

You're a very poor liar, Michael thought. Apparently Sarah was of the same opinion, because her expression for an instant turned from blank to skeptical.

"All right, Grandpa," she said in that same dead tone. She disappeared up the steps again, her shoulders so straight and proud that the sight made Michael's throat hurt.

A tense silence descended over the room once Sarah's footsteps had faded, as the three adults stood locked in their own private thoughts. And then Michael was moving, climbing the short run of steps to the main level and pulling open the door to the hallway of the main house. Briefly, he wondered why in hell he was doing this, and then Sarah's blank, resigned face rose before him, and the rage broke the surface, propelling him forward.

"McCready—" Abbott warned. "It's not your place to interfere."

Michael chuckled hollowly. "*Mister* Abbott, it's never been my habit to keep my place."

Mary's voice was kinder, though just as firm. "Michael,

please—" But that did no good either, and he was soon beyond her entreaties or her husband's commands.

As he searched, Michael peered through a half dozen doorways into rooms filled with muslin-covered furniture and a musty air. It was as though the house hadn't had a living resident for years, and all that remained were the ghosts of the previous owners.

He finally tracked Seward down in the library, a dark-curtained room whose walls seethed with books. The only light came from one weak table lamp and a roaring fire, before which Seward sat in a high-backed armchair.

"You're remarkably bad at following orders, aren't you?" Seward muttered, his gaze fixed on the fire. There was a whiskey glass in his left hand. He took a healthy sip while Michael watched.

"I've been told I don't take orders from you," Michael bit out. To his surprise, Seward only laughed at that.

"No, you don't, that's true," he acknowledged, green gaze rising to flicker over Michael like the light from the flames. "But you take orders from Thomas, and he's rather fond of me."

"I can't imagine why, considering the way you treat his granddaughter."

Seward's gaze fixed on him, remained steady. He held up the glass. "Would you prefer she see me like this?" he snapped.

Michael's jaw clenched. "You were the one who decided to start drinking."

"It seemed like a good day for it," Seward murmured, returning to his contemplation of the fire.

"If you're looking for some way to punish her because she chooses to spend time with me…," he began.

Seward glared at him. "Yes, that's it, you've uncovered my evil plan," he snarled. "You must think I'm an idiot as well as a cripple."

Michael cursed himself silently, realizing he was getting nowhere with this bull-in-a-china-shop approach. Unfortunately, he was so quick to anger these days that it was difficult to consider any other method. Taking a deep breath, he stepped between Seward and the fire, forcing his gaze upward again. "Listen. I didn't come here to antagonize you—" Seward snorted and took another sip of his drink, "—only to tell you Sarah obviously enjoys spending time with you. She's disappointed that you canceled her painting lesson."

Seward actually looked startled, which surprised Michael in turn. "Is that what you think it is?" He shook his head. "You couldn't be more wrong. I believe she's the one who's teaching me."

Michael frowned at the unexpected display of humility from a man he'd assumed to be completely arrogant. "Whatever you choose to call it, she relied on you, and you let her down."

Seward flinched at that before draining his glass. "She's better off not relying on me"—his gaze rose to meet Michael's again—"or on anyone."

Without realizing what he was doing, Michael took a step forward, looming over Seward with fists clenched. "That's easy for you to say, isn't it? You can't even cook your own damned meals, and you're going to lecture a child about self-reliance?"

Seward stared at him. "Get out," he spat.

Saluting smartly, Michael turned on his heel and strode from the room without looking back.

THE following week brought the first truly warm weather of the year, though Michael was still wary that a late frost might kill his seedlings, so he faithfully continued to stoke the fire in the greenhouse's small pot-bellied stove every night. Later in the week, the grass had grown so much that he had to take out the push mower and go over the entire grounds. It took him the better part of the day, and by the end of it his arms felt half-pulled from their sockets. The only remedy he could practice on himself was a hot bath, and he'd have that soon enough.

He was in the greenhouse near sunset, checking on the progress of his marigolds with Sarah, when she said softly and without ceremony, "I know he drinks."

Michael took a moment to gather his thoughts before answering.

"He wouldn't like to hear you say that."

She cocked her head at him. "It's not his fault. He was hurt. He needs to."

Michael shook his head, not wanting to argue with her. "There are other ways. Other solutions."

Studying a particularly healthy seedling that had already poked its head above the soil, she asked casually, "Do you know any of them?"

Michael sucked in a breath. "I used to."

Sarah looked up at him. "Then you can help him."

He wanted nothing more than to say *no*, but her gaze was filled with something he might have called hope, and he couldn't bear to destroy it outright. Instead he murmured, "I don't think he would welcome my help, Sarah."

"You have to be careful when you do it, that's all," Sarah said, with the confidence of one who had thought long and hard about this. "You make it seem like you're not really helping him, or that he's helping you. He doesn't like it if he thinks you pity him."

"No danger there," Michael muttered under his breath. Aloud, he told her, "Sarah, the war—whatever happened to him, it didn't only affect his body. Do you understand? He doesn't want to get better because it hurts him too much to try."

"That's why we have to try for him," Sarah said quietly. "The way Grandma and Grandpa did for me."

Watching her solemn face, upturned and hopeful, the ache that had settled in his limbs spread deeper, sapping his strength. Damn her.

"All right, I'll try," he heard himself promise, though he'd sworn to himself that he would make no more promises to himself or anyone. "I don't have the first idea of how, but I'll try." *For you, though, m'dearie*, he added silently, *not for him.*

BEFORE Michael could think of a way to fulfill his promise, however, Seward's aunt descended on the place like a plague of locusts, turning the household upside down.

She announced her imminent arrival in a telephone call to Abbott, who promptly ran around the room like a dog chasing its tail for several minutes before Mary finally shouted at him to sit down before he fell down. Having seen the state of the house, Michael could understand the source of the old man's anxiety, although he couldn't summon much sympathy.

"Michael will help you," he heard Mary say. "Won't you?" she asked, turning to him, though anyone who thought that might be a question should be committed. Her warm brown gaze had steel in it as it caught and held Michael's.

"Of course," he said, smiling. "I'd be glad to help."

The next morning he found himself scrubbing the dining room floor, knees soaked through with cold water and silently cursing his generous impulse. Mary and her husband did what they could, but the house had suffered from a general and lengthy neglect that no amount of dusting could cure. By noon, they'd come to the decision that it would be best to make two or three rooms sparkle and steer the dowager Anderson toward them than to have the entire ground floor in a state of shabby cleanliness. By late in the day, they were exhausted, but Mary was satisfied with their efforts.

"If he'd let more of us into the house to clean it once in a while," Mary grumbled, "we wouldn't have had to work our fingers to the bone on short notice."

"Hush," Abbott admonished, casting an eye down the hall toward the library.

But Mary only waved a hand. "He can't hear me," she groused. "And if he could, I wouldn't mind. You've coddled the boy long enough, Tom."

"Woman, be quiet," Thomas growled, loud enough to startle both Mary and Michael. "You don't know the half of it."

"I know enough," Mary said softly, turning her back on her husband before he could attempt to silence her once more. Robbed of its target, Abbott's ire trained on Michael, who ducked his head and followed the mistress of the house back to the kitchen.

"HELLO, Mister McCreeley. I trust you are well?"

Michael stepped forward to offer Seward's aunt a hand as she descended from the motorcar. She looked only a little worse for wear, which meant that either Abbott's driving had seen a miraculous improvement or she had too much ice water running through her veins to worry about dying in a road accident.

"I'm fine, thank you, mum," he said as her cool fingers gripped his. Noting the slight tremble in her hand, he decided she wasn't as calm and collected as she pretended.

Once she was on solid ground, she released his hand and turned her head slowly to take in the garden. "I see you've been working." She nodded pointedly toward the new patch off the kitchen. He'd planted seed potatoes there this morning.

"Yes, mum. I thought the place could do with a vegetable and herb garden." He left out mentioning that Mary had asked for it in case she disapproved.

"Did any of the old plants survive?"

"Some," Michael answered. "If this weather holds, I should know better next week."

"Good, good," she said, nodding briskly. "Between you and me, we'll soon have things set to rights around here."

Michael kept his expression blank, but privately it occurred to him that he didn't like the sound of that at all.

As she headed up the walkway ahead of Abbott, she turned and said, "Oh yes, and Michael, my nephew and I will be taking our luncheon on the terrace. Please carry the round table from the parlor outside."

Michael smiled tightly. "Certainly, mum." He could only imagine the look on Seward's face when she handed him *that* piece of news. In the weeks he'd been here, he'd never seen Seward venture outside.

Mary wasn't thrilled with the news, either. She'd spent half an hour setting the dining room table, and to find out they wouldn't even be seeing it made her grit her teeth so hard Michael feared they might crack. Grumbling about how the high and mighty could do with a lesson in courtesy, she bustled off to collect the china and silverware while Michael saw to the table.

An hour later, Michael was making himself busy in the garden when the wide glass doors of the parlor opened, disgorging Seward and his aunt. Abbott stood beside the table in his best suit—Michael knew it was his best suit because Mary had also grumbled about having to press it last night—practically wringing his hands as Seward, supported by his cane, made his slow way across the stone terrace to the table. It was a distance of no more than twenty feet, but Michael knew it would be difficult for him in his condition.

The truth of it was that he needn't have placed the table even that far away, but he'd wanted an opportunity to assess Seward's condition further. What he saw during that pained walk confirmed his earlier suspicions. Whoever had seen to his care had not put him through a regimen of rehabilitation, or if they had, it had been perfunctory at best and criminally negligent at worst. It confounded him that a rich man's son had received such cavalier treatment. Even if the army doctors had been incompetent, why had Seward not taken advantage of his position and gone for private treatment? If this house was any indication, he certainly could afford it.

Seward must have weakened, or his foot caught on the edge of a flagstone, because he stumbled just before he reached the table. Michael found himself moving instinctively, but before he could make a complete ass of himself, Abbott and Seward's aunt were flanking him, supporting Seward and helping him to his seat. There was no doubt that he was livid as he dropped into the chair like a lead weight; it was not possible to mistake that look once you'd been on the receiving end of it.

For that reason alone, Michael knew he should look away, but for more time than was wise, he stood transfixed, almost trembling under the weight of the knowledge he'd gained from that short, painful episode. He tried to tell himself he was unaffected, but he knew it was a damned lie. The spots of color high on Seward's cheekbones were testament to a pride that astonished and humbled him; Michael couldn't bear witness to that and pretend he felt nothing.

They soon settled down to luncheon, picking at dainty sandwiches and cakes and coffee while the old man fetched and carried for them. For his part, Michael kept himself occupied in the garden nearest the terrace, making a great show of preparing beds already well prepared. Soon he was within earshot of the conversation without appearing to take the slightest interest in it.

He told himself he was merely eavesdropping to learn how best to proceed with Sarah's request, and he had almost convinced himself of it when he heard Seward's low voice.

"Are you threatening me, Aunt Rebecca?"

"Oh, for heaven's sake, don't be ridiculous," sighed the aunt. "I'm not about to cut you off."

"You certainly could. Your support of this house—with me in it—is contrary to the will."

The woman snorted. "Your father left the money and the house to me; he never indicated to me what I was to do with it. The dispute between the two of you, whatever its cause, was none of my concern, and it's still not. I do as I please, and I please that you should continue to live here. The inheritance you received from your mother certainly won't pay for its upkeep, let alone its purchase price."

"True," Seward muttered. "Thank you for reminding me."

"It wasn't meant as a reminder, merely a statement of facts," the woman sniffed. "I do think you could be a little more grateful."

"I am grateful to you, Aunt Rebecca, but I hope you understand that you will find me even more grateful if I can be left alone—"

"I won't do that any longer," Mrs. Anderson interrupted. "This simply can't be permitted to go on. You've been home from Europe six months, and you haven't done a thing with this house. It's falling into a state of disrepair and decay."

"Much like its tenant."

"I'm only thinking of you," she told him. "People are beginning to talk. A rumor is circulating that you sit perched in one of the attic windows with a rifle, for heaven's sake."

"Sometimes I do," Seward returned. "I find the tactic marvelously effective for discouraging unannounced visitors." Michael bit his tongue to keep from laughing at Seward's dark humor.

"Nevertheless," Mrs. Anderson continued, undaunted, "George Seward's son is not going to live as a ghost in his own house. I'm sorry, John, but I cannot allow that to happen."

That prompted the same dry, bitter laugh Michael had heard the other day. "No, of course you can't. Why, the gossip would be *unbearable*. You wouldn't be able to hold your head up on the Avenue. We must honor the memory of your dear brother above all."

There was a pause. "I've never understood why you insist on referring to George as though he weren't your father."

"He wasn't."

"The things you say," the woman sighed. "I don't understand you anymore."

"You never did, Auntie dear."

After a moment of chilly silence, the woman said coolly, "John, I am not going to discuss this further with you. The grounds will be restored, and the house will be repaired and redecorated."

"It'll be a pretty setting for a lump of coal," Michael muttered.

There was a short pause. "Well, I meant to speak to you about that as well."

Michael risked a glance up and saw Seward's thin, sarcastic smile. "I'm to be restored along with the house, am I? I'm honored. Too bad it can't be done."

His aunt set her jaw. "You haven't tried," she said flatly.

"You're right," Seward returned, with equal sangfroid. "I haven't."

That statement brought Michael up short. It took a couple of moments before he recovered himself and remembered that his eyes were supposed to be on the garden, not on Seward's pain-twisted face. When he did, he heard Seward's aunt say softly, "Well. I'm sure you must have had your reasons, but there comes a time when we must buckle down and face the world."

"Now why didn't I think of that?" Seward sneered.

There was the sound of a chair scraping back. "I knew you wouldn't react well to the news. But in time I'm sure you'll see it's for the best." Another pause. "Thomas, I'd like a word with you in private."

Michael looked up to see Abbott's gaze darting furtively from Seward to his aunt. He must have received his answer, because he said clearly, "Of course, mum," and followed her into the house the way she and Seward had come.

As for Seward himself, he sat at the table for a few moments, and then Michael heard him say, "Well, did you get all of that?"

Michael looked up and met that direct, uncompromising gaze, but before he could formulate an answer, Seward waved a hand at him. "Never mind, never mind. After all, it's not as though I have any dignity left to preserve."

With the aid of the cane, he pushed himself to a standing position and made his slow, hobbling way back to the house, Michael's gaze riveted to his every step.

THE next month was a flurry of activity and work as Seward's aunt made good on her threat to improve the house and everything within it. Furniture was delivered, draperies and linens ordered, and an electric refrigerator—the new kind linked to a compressor installed in the basement—replaced the old icebox. Electrical wiring, ten years old, was deemed inadequate and new wiring was installed. Plumbers were brought in to update the bathroom fixtures; fresh cobblestones were installed in the driveway; cracks in the plaster were repaired throughout the house.

And every one of the hundred or so odd jobs that required a strong back rather than skill was relegated to Michael. Given new orders by Abbott, he cut his time in the garden so that he would have the opportunity to complete the various tasks that had been assigned him. He began by completing the cleaning of the interior of the house from top to bottom and ended with a repainting of the entire exterior that took him a full week. Along the way there was furniture to be moved, floors to be stripped and re-waxed, roofs to be patched—the list seemed endless. And throughout it all, he saw not a whisper of Seward in the house. Somehow, the man managed to avoid detection and yet remain a ghostly presence that prickled the hairs on the back of Michael's neck.

By late May he was exhausted, though no more so than the Abbotts, who were showing the strain of the extra work far more than he. Despite Mary and Michael's combined efforts, the old man had been involved in every step of the process, dealing with hired men and overseeing their efforts in accordance with Mrs. Anderson's wishes. Michael tried to remind him the men knew their jobs and could probably be trusted to do them, but Abbott shrugged him off and told him, predictably, to mind his own business.

"I appreciate what you're trying to do," Mary said one afternoon over coffee and cherry pie, in what felt like the first time they'd sat down all week, "but it's no use. He won't listen to me, either."

A month ago he would have shrugged it off, but her words did nothing but fuel Michael's anger. He was surprised to discover it bothered him to know that Abbott was ignoring his own health for the sake of what he perceived as his duty, but he reassured himself by reasoning that he was merely sympathizing with Sarah and Mary, who actually cared about the old bastard.

"At least the house is almost finished," Mary sighed into the ensuing silence. "Soon things can go back to normal around here."

Unfortunately, Mary's prediction proved to be overly optimistic, for the moment the house was standing resplendent in its new, glossy coat of paint and its tastefully modernized interior, Seward's aunt began the real transformation. It started with a seemingly never-ending stream of clothiers and haberdashers. One after another Michael saw them enter the house game and energetic, arms full of boxes and fabrics, and leave it dejected and battered. Watching them limp away with their tails tucked between their legs, Michael could not help feeling they should have at least been warned beforehand, although the outcome would still have been the same. Their opponent was fierce and battle-hardened, and he occupied an entrenched position that seemed impervious to attack.

Still, the parade continued for a full week, during which Abbott began to take on the appearance of a ghost himself. Never hearty, his already thin frame edged toward gaunt, and dark circles ringed his eyes.

"Sit down before you fall down," Michael said gruffly one night, when Mary was about to hand him Seward's supper. "I'll take it to him."

But Abbott merely shook his head stubbornly, too tired to lash out in words, and took the tray from Mary, who watched him go with worry in her gaze.

Sarah, who had fallen more and more silent as the weeks went past, despite Michael's efforts to keep her spirits up, looked at each of them in turn, then stood and headed up the stairs. Mary opened her mouth to speak to her, then closed it again.

Cautiously, Michael laid a hand on her arm. "All right, then *you* go sit down," he ordered gently. "I'll clean up." She looked up at him, startled, then nodded and moved to sit at the wide wooden table, settling into the chair with a small, soft sound.

He was halfway through the dishes when he glanced over and saw her blunt, sturdy fingers gripping her teacup with such force he was afraid it might shatter. He considered taking it from her but decided to leave her be. There were worse things, after all, than wrecking a teacup or two.

HAVING experienced a setback in remodeling his exterior, Seward's aunt, bloodied but unbowed, next turned her attention to the inner man. And that was the point at which things deteriorated completely.

Michael was carefully pruning the newly leafed trees in the front yard that morning when he saw the car drive up and emit a small, sturdy woman in a nurse's uniform. She carried a huge black grip and looked impossibly young, and Michael felt his heart sink.

By lunchtime she was sitting in the kitchen, her eyes red and puffy from crying, while Mary fussed over her and fumed at Seward. Her name was Emma, and she'd graduated from nursing school a month ago; this was her first job. She'd wanted to work in a maternity ward, but since no positions had been available, she'd accepted this one instead.

"I'm surprised the girl survived," Michael murmured, speaking quietly with Mary by the stove while Emma sat at the table spooning Mary's corn chowder into her mouth with a shell-shocked air. Seward's aunt couldn't have selected a less suitable candidate to handle her strong-willed nephew, though perhaps she'd been hoping the beauty of the young woman would cause him to magically forget the horror that had destroyed his body. She had only the most perfunctory training in physical therapy and no experience at all with war veterans.

"This has to stop," Mary whispered. "Thomas is as pale as death, Sarah is as quiet as she was when she first came to us, and I'm at my wit's end. That boy has to be made to see reason."

"If he doesn't want to regain his health, no power on Earth will convince him to apply himself," Michael said grimly.

Mary frowned. "Then what can we do?"

"If I knew the answer to that," Michael sighed, "I wouldn't be here right now."

THOMAS drove Emma to the train station that afternoon, and over the course of the following two weeks, he ferried three other nurses back and forth from the house. Two of them lasted barely longer than Emma, though the third made a valiant attempt, staying a full four days before giving up. Elizabeth was, Michael learned, a highly trained nursing sister from England, and she had considerable experience with convalescing patients. Her looks, Michael noted with some amusement, were best described as plain. Apparently Seward's aunt had finally abandoned her attempt to appeal to her nephew's aesthetic sense.

"I thought a bit of time in the country would do me good, but they're not paying well enough to put up with his cheek," Elizabeth told him as they strolled through the garden. "He needs an alienist before he needs a nurse."

"Did his aunt tell you anything about his injury?" Michael asked.

She eyed him speculatively, silently. Of course, it was not her habit to share her patients' medical histories with the gardener. Michael hesitated for a moment, reluctant to bring her into his confidence; then, his dusty conscience reminding him of his promise to Sarah, he took a deep breath and spoke. "I was in my first year of medical school when the war broke out. Before that I was trained as a rubber. I joined the ambulance corps and was at the front until 1917, then returned to England and spent the remainder of the war working in an American convalescent hospital, where I implemented physical therapy routines for the men."

Elizabeth came to a halt and stared at him. "Bloody hell," she said quietly, "I thought you looked familiar. I was stationed in a base hospital near Ypres in 1916. Were you—"

Michael nodded. "It's a small world, isn't it?" He didn't bother to tell her he didn't remember her. At the front, one had soon learned not to look too closely at faces. Each face you recognized was one that could be missed.

"Too small," she agreed. She looked away, contemplating the nearest flowerbed, and after a moment Michael joined her in her study of his work. Satisfied that the danger of frost had passed, he'd transplanted the annuals yesterday. Neat rows of snapdragons and pansies stretched out in front of them, the buds just beginning to sprout.

"Damn," Elizabeth murmured, arms wrapping around herself despite the warmth of the day. "Even flowerbeds remind me of cemeteries now."

Michael led her away gently, and they walked slowly toward the back of the property. Once they were safely in the wilder terrain, he saw some of the tension leave her body. "I'm sorry," she said.

"Don't be," Michael admonished her gently. "I know how it feels to have everything you touch seem tainted."

Elizabeth stared at him. "That's it. That's exactly it." She waved a hand to indicate the garden beyond the woods. "If I'm not being too forward, has this—working at something so completely different— helped you?" she asked.

"Not precisely," Michael hedged, thinking of Sarah's haunted eyes and Seward's broken body. "Though I suppose I was hoping it would at least be restful."

Elizabeth sighed. "I don't think you'll get much rest with that one under the same roof." Sobering, she said, "Why do you want to know about him?"

"I made a promise," Michael admitted, spreading his hands. "And like it or not, I have to do what I can to keep it."

Elizabeth raised an eyebrow at him. "Do you believe in fate?" she asked.

Michael's gut clenched unpleasantly. "No."

"Good thing," she told him firmly. "Because if he's your fate, you might as well jump in the river now and have it over with." She watched him for a moment longer before nodding. "All right. I have notes I made from the conference with his doctor. I'll leave them for you."

Michael thanked her graciously, although he knew what he was feeling was as far from gratitude as was possible.

THERE is little privacy or safety to be had in the trenches, and when Michael is moving among them, he is working, so the chances for the brief, furtive couplings that some men find between bombardments and gas attacks and assaults are limited. Even if there were opportunity, he has to admit he would not be tempted, because the last thing he wants is to defile his desires with the stench of desperation and death. Instead he stores them away and unpacks them during his periodic leaves in Paris, where there is always a willing partner for the evening if you know where to look.

Michael knows where to look, even before he can understand the language, because the world in which he moves is fluent in silences. The only significant difference from New York is that the entire city seems to be the Bowery or Greenwich Village, secrets kept in the open for everyone to see but not see, a wink and a nod the rule rather than the exception. He likes it there, likes the freedom and the spirit of the place, and every three or four months, he can spend a few days scrubbing the dirt and blood from his skin and enjoying the company of men who don't reek of gangrene and Belgian mud, men whose bodies are fine and firm and whole.

If he concentrates, he can almost forget there's a war by the time his leave is up.

Later on in the war, when Paris is living under the threat of the German long gun and the terror of the Zeppelins, its luster dulls sufficiently that it is no longer enough to rob Michael of his memories, even for a moment. When he comes buried deep in a sweet, rounded ass, vision filling with starry pinpoints as his blood flees his brain, he can no longer lose himself entirely in the comforting amnesia wrought by pleasure. The stench of death does not leave his nostrils, and the *vision of sightless eyes and orphaned limbs rises up before him, suffocating his desire.*

When he arrives in England, he can barely even stand to touch himself, let alone anyone else. His last potential fuck before the war ends sucks him for what seems like hours, and if he shuts his eyes he can forget that anyone is touching him, because he feels nothing, nothing, nothing.

Michael woke from the flood of reminiscences gasping and sweating, his throat tight and his fists clenched in the sheets. The first fingers of dawn light were beginning to slide in the open window. Below him, he could hear the faint murmur of voices. As he lay collecting his scattered thoughts, the voices rose, resolving themselves briefly into sharp, barbed words before fading away to nothing. A few moments later, he heard the sounds of movement, the squeak of bedsprings and creak of floorboards.

Abbott and his wife were arguing again, as they had been doing nearly every day since the dowager Anderson's visit. Michael had always thought marriage to be a prison—he'd never known a couple that had been truly happy—but at least until now the Abbotts had seemed such, despite the husband's less than winning personality. Obviously Mary saw something worthwhile in him, for she was doing her damnedest to keep the old coot from killing himself with overwork; too bad Abbott wasn't listening to any of her advice. Either he was one of those idiot servants who believed in duty above all else, or Seward had some mystical hold on him that Michael didn't understand. Whatever the case, he was a fool to be ruining his health for someone who didn't appreciate his efforts.

Clearly it would fall to Michael to try to come up with some scheme to get Seward back on his feet, but even after reviewing the information about his case, he didn't have the faintest idea of how to broach the subject with his prospective patient. He closed his eyes, Elizabeth's well-formed, precise script dancing behind his eyelids, efficiently summarizing a horror so vast it was a miracle that Seward was still breathing.

*Multiple fractures to all limbs; r. floating rib 12
    shattered and removed; collarbone cracked on r
    side; diaphragm punctured; no major organ
    damage*

*Remained unconscious for 8 d. after transfer to base
    hospital; believed possible brain damage for a
    time*

*Traction 12 wks. All bones healed; r. femur fracture
    bolted, retained some weakness for 8 mos.*

*Paralysis to lower limbs for 2 mos. after traction
    removed; may have been hysterical*

*Physical therapy attempted; atrophy of limbs
    advanced, patient nonresponsive, progress slow*

*Patient can walk with assistance of cane for short
    distances; no endurance*

*Last visit to doctor Dec 1918; prognosis for full
    recovery poor*

None of this was a great surprise to Michael; it did confirm that most of his initial impressions had been correct. However, the extent of Seward's injuries was far beyond what he'd been expecting. The rest of the report contained the doctor's suggestions for physical therapy, which he could easily see lacked any ambition. At most, they would keep Seward's body from deteriorating further, but they certainly would not improve his physical condition. Evidently even his high-priced doctors had given up on him, or they lacked an understanding of the latest techniques and exercises, or both. Whatever the reason, the hard truth was that the report left him no further ahead. He could hardly stroll down to Seward's library one day and suggest a regimen of massage and exercise. If the recommendations of experts fell on deaf ears, the suggestions of a gardener would seem ludicrous.

Sighing, he pushed himself out of bed, unwilling to face another day of Sarah's quiet reproach but not seeing any other option.

THE late spring day soon blazed with a heat to rival midsummer, and Michael spent the entire day in the garden, the sun baking his skin as he worked. By the time it was over, he was exhausted but satisfied with his efforts in a way he hadn't been in nearly a month. The grounds were finally starting to look the way he'd imagined, several of the early perennials in full bloom and a dozen varieties of herb and vegetable sprouting merrily in Mary's kitchen garden. From this perspective, the freshly painted house seemed peaceful and serene, a pale jewel in a living, breathing setting.

Eventually he returned to the house, having told Mary early on that he would satisfy himself with leftovers when he came in. Eating at the dinner table with the Abbotts was becoming intolerable to him, especially now that his frustration with the situation was reaching a head. It was all he could do to keep from ripping the tray from Abbott's hands every night, and he did not wish to be tempted today after the best day he'd had in weeks.

When he entered the kitchen just after sunset, he found Sarah and Mary at work at the kitchen table. Sarah was finishing a math lesson in her schoolbook, and both their heads were bent together as Mary murmured soft words of encouragement to her granddaughter.

As he shut the door, Mary looked up and smiled at him. "You look like a cooked lobster," she said, not unkindly. Sarah's gaze rose to his, then fell back to her book. "Supper's in that infernal contraption," she said, pointing to the refrigerator.

"Has he been gone long?" he asked. This was usually the time when Abbott returned from helping Seward prepare for bed.

Mary cast a glance at the door leading to the house, her expression grim. "Long enough," she said. "He should be back any minute."

Michael nodded, then retrieved and set out his own supper. He'd long since broken Mary of the habit of catering to him. She prepared his meals and washed his clothes, he'd told her; when her day was done, she didn't need to drop whatever she was doing to serve him.

Debating with himself for a few seconds, he sat beside Sarah, easing into the chair as smoothly as possible considering all of his joints were creaking like rusty hinges. As he ate his cold pork and potatoes, he watched her write her numbers slowly and carefully, with the painstaking precision of a child.

"Careful there," he warned when she made a small error in her multiplication. Her pencil stopped, hovered over the numbers for a moment; then she reached for the eraser and corrected herself.

"Thank you," she said without looking up from the paper.

"Not at all," Michael said, heart hammering against his ribs. Those were the first words she'd spoken to him in what felt like ages, and he was astonished that it meant so much to him.

Then she peeked up at him shyly, and he realized it wasn't so astonishing. Against his will, the little thing was burrowing into his shriveled heart; he was defenseless against her.

"I burn like that, too," she confided.

"Good thing you weren't out today, then, or your grandmother would have two lobsters for the pot."

This prompted a tiny smile from her, and he felt warmth diffuse through his limbs. The three of them sat companionably for a few minutes, the only sound the soft hum of the refrigerator's compressor and the *scritch-scritch* of Sarah's lead against the paper.

And then a muffled shout pierced the room, bringing Michael to his feet just ahead of Sarah and Mary. They raced for the hall door, Michael reaching it first and yanking it open.

Seward was hobbling toward them at a quicker pace than Michael had ever seen him manage, his expression stricken.

"It's Thomas," he said. "He's collapsed. I couldn't help him."

Behind Michael, Mary gave a soft cry. "Where?" Michael demanded.

"In the library."

Michael picked up his pace, running past Seward. "Is the nearest hospital in Hudson?"

"Yes," Seward shouted back as Michael reached the door.

He found the old man lying slumped in the wing chair near the fire. Kneeling before him, Michael felt for a pulse in the wrist. It was thready and fast, but it was still there.

Behind him, he heard footsteps. Not bothering to look around, he said, "He's alive." Mary whispered a brief prayer of thanks, and Michael loosened Abbott's shirt and removed his tie before lifting his slight body into his arms.

"I'm coming with you," Mary said, and Michael nodded.

"So am I." Michael turned to see Seward propped up against the door frame, chest heaving. Michael's jaw clenched as the rage at Seward's selfishness rose over his head, threatening to drown him. With a great effort of will, he resisted the urge to lash out at him. It would serve nothing, and only waste time Abbott might not have.

"If you aren't there by the time I have the car started, we're leaving without you," Michael said shortly, striding off down the hall with his charge without waiting for a reply.

IT WAS only a handful of miles to Hudson, but it took Michael twenty minutes over rutted dirt roads to reach the hospital. The car was a huge, ungainly beast, and it skidded several times as he took a particularly sharp turn.

Sarah sat with him in the front seat, grim-faced and silent, while Mary and Seward sat in the back with Abbott laid out between them. Michael had considered giving one of them instruction in how to check his pulse, then decided against it. His vital signs were weak enough that they wouldn't be detectible over the vibration of the car's engine, and if his heart stopped on the way, Michael doubted he'd be able to revive him. Their only hope was to reach the hospital in time.

Michael skidded to a stop outside the front doors of the main building, then bundled Abbott out of the car and up the front steps as quickly as he could, Mary and Sarah trailing behind him.

"I need help!" he shouted as he entered. Instead of bringing the hospital staff running, he managed only to startle the steel-haired woman behind the huge oak admitting desk. Her eyes widened, then rapidly narrowed in disapproval.

"Young man, please lower your voice," she said primly, rising to her feet.

"Where's your duty doctor?" he demanded. Shifting Abbott's weight in his arms, he rested the old man's head against his shoulder so that he could detect his breathing. The puff of air against Michael's neck was faint but steady.

"Making rounds on the second floor," she answered. "But wait! You must—"

"Sarah," he called behind him as he started up the wide staircase, "please tell the woman your grandfather's name and address."

The doctor came running at Michael's shout, boot heels clicking on the linoleum. He looked hardly older than Michael himself, blond hair neatly razored over his ears. "Yes? How can I help you?" he asked.

"Show me to an examining room," Michael snapped.

The doctor's deep blue gaze took a swift inventory of Michael's work shirt and dusty trousers. "Now wait a—"

"When you actually get down to work," Michael interrupted smoothly, "you'll find his pulse elevated and thready, breathing weak. It's possibly an embolism, but a mild myocardial infarction is more likely. That is," he added as the doctor's eyes widened, "if he's still breathing by the time you get off your high horse."

The young man's mouth worked for a moment, and then he nodded. "Follow me," he said, turning on his heel.

AFTER two hours that seemed interminable, Michael rose to go looking for the doctor when the doctor came to them, opening the door to the small waiting room and peering in. Mary looked up first, her face revealing nothing, only the tension in her knotted hands giving her away. When the young man did not speak right away, she put a protective arm around Sarah's shoulders, then met his gaze.

"We've done all we can," the doctor said. "He's, ah, resting comfortably, and it—it does appear he may have suffered a myocardial infarction. When he's strong enough, we'll have to perform tests on him to determine the extent of the—ah, damage...."

Michael's jaw twitched convulsively. Obviously, they weren't teaching tact at Columbia medical school this year.

"... and we do intend to monitor his progress throughout the night. Ah, I must also ask, forgive me, but how will you be paying for his care?"

Michael stood. "I'll be the one in his room monitoring his progress," he said. "As for payment, you need to talk to Mister Seward, who came with us."

The young man blinked. "John Seward? Doctor Seward's son?"

"That's right," Mary answered.

"Oh, well," the doctor said, brightening, "that settles things easily. Doctor Seward was Chief Surgeon here for twenty years. None of his relatives will ever pay for services at this hospital."

Michael watched as Mary opened her mouth, then shut it again. "Thank you," she said finally. "When may I see my husband?"

"I don't imagine he'll be awake until the morning. There's no point in your staying, really—"

"We'll stay," Mary said, and there was that same steel in her tone that Michael had come to respect.

"Ah, uh, well, of course, that's your choice," the doctor stammered, backing toward the door. "I'll be going off shift at 6 a.m. I'll introduce you to Doctor Peavey before I leave." And with a final nod, he removed himself from the room.

Mary snorted after the door closed behind him. "He has some growing to do yet." She squeezed Sarah's shoulders and kissed the top of her head. "How are you, my sweetling? Tired yet?" Sarah shook her head. "Well, when you get tired, lay yourself out on the chesterfield over there."

"I'm going to go watch over him," Michael said. "The nurses check him only once every half hour at most." Before he could rise to his feet, Mary's hand on his wrist stopped him.

"Find Johnny first," she said softly. "We haven't seen him since this started."

Michael was still reeling from the fact she'd called Seward "Johnny" when she added, "And don't be harsh with him. It's not his fault."

"How can you say—" Michael began hotly, but a gentle squeeze to his arm silenced him as effectively as a blow.

"You don't know all there is to know," she said simply. "Just—please make sure he's all right. Thomas would want that."

IT DIDN'T take long for Michael to find Seward. Once the battleaxe downstairs had coldly informed him no one fitting Seward's description had entered the hospital since they'd arrived, he'd walked outside and found him sitting on the front steps, elbows resting on his knees, smoking a cigarette. Seward's long-fingered hands were trembling visibly, although the night was warm.

"Mary asked me to find you," Michael said, sitting down beside him.

"You've found me," Seward murmured, taking another drag. "Now go away."

Fury slammed into Michael hard, making him forget Mary's words. "Not even interested in knowing whether you've killed him or not?" he sneered.

To his utter shock, Seward did not answer back as he usually did. Instead he stared at Michael for a moment, then crumpled before his eyes. He buried his head in his hands and drew deep, shuddering breaths. "If you imagine," he gasped brokenly, "that you loathe me more than I loathe myself, you're mistaken. Please, I beg you, leave me alone."

Michael sat frozen for a moment, suspended between new habits and old. The new man would stand up now and do as Seward wished, not out of courtesy or obedience but rather from a lack of interest. The man he had been, however, knew that was not what Seward needed. Finally, he heard his own voice say, as from a distance, "He's not out of danger yet, but chances are he's going to recover."

Seward's hands still covered his face, but at Michael's words he produced a small, soft sound, something dangerously close to a sob.

"Come inside," Michael said gruffly.

Seward lifted his head from his hands, wiping at his cheeks as he did so. "No," he said, shaking his head. "I won't set foot in that place."

Michael sighed. "Suit yourself," he muttered. "But you'll be staying out here all night."

Seward studied the cigarette stub between his fingers, then dropped it on the step and crushed it beneath his left foot. "It's all right," he answered as he reached inside his jacket for another one. "It's not the first time I've done it."

MICHAEL watched Abbott through the night and well into the next morning. He gratefully drank cup after cup of coffee brought to him by the young duty nurse, whose sympathetic green eyes were the exact color of Seward's.

Abbott began to stir around eleven, and Michael rushed down the hall to retrieve Mary and Sarah, who were fairly vibrating with worry and frustration by this time. They allowed Mary in first; she emerged from the room a few minutes later, her cheeks rosy, tears bright in her eyes. She placed an arm around Sarah and tried to lead her inside, but the girl flinched and darted away from her touch.

Mary's face reflected several emotions that came and went too quickly for Michael to identify. Finally she murmured, "All right, we'll wait until you're ready," and smoothed a hand over her granddaughter's hair before motioning for Michael to go inside. "He wants to see you." As puzzled by her words as by Sarah's odd reaction, Michael complied.

Abbott was propped up in the bed, looking weak but much better than he had the night before. He nodded to Michael as he drew nearer.

"Mary says I have you to thank for saving my life," he said shortly.

"I don't know about that," Michael replied. "You're a tough old bastard. It would take more than this to kill you."

Abbott stared at him for a moment, then began to laugh, the sound like dry leaves crackling underfoot. "Well, that much is true," he acknowledged, sobering. "But I still want to thank you." He extended his hand, and Michael took it.

"Is John still outside?" the old man asked softly.

"That's where I left him last night," Michael said shortly.

Abbott narrowed his eyes at him. "Were you in the war?"

"Yes," Michael answered. "I was there."

Abbott appraised him with that piercing gaze for another span of heartbeats before seeming to reach a decision. "I lost my son at the battle of Belleau Wood. I'll never see the ground where they buried him. Sarah's mother died nearly a year to the day after that of the influenza. When Sarah came to us, she woke screaming every night. That was the only time we heard her voice." He turned his head toward the window, the sunlight streaming in and sharpening the lines in his face. "I have worked for the Sewards for thirty years. Mary and I raised John. Frank was a big brother to him. When John was wounded, I...." He trailed off, mouth working in silence for a few moments before he could continue. "I couldn't lose another child. Do you understand?"

"Yes," Michael said again, because dear God, he did, for the first time in weeks he did.

"We thought at first he'd be able to make a full recovery—the doctors had hopes—but something happened to him over there, something no one understood. Everything we did seemed to make things worse, make him retreat further and further inside himself. He cut himself off from Mary because she tried to force him to see reason. After that I feared if I didn't hold my tongue, he might do—something—to himself. It wasn't overwork that did this to me, McCready. It was seeing him every day and knowing how goddamned useless I am to him. He's going to waste away to nothing, and I—"

Without being aware of it, Michael took a step forward and reached up to grip the old man's bony shoulder, stopping him before he became too overwrought. "No," he said firmly. "He's not going to waste away. Leave it to me."

The old man looked up at him with a mixture of disbelief and some small spark of hope, and Michael realized with a rising sense of dread that he was developing a nasty habit of making promises.

As he watched the old man settle into peaceful sleep, however, it occurred to him that he might finally have thought of a way to deliver on them.

"MY BOY, it's very good to see you again."

Michael took the proffered hand and shook it warmly. "Thank you so much for coming, sir."

Doctor Parrish waved away his thanks. "Not at all, not at all. Just between us, I was near desperate to escape the city for a day. And it's so pleasant here, isn't it?" He took in the grounds and smiled that huge, infectious grin that Michael remembered so well, even though it had been months since he'd seen it last. "You've done well with your garden. It's hard work, but it's God's work, isn't it?"

Michael's mouth quirked as he took the doctor's heavy bag from him. Parrish had always been Episcopalian to a fault. "I suppose it is," he conceded, not wanting to get into a theological debate with his old mentor.

Parrish looked at him sidelong as they walked together toward the kitchen entrance. "Well, that's all right, my boy, that's all right. He believes in you." He smiled. "You can't tell me you don't see the hand of fate in your arrival here."

Michael rubbed at the back of his neck. "I definitely see the hand of something," he muttered.

Parrish laughed. "Say what you want, but this man needs you, and not because you can make daisies grow. Whether you like it or not, this is a call to action."

Michael shook his head. "I'm only doing a favor for friends.

When I'm done with this… obligation, I'll be returning to the garden." *Or the bathhouse, if I can manage it. Paddy be damned, I'll probably need it once this is over.*

Parrish was silent for a few moments. "I'm very sorry to hear that," he said softly. "But perhaps working with this young man will change your mind."

Michael barked a sharp, dry laugh. "When you meet him, Doctor," he murmured, "I think you'll see how unlikely that is."

TO SAY Seward was less than thrilled at the sudden appearance of another medical professional in his midst was akin to saying that the Johnstown Flood had been a minor inconvenience. Of course, the fact that Michael had given him no warning of Doctor Parrish's arrival hadn't helped, though he doubted that foreknowledge would have improved Seward's mood a great deal.

Seward looked up from the letter of introduction Doctor Parrish had given him. "Your credentials are most impressive, Doctor, but I'm unsure as to why Doctor Daniels saw fit to send for you. He and his colleagues have already made their prognosis, and I thought the matter was settled."

Parrish glanced at Michael, who remained silent. "As that letter shows, Doctor Daniels and I are acquainted. However, I was not sent by him," Parrish said carefully, "but… asked to consult by another party."

Seward sighed. "My aunt, then. That woman will never learn—"

"Nor was I sent by your aunt." This time Michael could feel the weight of Parrish's gaze on him.

"If my dear aunt didn't send for you, then who did?" Seward demanded, his veneer of civility wearing thin.

"I did," Michael answered.

Seward's astonishment briefly surpassed his anger. "You did?" He snorted. "Unless I'm sorely mistaken, you were hired to prune the rosebushes, not meddle in my personal affairs."

"I can assure you that Michael is well qualified," Parrish said kindly. "He worked under my supervision for a year, and I have every confidence in his skills as a therapist."

"Oh, for God's sake," huffed Seward, glaring at Michael. "Did Aunt Rebecca hire you to insinuate yourself—"

Michael shook his head, his low chuckle startling Seward into silence. "There's no evil conspiracy afoot, Seward. Your aunt doesn't know me as anything but a half-witted Mick gardener. And believe me, she couldn't have tempted me to do this if she'd offered me every last dime of her fortune."

"Then what gives you the right to—"

"Sarah gives me the right," Michael snapped, cutting him off. "She came to me weeks ago asking me to help you, and I promised to do what I could. She cares about you, and now she's worried sick about her grandfather. She doesn't want anyone else she loves to die. Can you blame her?"

Seward said nothing, merely gripped the arms of his chair and stared at the empty hearth. Michael stepped forward and crouched down in front of him.

"Personally," he said, voice low, "I think you're just like the rest of those selfish bastards I treated in England who told themselves it would be fine and noble to slit their wrists or swallow a bottle of pills rather than face the risk that no one would want what was left of them if they came home. You're going to do it more slowly than the rest, but the result will be the same. I'm not sure if that makes you more or less of a coward."

Seward's eyes flashed at that, but Michael held up a hand to forestall him. "That old man is lying in a bed upstairs because he loves you, and because you're the only son he has left, and he doesn't know how to make you want to live. I don't know how to make you want it either, but I know that you care about him, and I know you don't want him to destroy himself over you. But he will, Seward, and right now you're the only one who can prevent that."

Seward shut his eyes and sucked in a jagged breath. "You don't understand," he insisted. "I can't regain my strength. It's not possible."

"That's not strictly true," Doctor Parrish offered gently. "I've read the reports from your doctors. It's clear they've never challenged you the way they should have. You've lost muscle mass, joint range of motion, reflexes—not to mention hope—as a result, but the trend is not irreversible."

"Forgive me, but all doctors are alike as far as I'm concerned," Seward said coolly.

Parrish only chuckled at that. "If only that were true. But while many of us are eager to learn new techniques, many others remain hidebound and reactionary. I know your doctors, and forgive *me*, but they fall into the latter group."

Seward huffed out a breath. "That requires no apology. You're talking about my father's closest friends; I could have told you as much."

"Yes, well, my point is that you haven't yet seen all that medical science has to offer. Homeopathic healing and physical therapy have made great strides in the past several years, and Michael and I have a wealth of experience in both. I'm sure that we can develop a regimen for you that will address your specific needs. I'm willing to work closely with Michael to oversee your progress."

Seward frowned. "Why would you do this?"

Parrish smiled. "Purely selfish reasons, my boy. If I tempt Michael back into medicine, I am assured of a very great reward in heaven."

Michael glanced up at him. "I knew Protestants had to bribe their way past Saint Peter, but I think you'd better try for something more attainable," he murmured.

Parrish laughed. "Well, shall we start?" he said, clapping his hands as though the matter had been settled to everyone's satisfaction. "I'm sure this young man will be happier to see the end of me sooner rather than later."

Michael rose and stepped back as Parrish stepped forward. "Now," the doctor said bracingly, "let's start with something simple. I'd like you to stand for me, please. Use whatever supports you would normally use, and try to keep your motions as natural as possible."

Seward's gaze shifted back and forth between Michael and Parrish as though he were searching for some way to regain control of the situation. Apparently finding none, he set his jaw and reached for his cane.

"There's a good fellow," Parrish said kindly. Michael bit his tongue to keep from smiling. Then he looked up and saw Seward struggle to his feet, swaying a little as he reestablished his balance, his brow furrowed in concentration, his hand white-knuckled on the cane, and all traces of humor left him. Folding his arms, Michael leaned back against the wall and tried to focus on the task ahead.

BY THE time Doctor Parrish had completed his examination, all three of them were exhausted, but Michael could tell the results were significant. Few had been able to resist Parrish's gentle yet firm cajoling, and Seward was no exception. He'd put genuine effort into the tests, attempting everything Parrish had asked of him, even if it had caused him pain.

For there was no doubt now that Seward was in a great deal of pain—more than Michael would have guessed. The retraining of his muscles would be a slow and difficult affair because of it, for like other severely injured men, Seward had developed many largely involuntary reactions to minimize that pain. He favored some muscles over others and in so doing had hastened the atrophy of the disused muscles and tendons, particularly on his more devastated right side. Rehabilitation would not be a short or easy process for any of them.

"If he can commit to his recovery, anything is possible," Parrish said cheerfully as Michael walked him back to his car. "I have to attend a conference Monday, but I should be able to get a plan to you by the middle of next week. In the meantime, you know what to do."

Michael nodded. Massage was the initial key to improving circulation, especially in a patient so weak.

"Just a basic one today, but give him a full treatment tomorrow, and every day thereafter." He cast one more glance around the grounds. "How I wish there were a pool. And you say you can't persuade him to go to the hospital?"

"No," Michael said. "I wouldn't even get him over the threshold."

"That's too bad. They have a fairly decent exercise room in Hudson. Well, I'll make my appeal to his aunt and see what that gets us." At Michael's raised eyebrow, he said, "Daniels owes me a favor. I'll have him introduce me to her as a specialist he's consulting on the case. Perhaps I can convince her to provide you with some equipment. As for you… if you can wire me the bare bones of your curriculum vitae, I'll have my secretary type it and make it presentable."

Michael shook his head. "You're much too conniving to gain admittance to heaven, I think." He handed the doctor's bag to his driver, who stood waiting.

Parrish laughed and patted his arm. "All in a good cause, my boy." Pausing, he added, more earnestly, "You had such a marvelous way with the men. They all missed you terribly when you left, you know." As Michael stood reeling from this, Parrish shook his head. "I am a doddering old fool. Of course you didn't know that." He sighed. "Michael, I hope—well, you know what my hopes are regarding you." He smiled up at Michael with a fondness that brought an unexpected lump to Michael's throat. "I can't tell you how pleased I am to be working with you again."

"I—" Michael began, faltering as the doubts he'd been holding back unexpectedly flooded through him, joined by memories he'd done his damnedest to bury beneath months of selfishness and mindless pleasure.

The breaking point comes without warning.

At the front, it is a gradual thing, a slow realization that a month, two months more of the constant shelling, the cries of the men, the stench of death will send him down the path that so many others have already taken. He is not stupid. He can feel the madness building in him and takes steps to escape as quickly as possible. Surely, he reasons, a change was as good as a rest.

He soon finds out he could not have been more wrong, for at least at the front he can distance himself from each individual man, let his focus blur until they are simply a murky sea of indistinct faces and bodies. Here each man has a name, a story, though not every one has a face. Half of David's was blown off somewhere in Belgium; they are trying to grow him a new one using an experimental treatment that has more in common with the realm of nightmares than medicine. There is a long column of flesh, blood, and skin leading from his shoulder to his rebuilt jaw, a bridge between the living and the dead.

Although he has perhaps the least reason to be so, David is easily the most cheerful of the men under Michael's care, constantly joking and jollying along the others, some of whom have much less cause to be dispirited.

"I think I'm going to be even more handsome than ever," David tells him one day, turning this way and that in front of the hand mirror Michael holds for him, preening like a debutante before her coming-out party. "What do you think?"

And suddenly Michael's chest constricts, stopping his breath, and he knows he cannot force another lie from his throat. He has told so many damned lies over the last year that he is drowning in them, and in the end they have done no good. Either the men survive on their own, or they succumb to despair. He cannot change them, change this, change himself. He rises on trembling legs and staggers away, pursued by David's concerned questions.

Parrish finds him a little while later in the staff lounge, deserted this time of night, where he has curled into a ball on the chesterfield like one of the patients from the mental ward two floors down.

Perhaps he will end up there. It would be fitting, he thinks.

A comforting hand rests on his back and begins a gentle circling motion. It only makes him sob harder. "I'm sorry, my boy," Parrish murmurs. "I should have seen the signs that all was not well with you. Forgive me."

Michael shakes his head but can make no more answer than that. Within two weeks he is bound for New York, his failure a second skin that insulates him from the cold North Atlantic winds.

Michael blinked rapidly and took a deep breath. "Yes," he managed, voice ragged. "Good to be working with you, too, sir."

With a final smile and a paternal squeeze of Michael's arm that his own father had never bestowed on him, Doctor Parrish stepped into his large black sedan and drove away.

MICHAEL trudged back up the stairs, intending to ask Seward when he wanted his supper, only to find the man fast asleep. He lay on top of the quilt, curled on his left side, his dark hair askew and falling over one eye like a mischievous boy's.

Jaw clenched, Michael walked next door and began pouring a hot bath. He searched the linen closets for mineral salts; finding none, he made a mental note to seek some out on the next trip into town. When the tub was filled, he returned to Seward's room and shook him gently.

"Nnnnpphh," Seward said.

"Same to you," Michael replied, shaking him again. "Get up, please."

Seward tried to move an arm and immediately winced. "Leave me to expire in peace."

Michael sighed. "Believe me, I wish I could."

With slow, deliberate care, Seward pushed himself to a sitting position as Michael helped him. "Neither of you really knows anything about medicine, do you? That was just one of your gardening friends helping you play a prank."

Taking hold of Seward's legs, Michael swung him around slowly so that his feet were dangling off the edge. With great care, he slipped an arm around Seward's back and supported him as he stood.

"Where are we going?" Seward demanded as Michael guided him out of the room.

"You're getting a hot bath and a massage." Seward stiffened against him. "You need both, or you'll be in even worse pain tomorrow."

When they reached the bath, Michael propped Seward carefully against the edge of the tub, then reached for the fastening of his robe.

Seward shoved his hand away.

"I can do it," he gritted.

Michael nodded, stepping back cautiously, yet still ready to spring forward if Seward lost his balance. Seward loosened the belt, then hesitated. "Are you going to stand there and stare at me the entire time?"

Michael sighed. "You've just exercised more than you have in months. I'm only here to ensure you don't fall and crack your skull."

Seward remained still. "I don't—" he began, then shook his head, gaze shadowed.

"I can guarantee you I've seen worse," Michael said, with a gentleness he thought he'd forgotten. He'd been present for Parrish's examination, but the doctor hadn't required Seward remove his undershirt or shorts for the tests, and Michael knew from the reports that the worst of the scarring would be over his torso, front and back.

Seward snorted. "Is that supposed to reassure me?" he sniped.

Michael shook his head. "No," he said simply.

Seward held his gaze for another moment, then turned slowly and shrugged out of the robe. When he tried to remove the undershirt, however, he hissed in pain as he tried to raise his arms past his shoulders.

"Here," Michael said when the second attempt ended unsuccessfully. "Bend over while you rest your hands on the edge of the tub. Like this." He stood beside Seward and demonstrated.

Seward opened his mouth as though he were about to protest, then closed it and obeyed. "Slowly," Michael instructed. He could tell the motion was still painful, but at least Seward's arms were no longer fighting gravity. As soon as he was in the position, Michael efficiently pulled the shirt up and over his head and arms, then helped him up.

Michael tried not to let his gaze wander, but as Seward straightened, he couldn't help but see the angry, puckered scars that adorned his chest and belly. The largest one was the surgical scar from his rib operation, but there were others, at least a dozen, probably the calling cards of a shrapnel bomb.

Yes, he'd seen worse; that certainly was no lie. But the implication that he would be indifferent to the evidence of Seward's suffering had been completely false, and Michael had known it from the start. As much as he'd tried to harden himself against Seward, he had never been able to look at a broken body and see only a body, to remain impartial or unaffected. In that respect, he was no more help to Seward than a little chit fresh out of nursing school whose only ambition was to cuddle babies.

Returning to himself after God knew how long, Michael realized that Seward was staring at a place off Michael's left shoulder, his cheeks pink with exertion and embarrassment. Feeling ill at his own unprofessional behavior but trying mightily to keep the reaction from showing on his face lest it be misinterpreted, Michael hastily stepped back, dropping the shirt over the back of a chair. "I'll let you take care of the rest," he murmured.

"Thank you," Seward bit out, sarcasm dripping from his voice. Michael kept his gaze focused on the other man's back as he unbuttoned his shorts and let them drop to the floor, then sat on the edge of the tub and gradually swung his legs over it. The tub itself was one of the more rectangular, modern types with a low, wide rim. Seward had probably had the original model replaced so that he could be more self-sufficient.

Promising to return in half an hour, Michael left the room as quickly as possible, cursing himself soundly as he went. He spent the time pruning the apple tree behind the house while Sarah lopped the heads off the dying day lilies, watching him out of the corner of her eye. It occurred to him that they were both a little too ruthless in their tasks, but he couldn't find it in himself to care.

"Did he tell you to go away?" Sarah asked him as she brushed the dirt from her skirts.

Michael smiled. "More or less," he said.

"You're not going to listen to him, are you?"

"No," Michael answered.

Sarah looked at him through her lashes and smiled tentatively, and the fragile hope in it was nearly his undoing. "Well," he said gruffly, squeezing her small shoulder as they walked toward the house together, "don't worry about it, m'dear. Rome wasn't built in a day."

When Michael returned to the house, Seward was back in bed, the quilt pulled up over his body this time, revealing only his head, neck, and the curve of one bare shoulder as he slept. Sighing, Michael decided to retire from the field for the day, giving them both precious time to regroup. Tomorrow would be soon enough for the next battle.

IN THE morning when Michael went outside to start the car, he found Sarah already busy weeding the vegetable garden.

"You'll dirty your dress," he scolded, because he imagined it was something Abbott would have said.

She shrugged. "I don't mind. The teacher doesn't strap you for that; she only makes you write lines on the board." Tugging another plant free and tossing it on the pile, she said, "School will be over tomorrow. I can weed all the gardens for you, if you like."

He felt unaccountably touched by her offer. "I'd appreciate that. Thank you." The weeding was light work, but it was fiddling and time-consuming. If Sarah took it on, it would give him time to work with Seward each day and probably keep him from going mad trying to juggle both jobs.

Nodding, Sarah stood and brushed the worst of the dirt off her skirts, then removed the gloves and laid them on the pile. They walked together in silence to the car.

AFTER driving Sarah to the school, he stopped in town at the pharmacist's, where he confounded the man with his purchases of mineral salts, Vaseline, cocoa butter, lanolin, saw palmetto extract, and cajeput and sassafras oil. He still remembered the proportions needed for the mixture the physical therapy staff had used at the convalescent hospital to develop muscle tone in recovering patients. There had been some who'd recovered, he reminded himself; not nearly enough, but there had been some. He had to remain focused on that if he was to be of any use at all to Seward and fulfill his promise to the Abbotts.

When he returned to the house, Mary's sour expression told him all he needed to know. "He's in a fine mood," she remarked. "Keep your fingers away from his mouth. He's liable to bite them off."

Michael attempted a smile. "I'll be careful," he murmured as he climbed the stairs with his sack of supplies.

He found Seward at the desk in his bedroom, which sat before the wide windows overlooking the front lawn. Brushing away memories of a moonlit night and the feeling of being watched, Michael stood still and silent in the middle of the room until Seward made an impatient noise and glared up at him.

"Well? What fresh hell do you have planned for me today?"

"A massage," Michael said smoothly. "The one we missed yesterday."

"I've had massages," Seward snapped. "They don't help."

"You haven't had one of mine," Michael answered, forcing his tone to remain light. "This one will be fairly superficial, to begin improving your circulation. We won't go deeper until you're ready."

Seward's jaw clenched convulsively, then relaxed. "All right, then," he muttered. "Let's get it over with." Reaching for the cane propped against the desk, he levered himself to his feet. Recovering quickly from his surprise at the sudden capitulation, Michael moved to the bed and stripped it down to the sheets.

When Seward was seated on the bed, he took off his dressing gown, revealing an Oxford shirt and trousers. He shucked off shoes and socks, then swiftly unbuttoned the shirt; Michael noted he wore nothing underneath this time. Standing again, Seward dealt with the trousers, then stood in his shorts, his green gaze direct and challenging. "Is this sufficient?" he demanded.

"Yes," Michael answered, keeping his eyes level this time. Nodding, Seward sat down again, then made to swing his legs up onto the mattress.

"No, I'd like to start with you in that position, if you can hold it," Michael said, stopping him.

Seward nodded again, and Michael hastened to retrieve the jar of cocoa butter and open it as he sat on the low footstool beside the bed. Scooping out a small amount of the thick stuff with his fingers, he took Seward's left foot in his hand and began to stroke the sole.

Seward twitched when the cool butter touched his skin but relaxed gradually as Michael continued his work along the sides and up toward the ankles. Using nothing more vigorous than strokings and frictions, Michael worked his slow way up to Seward's knees. When he was finally satisfied, he released the left foot and made to grasp the right.

Not surprisingly, Seward flinched at the first gentle pressure on his damaged foot. "It's all right," Michael said, easing his grip even further. "I know. Just let me know if I'm hurting you."

"You'll be the first to hear," Seward drawled, but that was the last time he gave any indication that Michael was causing him pain. Watching Seward's stoic face from time to time as he worked, Michael saw the square jaw set against any betrayal of discomfort.

Returning his attention to his task, he kneaded Seward's calf gently but firmly, finding evidence of numerous fibroses between the weakened muscles. Employing the tips of his fingers, he palpated them with care. It would take time and a variety of treatments to reverse the damage. Luckily, he had confidence in Doctor Parrish's powers of persuasion. If anyone could convince that old bat to spend her money on a noble cause, it would be his former mentor.

By the time he'd finished his work on Seward's lower legs, he noticed the other man was trembling visibly in an effort to hold his torso upright. Standing, he said, "Prone position now, please." He helped Seward roll onto his stomach, then began working on the backs of his thighs, encouraging the circulation of blood with wide, circular motions of his palms.

He debated about asking Seward for permission to work on the gluteal muscles; all of the muscle groups involved in locomotion required attention, but Michael finally decided against it, at least until his patient was more comfortable with him. Seward was humiliated enough already by this degree of exposure. There was no sense in pushing him past his low tolerance level and risking sabotaging their program—and Michael's promise. He would fight only the battles he had a chance of winning.

Instead, he began long, sweeping strokes up Seward's back, pausing now and then to rub and gently knead the muscles. When he came across a scar, he stretched the skin carefully and circled the puckered flesh with his fingertips, finishing off with soft strokings. As he proceeded, he was relieved to find himself falling into a familiar rhythm, one that he knew well from nearly a decade of work as a rubber. He began to believe he could do this. He could maintain his distance and do the job.

Seward had been silent since Michael had started on his back. Curious, Michael leaned over him and found that his eyes were closed.

"Hey. Time to turn over," Michael said softly.

Seward started, then pushed weakly at the mattress in an attempt to roll himself over. With help from Michael, he was soon on his back staring up at the ceiling.

"How are you feeling?"

"Fine," Seward gritted, his face an unreadable mask. "Get on with it."

Biting back a retort, Michael wrapped one hand around Seward's wrist and raised his arm carefully, then began stroking his forearm with the other hand.

Well, there was one benefit to treating a man like Seward, he thought wryly: at least he wouldn't be required to polish his rusty bedside manner.

THEY continued on in that fashion for nearly a week, and soon Michael's days began to assume a regular pattern. He'd rise early and work with Sarah in the garden for the morning. After lunch came Seward's massage, with a bath every other day to further encourage the restoration of his circulation. When Michael was done torturing them both, he'd check in on Abbott and help him with the exercises that his doctor had prescribed to assist in his recovery. The old man was on his feet now, but he was still weeks away from resuming even a portion of his former duties.

Throughout it all, Seward remained completely aloof. He surrendered his body to Michael's ministrations readily enough, but every time Michael placed his hands on Seward's skin, he could feel the tension that Seward stored in every joint and muscle and tendon. Worse, as the days wore on, Michael began to understand that Seward's acquiescence was nothing but a sham. He was no more active a participant in his own recovery than he had ever been, and perhaps less so. Michael didn't have the first idea of how to deal with this passive resistance. He only knew that every day, his frustration at seeing Seward's pliant body laid out before him was swiftly increasing.

Saturday morning dawned clear and warm, and Michael decided it was time to risk introducing another facet of Seward's treatment. After breakfast, he intercepted Mary before she could take Seward his meal. She looked on him with pathetic gratitude as he plucked the tray from her hands.

When he arrived at the bedroom door, he found Seward already dressed and seated at his desk. He scowled when he spied Michael in the doorway.

"What's wrong with Mary?" he barked in lieu of a greeting.

"Nothing," Michael said pleasantly, striding forward and placing the tray on the desk.

"Then—and I'm certain I'm going to be sorry for asking this—why are you here?"

Straightening, Michael said matter-of-factly, "It's going to be a beautiful day, and I think it's time you began taking some sun."

Seward stared at him, clearly nonplussed. After a moment, Michael elaborated. "It's called heliotherapy, and it's an important part of your rehabilitation. The healing properties of the sun's light and warmth are well documented."

Seward pursed his lips. "I don't see the point of it."

Michael sighed inwardly. He might have known Seward wouldn't make it easy for him. "The only substitute for natural sunlight is ultraviolet treatments."

"I know," Seward growled. "They stuffed me into one of those damned light cabinets every day at the hospital in England for weeks. Idiots gave me blisters over half my body before they decided it wasn't working."

Michael shook his head. That went a long way to explaining why Seward was fed up with the medical profession. There was a reason why the wounded men had called them "ultraviolent treatments." "Doctor Parrish had all the ultraviolet machines thrown out of our convalescent hospital. He insisted the men spend time outside in fine weather and had a glass atrium built for the winter months." He spread his hands. "Listen, we don't know all of the reasons why it works, only that it does. It speeds up the healing process and improves health in a general sense." Exposure to sunlight had also been proven to improve the mood of recalcitrant patients, though of course Michael kept this to himself. "I'm only asking you to give it a try for a few days. You can sit and relax while I work, and I'll take you back inside after an hour or two. If you don't see an improvement by the end of the week, you can discontinue it."

Seward glared at him for another few moments, then huffed out a breath. "All right. Come back in half an hour and I'll be ready."

Michael nodded and left swiftly, the taste of even this small victory unexpectedly sweet.

THE warm day drew everyone outside. As soon as she had finished her indoor chores, Sarah came out to help Michael with the weeding. Mary emerged a short time later, her sleeves rolled up and a heavy apron covering her skirt.

"I don't see why you young folks should be the only ones to have fun getting dirty," she said, and set to weeding and watering her kitchen garden. When she was done, Michael watched her gaze upon her small plot of earth and smile a quiet, private smile. It had never been in his nature to become attached to a particular place, for he had never had so much as a patch of weeds to call his own. However, it was clear that it meant a great deal to her, and for that reason he was pleased and strangely humbled by her obvious pride.

To his surprise, Abbott hobbled his way out of the house around ten, his steps slow but surer than they had been a week ago. Michael jogged over to help him, but Abbott waved him off. "I'm not at death's door," the old man grumbled without rancor. "Just let me take my time."

Sarah came bounding up to him, her cheeks dirty and her dress grass-stained. She waited patiently until Abbott took her hand and smiled down at her. "Come along, child," he said, "let's you and I pay a visit to Mister Seward."

Michael watched as the two slowly made their way across the lawn to the terrace, then began to mount the steps. Seward had spotted them by now and was on his feet. He limped over to meet them, his face grave.

Michael went back to work, deliberately choosing a bed far from the house so that he could not eavesdrop unintentionally, though his curiosity soon got the better of him and he was tempted to take a look. What he saw confused him. Seward was heading back toward the house, his back stiff, his entire body a taut bow. Abbott was still holding on to his granddaughter's hand, his own back ramrod straight, his eyes flashing with something Michael couldn't identify from this distance.

Deciding that discretion was vastly overrated, he walked up to the house and met Abbott and Sarah descending the stairs. "What's the matter?" he demanded as the glass doors closed behind Seward. The bastard had promised Michael an hour or two; he'd lasted precisely fifteen minutes.

Abbott shook his head once, jaw tight. "What else? He still blames himself for what happened to me," he said.

That would explain why Seward hadn't been to see Abbott since the old man had been released from the hospital. "What did you say to him?"

Abbott hesitated, then said, "I told him it was my fault, not his."

Michael rolled his eyes. "Now I know where he gets it," he

muttered, jogging up the flagstone steps and following Seward into the house.

He found him, predictably, in the library, where Seward had just finished pouring himself a bourbon. Before he could think about what he was doing, Michael strode forward and plucked the glass from his hand.

"You—" Seward began, indignation flaring in his eyes.

"You'll never recover if you keep trying to pickle yourself," Michael told him shortly. "And you'll kill yourself too slowly for it to be of any use to the rest of us, so I'll be confiscating these for the duration of our time together."

Michael had the satisfaction of bringing Seward up short. He stiffened, then leaned back in his chair. "You're—what?"

"You heard me," Michael said, snatching up the bottle before Seward could reach for it. "Consider me your own personal Temperance movement." He indicated the box on Seward's table. "The same goes for those cigarettes."

Seward's eyes grew round. "I have these imported from France," he protested, as if that fact would spare them.

Michael only snorted. "No wonder they smell like shit. Hand them over."

"Your hands are full," Seward sneered.

Michael raised the glass to his lips and gulped down the contents. Dropping the empty tumbler on the table, he picked up the cigarette box. "Not anymore."

The look that Seward turned on him then was pure, untrammeled hatred. Michael only smiled benignly. "I'll see you this afternoon," he said, saluting jauntily by raising the bottle to his temple before heading for the door.

"I'll see you in hell first," Seward shouted.

"Why not?" Michael fired back over his shoulder. "I hear it's only a short walk from this bloody place."

IF MICHAEL had been a religious man, he would have seen the arrival of Doctor Parrish's letter scarcely an hour later as the hand of Fate intervening on his behalf. As it was, he merely took the fat envelope and signed for it, ignoring the frankly speculative leer of the excessively pretty boy who delivered it.

Parrish's letter was attached to a detailed therapy plan for building Seward's strength and endurance, particularly in his atrophied right limbs. Even though he was intimately familiar with the doctor's work, Michael couldn't help but be impressed by the thorough and aggressive course of treatment. It was as though he'd sensed Michael's mood as well as Seward's physical tolerance and developed the plan accordingly.

> *My colleagues would no doubt blanch at the shortened timetable for this patient, but I believe that if Seward does not see results—and quickly— he will abandon the treatment.*

Michael snorted; truer words had never been expressed.

> *For that reason, I also met with Mrs. Anderson this past Tuesday. A truly formidable woman. She was surprised when I vouched for your skills as a therapist, of course, since she only knows you as a gardener. However, by the time I was done listing your many virtues and accomplishments, she had quite fallen under your spell.*

Michael laughed aloud at that, earning a strange look from Mary. The idea that Seward's aunt could fall under anyone's spell was ludicrous. If anyone could bewitch her, however, it would be Parrish.

> *I impressed upon her the importance of gymnastic equipment to her nephew's recovery, and she*

willingly agreed once the benefits were explained to her. I believe she has her own reasons for wishing the boy hale and hearty, but as we are all working toward the same goal, I feel we need not delve too deeply into any of our motivations.

At any rate, I had already ordered most of the equipment before our meeting (I was, shall we say, confident of a positive result), and so it will be delivered to you on Monday morning. I have enclosed a sample floor plan based on a twenty-by-fifteen-foot room, but you of course may have to adjust for the dimensions. You know what to look for; it should be a well-lit space, preferably with southern exposure. As he is the only one inhabiting that cavernous house, I would imagine there must be a suitable room that could be converted.

I should be up for a visit in about a month's time, unless you call for me sooner. I have absolute faith in your ability to implement my instructions. Feel free to adapt them where you see fit to suit the situation. Until then, all my best.

Michael folded the letter carefully and tucked it in his pocket, then spread the plan out before him and studied it. After a few moments, he felt Sarah come up behind him to stand at his shoulder.

"What's that?"

"A plan for our new gymnasium," he told her. "Here are the mats, and here are the parallel bars—those are bars about so high"—he placed a hand on top of her head—"that help you walk." He pointed at the diagram again. "And here's the shoulder wheel and the wrist rollers and the finger board. And you'll see what all of those are on Monday."

"Where are you going to put it all?" she asked, and Michael smiled, enjoying her open curiosity.

"I think I know just the spot. Would you like to come see it?" She nodded eagerly. "Good." He rose to his feet, and she followed him.

From the moment Parrish had suggested the construction of a gymnasium, Michael had known that the room in which he'd first met Seward was perfect for their purpose. It once had been a ballroom of some sort but was now host only to a few dusty chairs and settees and the easels and painting supplies Michael had seen Seward and Sarah use. Huge glass doors and windows stretched from floor to ceiling, flooding the room with light.

"I don't think he'll like it if we use this room," Sarah said uneasily. "This is where he paints."

Michael inspected the artwork more closely. "I don't think he's done much painting since the last time you were here with him," he said. "There should still be room for the easels over in one corner. And with the weather improving, I'm sure he'll want to work outside." Sarah looked at him skeptically but said nothing. Michael jerked his head. "Let's get this furniture moved out, hm?" he said cheerfully, and she nodded and moved to obey.

He was backing his way through the ballroom door, the two of them carrying one of the settees between them, when Sarah's eyes widened. He craned his neck and saw Seward standing directly behind him, his face livid.

"Would you mind telling me what you're doing?" Seward demanded, voice tight.

Michael nodded at Sarah, and together they lowered the settee carefully to the floor. "I received a letter from Doctor Parrish. There's a room full of exercise equipment on order in New York, and it should be here on Monday."

"And you need this room, of all the rooms in this house?"

Michael nodded. "It's the best choice."

Seward's gaze flickered from Michael to Sarah and back. "May I speak with you in the library, please?"

"Certainly," Michael said, following Seward as he limped down the hall. The limp did seem a little less pronounced, he noted with some satisfaction. However, as soon as he stepped inside the library and shut the door, that feeling quickly evaporated.

"I'm not going to waste time explaining this to you," Seward growled, "so I'll get it over with quickly. I will no longer be requiring your services."

While Michael hadn't exactly seen that coming, he wasn't shocked by it. Folding his arms, he said, "My services aren't subject to your whims, Seward. I work for your aunt."

"As a gardener!" Seward snapped. "I'm sure she has no notion you've completely switched professions to—"

Drawing Parrish's letter from his pocket, Michael found the appropriate section, then handed it to Seward. "Fifth paragraph," he said brightly.

Scowling, Seward scanned the letter. Michael could tell the exact instant he read the relevant passage, because his expression cycled through shock to fury to defeat and back to fury. He raised his eyes to Michael. "You're brighter than I gave you credit for," he snarled.

"Thank you," Michael said, smiling. "You're a much bigger pain in the ass than I gave you credit for."

Seward flushed. "This is a new form of therapy," he said hotly. "Insulting the patient—"

"Let's get one thing clear," Michael interrupted. "You're not my patient, and I'm not a therapist any longer. I'm doing this because I care about those people, and they care about you, for some unfathomable reason. They've drowned you in kindness and compassion, and that's gotten all of you precisely nowhere. Well, if you don't want kindness and compassion, that's fine, because the truth is, I'm fresh out of both. I'm perfectly happy to peel off the gentleman's gloves and go bare-knuckles with you; it's much more honest. And at least if you're fighting me, you'll get some exercise out of it."

Seward stared at him. "You're mad."

Michael bared his teeth. "Then I'm in good company." He walked to the door, turning as he reached for the knob. "I'll be back later for your bath and massage. Three o'clock sharp. Be ready or I'll strip you and throw you in the damned tub myself."

When he returned to the ballroom, he found Sarah perched on the settee. She rose to her feet when she saw him approach and looked up at him with wide, apprehensive eyes.

Michael winked at her. "Still lots of work to do," he said as he picked up his end of the settee, "but we're getting there."

Sarah hesitated for a moment, then leaped over to the opposite arm and hoisted it as high as she could. Michael grinned, pleased to have at least one staunch ally at his side.

THE truck loaded with the promised equipment arrived at noon on Monday, and Michael spent the rest of the day securing the finger ladder, shoulder wheel, and stall bars to the wall, setting up the pulleys and weights, and affixing the metal supports for the parallel bars to the floor. He doubted Seward's aunt had envisioned the conversion of her country estate's ballroom to a gymnasium, but he couldn't muster up any sympathy for her plight.

Seward grumbled all the way down to the gymnasium the next day, though he did seem slightly surprised at the extent of the transformation and the variety of equipment. Michael introduced him to each machine and activity over the next couple of days, then swiftly started him on a routine that addressed the weaknesses in his atrophied muscles without overtaxing them.

Seward's attitude had taken an about-face. Where before their argument he had been quiet to the point of stoicism, now he complained at every possible opportunity. Michael much preferred this new attitude, because silence told him nothing, and he quickly learned to distinguish when Seward was honestly in pain as opposed to merely enjoying the sound of his own rebellion. He matched him insult for insult, pushed him and prodded him, and Seward responded, shoving back with all his might. As the days rolled into weeks, the strength of that shove grew by leaps and bounds.

"All right, try it again."

Sweating profusely and sprawled on the mat where he'd fallen,

Seward lifted his head and glared at him. "You must be joking."

Michael smiled and squatted down in front of him. "Come now. You know me better than that."

Groaning, Seward rolled to his side and pushed himself to a sitting position. He began to rise, transferring his weight to his left hip and leg.

"How many times do I have to tell you? Use your right side, your right!" Michael lunged forward and slapped Seward on his right hip. "This side."

"I know my right from my left, thank you," Seward gritted.

"You don't act like it," Michael shot back. "Get up properly."

Seward's expression would have burned poor little Nurse Emma to ash. Michael only glared back until the other man looked away and shifted his weight onto his other hip. Michael's feeling of triumph was tempered by the flash of genuine pain that swept across Seward's features when he taxed his weaker side as Michael had insisted. The thought that he was demanding too much of Seward nagged at him for the hundredth time since they had started, but he pushed it away. Although he knew it defied everything he'd ever been taught, it was better to risk pushing him too far than not far enough. Parrish was right; if Seward didn't begin to see concrete results, he would give up completely, and Michael would be unable to fulfill his promise.

"That's enough for today," he said, purposefully keeping his voice harsh. "Time for your rubdown."

Seward said nothing, but the slight sag in his shoulders told Michael everything he needed to know. He had reached his limit for the day, and once again Michael had shoved at him until he was leaning over the precipice. His hands itching to offer support, he allowed Seward to walk out of the gymnasium ahead of him while he automatically catalogued the minute but visible improvements to his gait. Those observations would later be recorded in the journal he was keeping for the purpose of chronicling Seward's therapy, but for now he only found himself savoring the small yet astonishing feeling of satisfaction it gave him.

Michael remained in the gymnasium, straightening up equipment that didn't require straightening, until he was certain Seward would be ready for him. When he entered the bedroom, however, Seward was just removing the last of his clothing. Even though he'd seen Seward's naked body a dozen times by now, there was an intimacy to walking in on him when he was unprepared, as if by crossing the threshold he'd overstepped the bounds of their fragile working relationship.

Evidently Seward felt it as well, for he turned and stared at Michael, his face and upper torso flushing with embarrassment, his expression strangely vulnerable. Recovering swiftly, he turned his back to Michael and reached for a towel, hastily wrapping it around himself. They came together in silence, Seward moving stiffly to lie facedown on the bed, Michael pulling up the stool and reaching for the jar of lotion, feeling the greasy stuff coat his palms and cool his fingers.

He started in with gentle strokings, but even after progressing to a deeper massage, Seward's muscles were still knotted and unyielding. When he felt the frustration begin to dictate the movement of his hands, he stopped immediately. Otherwise he would risk doing Seward an injury.

"Why are you stopping?" Seward demanded.

"Because you're supposed to work with me, not against me," Michael snapped.

"I don't know what you're talking about," Seward shot back. "I've been doing everything you ask me to. You have no reason to complain."

Michael closed his eyes and counted to ten. This state of undeclared war was getting them nowhere. At some point they had to acknowledge the need for honesty between them, even if neither of them truly wanted it. Now, Michael realized, was as good a time as any. "Look," he sighed, "I can tell you're tensing. You have to let go."

"I'm fine," Seward hissed, forehead resting on his arms. "Just do your job."

Michael's fingers dug into the flesh of Seward's shoulders; the muscles jumped and twitched under the skin. "I can't do my job if you're going to fight me like this." Using his palms this time, he began a more soothing effleurage over the same area. "Relax."

Seward's body shuddered briefly, muscles fluttering under his hands before they tightened again. Michael redoubled his efforts, stroking lightly down his back on either side of his spine. "Relax," he repeated, more of a request than a command this time.

"I…," Seward began, and Michael leaned closer.

"Yes?"

But Seward only shook his head and tensed once more. Debating with himself for a moment, Michael slid his hands to Seward's sides, his touch now feather-light.

The tremors came suddenly, beginning in Seward's legs and spreading like wildfire until they seemed near to consuming him. Horrified, Michael hastily removed his hands, but when the shuddering only grew worse, he spread them over as much of Seward's back as he could. Seward buried his head in his arms and drew in a deep, shuddering breath that turned into a sob on the exhale.

Acting on instinct, Michael bridged the distance between them and draped himself over Seward's back, whispering his apologies into Seward's skin. His hands moved constantly, trying to impart some of his own strength despite feeling weaker than a baby himself, shaken and bereft.

After a time that might have been minutes or hours for all Michael knew, Seward shifted under him and groaned. Realizing the tremors had stopped, Michael pushed himself off Seward's sweating back. Neither of them spoke for some time.

"Was that what you wanted?" Seward demanded, though there was more exhaustion than heat in it.

Michael rested his hands on Seward's shoulders for a moment before withdrawing completely. "No," he answered softly. "I'm sorry."

"Don't be," Seward murmured. "You were right." He shifted, turning his head toward the wall. "I've been in pain for so long, I don't know how to let go of it."

Michael felt his heart lurch in his chest at the unexpected confession. "I think perhaps you just did," he said, the words thick in his throat.

"I hope so," Seward murmured, closing his eyes. "God, I hope so."

Michael had no idea how long he stood there, gaze fixed on the sweep of Seward's eyelashes and the dark crescents below them, before he registered that the other man was fast asleep. He did not even consider waking him for the rest of his massage; instead, he drew the curtains, covered Seward with a light blanket, and let himself out of the bedroom as quietly as possible.

THE next day was beautiful, warm and sunny, and Michael spent far too much of the morning in the garden. The time for Seward's exercises came and went, and still he worked, willfully ignoring the voice that called him a coward.

He'd been so certain for a while that he could maintain the distance established by mutual agreement, assuming that the part of himself he'd buried, that eager young idiot determined to save the world, wouldn't rise from the dead. He couldn't have been more wrong. Worse, his original assumptions about Seward were crumbling before his eyes. He had no idea what he would see when the dust settled, but he had a suspicion he wouldn't like it. Or perhaps he would like it too damned well for his own good.

He was still mired in indecision and frustration, unable to force himself to go into the house, when Seward—in yet another extraordinary move—came to him.

Sarah emerged from the house first, opening one of the mullioned glass gymnasium doors and waddling out with one of the easels clutched in her hands. It was taller than she was and unwieldy, but she managed to get it outside without breaking anything and unfolded it carefully on the terrace before bolting back inside to fetch the other one. When she had them both set up, she brought out two blank canvases and propped them up so that the artists could face the garden.

Seward emerged from the house with the painting supplies. Michael couldn't help but notice that his limp seemed a good bit less pronounced than it had the last time he'd seen Seward set foot on that terrace. The other man handed the girl one of the palettes, then surveyed the lawn with his deep, watchful gaze.

When it settled on Michael, he felt the weight of it like a blow. He met and matched it, then looked away, unwilling to see even the slightest measure of disappointment or reproach. He reminded himself he didn't give a damn about Seward's opinion, but that didn't seem to help.

When he looked up again, Seward's eyes were trained on the canvas. As he watched, Seward lifted his hand and made a firm, broad stroke across the pristine surface.

Shivering from a sudden chill in the air, Michael turned back to his work, uprooting weed after weed, inadvertently digging up three marigolds in his haste to finish.

THAT night a fierce thunderstorm swept overhead, hail pelting the roof above Michael's head like fistfuls of rocks hurled by an angry giant. When Michael awoke in the morning, his worst fears were confirmed when he saw half of the plants he'd nurtured lying ground into the dirt where they had once lifted their eager heads to the sun.

He spent most of the morning in the garden, uprooting the dead flowers and flinging them into a wheelbarrow. The ground was soggy enough from the storm that various parts of him were liberally coated in mud after an hour. The smell of the living earth filled his nostrils as he worked.

He was nearly finished when he looked up to see Sarah and Seward crossing the lawn. Sarah's hand was engulfed by his large one as they walked slowly but steadily toward him. Wiping off his hands, Michael met them halfway, beside the ruins of one of the annual beds. "I was about to come in," he said, more testily than he'd intended.

"I wanted to see the garden," Sarah said, looking up at Michael. "And Mister Seward said he would come with me." Her head turned slowly, taking in the devastation as she clutched Seward's hand. "Oh. It's bad, isn't it?"

Silently berating himself for not considering her feelings, Michael hunched down in front of her. "It's not so bad. The older flowers are mostly fine, and your roses are still in good shape. And we can put the seeds right in the ground this time. We should have flowers again before the end of the summer, if we're lucky."

"Can I help you plant them?" Sarah asked shyly.

"Of course you can," Michael said. "I'm counting on you. In fact, I wondered if you could fetch the seeds from the greenhouse. We'll see what we've got left, and you can tell me where you'd like the flowers to go. And while you're at it, check and see if any of your grandmother's lettuce seeds are still there."

Eyes widening, Sarah nodded and released Seward's hand, then took off across the lawn as fast as her legs would carry her. Seward watched her go with what could only be called a wistful expression.

"She came to me when she was too afraid to go outside by herself," he murmured.

"I'm sorry," Michael said, bringing Seward's attention back to him. "I didn't think of what it would do to her. She's worked hard on this garden."

Seward's gaze shifted to the garden. "It's a shame this has to be taken from her, too."

Michael frowned. "The garden can be restored," he murmured. "Good as new."

Seward said nothing, merely turned around and began hobbling back toward the house. Michael noticed he seemed to be relying on the cane less for support than for reassurance.

"Have you tried walking unassisted on uneven ground?" Michael asked softly. They had tried having Seward walk without support a couple of times on the smooth floor of the gymnasium, but never outdoors.

Seward turned back and stared at him. "No."

Michael walked up to him and held out a hand.

Hesitating, Seward regarded his cane, then Michael. Sighing, he thrust the walking stick into Michael's outstretched palm.

"Try it," Michael urged gently. "Only to the terrace steps." The distance was no more than a hundred feet; it would be challenging but not impossible.

Seward started slowly, watching his feet take each step, obviously nervous about his balance. "Don't think about it," Michael called. "Just let your muscles compensate."

"Easy for you to say," Seward shot back, though Michael saw his posture relax somewhat. He jogged to catch up with Seward, then walked a few paces behind him.

Seward was about ten feet from the steps when he stumbled, his right ankle turning traitor and giving way as he tried to lift his foot. Michael watched as Seward's toes dragged against the ground and his body pitched forward. Although Michael was not able to catch him, he was on his knees a moment later, hands closing around Seward's arms and helping him to rise. "I'm sorry, it was too much to ask of you," Michael murmured, savagely angry with himself. He'd allowed his own selfish need to win over his best judgment, and he'd distanced himself from Seward. Now the man under his care had suffered for it.

And then Seward's head jerked up suddenly, nostrils flaring as he inhaled a sharp breath. His eyes grew wide and wild, and Michael's grip on his arms tightened.

"Are you hurt?" he asked, looking over Seward's body for some sign of injury.

Seward shook his head mutely and twisted, breaking Michael's hold on him.

It was then that Michael realized he'd forgotten to take off his gloves. There were dark brown rings on the arms of Seward's white shirt where his hands had been, and Seward was staring at them with something akin to horror.

"Damn it," Michael muttered, stripping off his gloves and reaching up to wipe at the mud with the sleeve of his own shirt.

"No!" Seward shouted, shoving himself backward, out of Michael's reach. He scrabbled backward on his hands, crablike, heels digging into the wet grass as he tried to escape.

Heart hammering, Michael held up his hands in what he hoped

was a placating gesture and leaned away from Seward, trying to prove he was no threat. He hadn't the faintest idea what the hell was going on, but he'd seen enough shell-shock victims to realize Seward was in the middle of an attack. The other man's face had gone as pale as his shirt, and he was panting as though he had been running for miles. Once he was flat on his ass, he raised his trembling arms and stared at the mud, then began brushing futilely at the stains. A low, desperate sound emerged from his throat, twisting Michael's heart.

It sounded like the cry of a dying man.

Michael tried to help, but whenever he attempted to get closer, Seward would grow even more agitated and distressed. It was clear that he was locked inside some terrible, vivid memory, but he retained enough of an awareness of the outside world that he could react to it. Unfortunately, it was the reaction of an unreasoning animal rather than a thinking man.

Michael sat there helpless for another few moments, trying to think of an approach that might get through to Seward, when Sarah came running up to them. Before he could warn her off, she stopped a few feet from Seward and dropped to her knees, crawling slowly toward him.

"Sarah…," Michael began, but the girl only shook her head and kept crawling.

"It's happened before," Sarah said, tone confident. "I know what to do."

Michael tensed as Sarah approached Seward's violently shaking body. She knelt beside him and leaned forward, speaking in his ear so softly that it could not be heard over the sound of Seward's keening.

After a few tense seconds, Seward subsided abruptly into silence, and Sarah's voice finally drifted to Michael's ears.

She was singing. The haunting old song was strangely sweet and pure when delivered in her small clear voice, and she sang it with the confidence of long familiarity. Michael wondered if Mary had sung it to both of them at one time or another:

I'll sell my flax, I'll sell my wheel,
Buy my love a sword of steel,
So it in battle he may wield,
Johnny has gone for a soldier.

When he had calmed sufficiently, her small hands pried Seward's free from his own arms, then stroked his hair back from his face with the tenderness of a mother for her child. Seward drew in a ragged, gulping breath, and Michael could see the tracks of tears etched into his cheeks. When she stood, the fingers of both hands wrapping around one of Seward's wrists, Michael scrambled to his feet to help them, his own eyes stinging.

PARRISH arrived on schedule a few days later for Seward's one-month checkup. Michael banished himself from the examination, citing pressing work in the garden, though it was a bald-faced lie. He and Sarah had already done the replanting. All that remained for now was to sit back and watch it grow.

The lunch hour came and went, and still Parrish did not emerge. Michael was ready to chew off his own leg by the time he'd drunk the last of his coffee.

As though she sensed his need for distraction, Sarah turned to him when they were finished with the dishes and took his hand, looking up at him with patient, solemn eyes until he relented and followed her.

She led him, strangely, to his own room. When he opened his mouth to ask a question, she darted inside and ran to the locked door at the far end that he had guessed opened onto the rest of the attic. Kicking off her shoes, she indicated with a pointed look that he should do the same. He obeyed, still puzzled.

Reaching into her pocket, she produced a small key and used it; the door creaked on its hinges, and then she was beckoning him to follow her. He suspected that she had acquired the key through less than honest means, but he wasn't inclined to question her about it.

The attic was predictably dusty and dark, not to mention hot from the June sun beating against the roof. Unlike Michael's room, this space was completely windowless. Sarah flicked a switch, and the darkness was banished by the yellow light of a half dozen bare Mazda lamps attached at regular intervals to the roof beams. There were steamer trunks from the more sedate European adventures of a previous century and old wooden chairs with the seats torn or the legs broken. For the most part, the attic was littered with the relics from a lost childhood, though Michael noted absently that the hobbyhorse's mane was carefully groomed and the seat was free of dust, and over in one corner a set of tin soldiers stretched in a neat line, saluting at nothing.

Sarah continued until they had almost reached the far end of the house, passing another set of stairs that doubtless led to the bedrooms below. His thoughts strayed to Parrish and Seward and the examination that was still going on. He was both desperate to know the results and afraid of the verdict, like a prisoner waiting in the dock for his sentence.

He and Seward had not spoken of the incident in the garden. In fact, over the past few days, they had hardly spoken at all. Their sessions together had been productive but mechanical affairs, like recitations of the multiplication tables by talented schoolchildren, and Michael had grown more restless and impatient with the polite silence that hung between them.

As much as he hated to admit it even to himself, he could no longer deny that he was curious about Seward. He wanted to understand the nature of the horrors he had endured. He wanted to know how he could look on Sarah with such warmth one moment and snap like a dry twig the next. He wanted to know far more about Seward than Seward was ever likely to tell him, and for that reason and a hundred others, he knew it would be best to stifle his newfound interest as quickly as possible.

"Here they are!" Sarah exclaimed with hushed delight, smiling as she flung herself on the floor without regard to the layer of dust and began flipping through a stack of oil paintings leaning on their edges against the wall.

"Look at this one," she instructed, lifting one of the smaller paintings, and Michael reached to pluck it from her hands. He could tell it was one of Seward's pieces from the signature, but apart from that it bore virtually no resemblance to the dark, brooding work that had been all he'd seen of Seward's art until now.

"That's my grandfather," Sarah said, unnecessarily, because the resemblance was clear and striking. Abbott's features were faithfully rendered in oils, but there was more to the work than that, for Michael could feel the presence of the old man in the direct, unflinching gaze staring back at him from the portrait. Sadly, he also felt the presence of a much younger man, not so much in years but in burdens. The painting must have been executed several years ago, before the losses and worries that had done their best to crush him.

Sarah handed him another painting, then another, each one more accomplished than the last. Seward's strength was portraiture, though there were also fine examples of still lifes and landscapes, obviously inspired by local scenery. He had rendered a few scenes of New York City as well. Michael was startled to recognize familiar streets in the Bowery and the Lower East Side, particularly the garment district. There was a series of portraits of young women, presumably some of the garment workers, dressed in shawls and long dresses, dark eyes huge in faces that were old before their time. Somehow Seward had managed to avoid condescension or melodrama in the tone of these works, infusing his subjects with a dignity and power he wouldn't have believed a rich man would be able to see in such faces, let alone convey.

"There are more over here," Sarah said, running over to another grouping a few feet away. Reluctantly drawn in by Sarah's enthusiasm and the striking artwork, Michael moved to get a better look at this batch.

These paintings were all portraits of one particular subject, and Michael presumed that was the reason they'd been stored separately. They depicted a handsome young man with blond hair and blue eyes who seemed strangely familiar to him. He was no more attractive than any of a hundred men Michael had known, but he was extraordinary in that the painter obviously saw him as some sort of ideal, the way Pygmalion had placed his Galatea on a pedestal. There was an aloof air to the subject, as though he had not been a man but a marble statue, untouchable and perfect. Looking at him made Michael strangely, inexplicably angry.

"I wish I knew who he was," Sarah said quietly, her gaze fixed on one of the paintings.

"His brother?" Michael offered.

Sarah shook her head. "He doesn't have any brothers or sisters. Just like me."

"A friend, then."

"He looks so sad," Sarah said. "Don't you think he looks sad?"

It was an odd observation, but after studying the painting, Michael realized it was possible to interpret it that way. "A little," he admitted finally.

Sarah shook her head, a frown creasing her brow. "Why do people have to be sad all the time?"

Michael stroked her hair. "Are you sad all the time, m'dearie?"

Still frowning, she cocked her head, thinking about it. "No. I used to be, though."

Feeling an unexpected buoyancy lighten his soul, Michael smiled. "Me neither," he murmured, leaning in like a conspirator. "And me too." Gently, he took the canvas from her hands and turned it to the wall, then took her hand and walked back with her the way they had come.

DOCTOR PARRISH did indeed pronounce Seward's rehabilitation to be progressing even beyond his high expectations. Together, he and Michael spent some time planning out the next phase of Seward's treatment, which involved more work outside the gymnasium and more emphasis on encouraging his independence.

"The painting is a good sign," Parrish said. "You need to do everything you can to promote that."

Michael thought about the portraits lying in the attic, remnants of another life; aloud, he sighed. "I'm not an alienist," he said curtly.

"Occupational therapy, my boy," Parrish rejoined, lifting an eyebrow. "Surely you've heard of it?"

Michael gripped his knees under the tabletop. "I'll do what I can," he murmured.

Parrish smiled. "And his social reintegration? How's that proceeding?"

Michael cast a glance at Mary, who was trying to appear as though she were not eavesdropping and failing miserably. "Poorly," he said. "Sarah is the only one who can put up with him for extended periods."

"Well, I'm sure that once he regains more of his strength, he will feel more inclined to renew old friendships," Parrish said brightly.

Michael conjured an image of Seward crumpled on the lawn,

tears streaming down his dirt-smudged face. "Let's hope so," he said dully.

Parrish remained silent for a few moments, and when Michael turned to look at him, he was confronted by that warrior's gaze, perceptive and knife-sharp. "He spoke well of you, you know."

And that was so startling that Michael could think of nothing to say.

Parrish only smiled and patted his arm. "There, that's better. I was beginning to think you had all the mysteries solved, and what a dull world that would be, hm?"

CONTRARY to all of Michael's expectations, Seward did indeed show some inclination to "renew old friendships" over the next few days. Michael noticed that he and Abbott actually spoke to one another now when the old man came out to share the sun on the terrace. There was a tentative, halting quality to their interactions, but it was a beginning, at least. It was clear from the way Sarah watched them both that she was interested in the outcome, and both men seemed more at ease when she was with them, so Michael made a point of releasing her from her commitments in the garden whenever he saw them together.

His work with Seward occupied more and more of his days, since Seward's exercise routine was growing in both variety and duration. The August heat meant that Seward could spend more time outdoors engaged in walking and calisthenics. At first he balked at wearing his athletic gear, but Michael only folded his arms and informed him that since there were no ladies in the vicinity who were interested in ogling his skinny ass, there was no need for modesty.

Seward glared at him darkly but eventually obeyed. All insults aside, Michael noticed that Seward was beginning to gain some muscle mass, though there was no chance he would be mistaken for a prize fighter in the near future. Still, the exposure of his limbs to the sun increased the benefits to his health. Soon he was tanned and looking heartier than he had since Michael had known him.

Seven weeks into his rehabilitation, Seward made an entire circuit of the grounds without the aid of his cane, Michael and Sarah walking on either side of him, bearing silent witness. By the time they reached the house, the sweat had plastered Seward's shirt to his back, and his legs were so unsteady Michael was sure he would topple at any moment.

And then Michael looked up and saw Mary standing at the kitchen door, tears brimming in her eyes. His own throat tightening, he cast a glance at Seward, who propelled himself forward with a new reserve of energy, his gaze never wavering from her.

When he finally stood trembling before her, Mary reached up and stroked his cheek tenderly, her action stealing the breath from his lungs with a sound like a sob. As if by instinct, they moved into one another's arms, Seward crushing her to him with a strength Michael would not have believed the other man possessed.

"We're so glad to have you back with us, Johnny dear," Mary whispered, and Seward hugged her a little harder, his shoulder blades jutting out like the broken stumps of wings.

MICHAEL was never sure how the change had come, but after that Seward took all his meals with the Abbotts, which meant that Michael saw even more of him. Seward was no longer snappish with Mary, Abbott, or Sarah, conducting himself as a well-behaved guest might. He was clearly not entirely at ease with them yet, but he was also just as clearly not the man he had been two months ago. Whether this was due more to Michael's ministrations, Sarah's quiet camaraderie, Abbott's approval, or Mary's welcoming arms, Michael couldn't say; doubtless it was an ineffable mixture of all four factors.

As for Seward's treatment of Michael, Michael noticed that while his interactions with Seward at the dinner table were civil, if not warm, his interactions with him in the exercise room or during massage still remained adversarial at best and hostile at worst. Michael was finding it more and more difficult to reconcile the man who helped Sarah so patiently with her reading and the man who battled with him daily in the gymnasium.

"Push harder."

"I am… pushing," Seward said testily, his calf muscles bulging with the effort to raise his leg as Michael applied a downward pressure. Seward lay on his stomach on the mat, his head pillowed on his folded arms. Looking back over his shoulder, he glared at Michael as best he could.

"This isn't as much as you gave me yesterday," Michael snapped back.

Seward's leg shuddered against the palm of Michael's hand. "You hadn't tortured me for an hour with those—damned—pulley weights yesterday."

Michael only kept up the pressure, hearing Seward grunt low in his throat as he struggled. For a span of a few heartbeats, Michael could feel Seward's muscles straining to overcome the downward force before the leg collapsed under his hand.

"God damn it!" Seward swore, fists slamming uselessly against the mat.

"Try it again," Michael said tightly.

"I can't!"

"You can," Michael insisted, as mildly as he could considering that his blood was pounding in his ears and he was suddenly, inexplicably furious.

Slowly, painfully, Seward turned himself over. Michael watched a bead of sweat roll from Seward's temple into his hair as he lay panting up at him. Something of Michael's rage must have shown on his face, because Seward's eyes widened. He pushed himself up on his elbows.

"Don't get up," Michael murmured, voice deceptively calm. "We're not done."

Seward blinked at him. "I beg your pardon?"

"You can rest for a minute or two, but we're going to try it again. And this time you're going to show some effort."

Seward's gaze hardened. "You're insane."

Again, it was not the first time Seward had leveled a similar epithet at him, but it was the first time it made Michael's palms itch to hear it. Seward made to sit up, and the next thing Michael knew his hand was splayed out across Seward's ribs, preventing him from rising.

"What do you think you're—" Seward began, his eyes growing round.

"Try. It. Again," Michael growled, leaning closer until he was mere inches from Seward's reddened face.

Seward glared up at him, his chest heaving, and Michael felt his hand grow damp from the sweat he encountered there. Gaze wandering, he studied his own hand, the thin, clinging cloth of Seward's undershirt, the taut quiver in his stomach. He remembered the nurse's matter-of-fact notes from her consultation with Seward's doctors:

Floating rib 12 shattered and removed

Before Michael was aware of his own actions, his fingers slid slowly downward until they were gently tracing the phantom line of the rib that no longer existed.

He is three months at the base hospital, only three months, but it feels like a lifetime. Ambulance drivers deal with smaller numbers, the casualties of a company or two, but orderlies at the base hospital wade through the living and the dead of a whole battalion or more. The worst is after a battle; the screams and moans of the men waiting for attention from the doctors and nurses rising in a hellish chorus, the inescapable stench of blood and shit, the dustbins overflowing with the amputated limbs. Michael helps the men—usually Negroes—whose job it is to bury the pieces, carrying them outside so that they can be hauled away or burned at the incinerator. It gives him an excuse to take a moment to breathe in fresh air, though the stink is on him, in him, and when he tries to smoke, his hands shake too much to hold his cigarette.

I might have thrown away a piece of you, Michael thought,

staring at his fingertips as they stroked back and forth, as if they were trying to conjure the bone back into existence.

A small lost sound from Seward brought him back to the present instantly. He blinked and raised his eyes to Seward's wide-eyed, startled face. Seward's skin was sheened with sweat, and his mouth was slightly open, as though he could not draw enough oxygen, as though Michael had been standing on his chest rather than touching it with the lightest pressure.

Jesus Christ, thought Michael, hands jerking away from Seward's body as though the contact had burned him. He averted his eyes, but he could feel the heat of Seward's gaze on his face, branding silent questions into his skin.

"I—I'm sorry," he murmured, rising swiftly to his feet. "That won't happen again."

Seward was silent for a long while before Michael heard him grunt and sit up.

"That's what I used to tell myself," he muttered. "I hope that you have more luck."

EVERYONE—including Seward, apparently—was surprised when his aunt decided to pay a surprise visit to the house a few days later. Mary fussed and complained and promptly insisted that Michael accompany her to Hudson, where she purchased fine cuts of meat and fish for their guest.

"The nerve of that woman," Mary huffed as she selected a salmon for the master's supper and a pork hock for the rest of them in the new grocery on Warren Street. Even when Seward had taken his meals alone, he had always eaten the same food as the Abbotts. It was out of the question, however, that Rebecca Anderson would eat pork stew and dumplings. "Coming here without a word of warning."

"She is the owner of the property. I suppose she can do whatever she likes," Michael answered mildly.

Mary cut her eyes at him. "The thief of the property, you mean," she sniffed, leaning in. "Johnny should have inherited that house."

Michael frowned, irked that he was interested in the question he was about to ask. "And why didn't he?"

Mary shook her head, her expression strangely shadowed. "Johnny and his father often… disagreed."

"That wouldn't be cause for disinheritance."

"There was a terrible argument just before he sailed for Europe," Mary elaborated as the fishmonger handed the wrapped salmon to Michael. Mary paid him, and they proceeded on to the butcher's stall. "His father didn't want him to join up, especially after he refused any… special consideration. In fact, he asked to be sent to the front."

Michael nodded. In the neighborhood in which he had grown up, everyone knew that rich men's sons were not drafted, and if they enlisted in the army, they were swiftly given commissions and relegated to safe positions far behind the lines. Learning that Seward had requested active duty was like hearing the moon really was made of green cheese.

"And his mother?"

Mary shook her head. "She died when Johnny was a boy hardly older than Sarah is now."

Michael was struck dumb at this, his thoughts churning. It was not the first time he'd considered the strange bond between himself, Seward, and the little girl. They were, in their own peculiar ways, intimately acquainted with loss and loneliness. Now it seemed they had one more thing in common.

As though she'd been conjured, Sarah flew up to them and showed them a brightly colored handbill. "A man gave me this!" she exclaimed, as near to excitement as Michael had ever seen her. "Can we go?"

Mary took the paper from her and eyed the bold print as Michael peered over her shoulder. It was an advertisement for a Labor Day celebration on the riverfront next week, promoting games, fun, and frolics of all kinds.

Mary frowned pensively. "I will have to consider it, Sarah. With your grandfather still not feeling as fit as he might, and Mister Seward…."

"We can help them," Sarah said, her eager gaze darting from Michael to Mary and back again. "Can't we? There are going to be races and prizes and fireworks, and a parade with lots and lots of music."

Perhaps it was the girl's uncharacteristic childishness that melted Mary's heart, but whatever the cause, she smiled and curved a hand over the back of her granddaughter's head. "We'll see, sweetling," she said warmly. "We'll see."

Solemnly, Michael tapped the girl on the shoulder. "Hold my fish," he told her, thrusting the salmon into her hands. When she grasped it, he swung her up onto his shoulder, making her giggle.

"Well," Mary said briskly, taking the pork hock and the change from the grocer, "at least now we have hope for Johnny. We have you to thank for that."

"Don't thank me," Michael said. "I'm only—"

Mary's hand gripped his arm, squeezing. "I'll thank who I please," she said tartly, though the smile still played about her lips. "And I please to thank you."

The corners of Michael's mouth twitched in spite of himself. "Yes, ma'am," he replied, hearing her chuckle as he held the door for her before stepping out into the warm summer day, ducking as he crossed the threshold with Sarah held fast in his arms.

SINCE Abbott was still on the mend, Michael was charged with the tasks the old man would have normally carried out at the supper that evening. He picked up all he needed to know about table service from a half hour at Abbott's knee, and then he was thrust into the dining room to perform his duties.

It was more than odd acting as the butler to a man who had been sharing every meal with him for the last week, not to mention the nearly two months Michael had spent nagging and prodding him incessantly into pushing his body beyond the limits of its endurance. He'd never had much patience with class distinctions and had always chosen jobs where his Bowery Irish upbringing hadn't been a hindrance to him. Ladling out soup and pouring wine while Seward and his aunt enjoyed their lavish meal was his idea of purgatory.

It soon became evident, however, that Seward was as far from enjoying the experience as Michael was, perhaps more so. Throughout the meal, he watched the tension in Seward's shoulders increase until his hands ached to ease it.

"I don't see why you needed the ballroom," sniffed Mrs. Anderson, picking at her salmon while Michael waited to clear away the dishes. "There are many rooms in the house—"

"Your precious house will eventually be restored to its former glory," Seward said patiently. "Never fear."

"Well, of course I'm not fearful, it's only that—oh, well, never mind," she said. "I suppose it is an excellent room for the purpose. And it's certainly yielding results. You look better than I've seen you since you came back from overseas."

"Thank you," Seward said mildly, though Michael could hear the scorn lying underneath.

Seward's aunt, apparently, took him at face value, for she smiled patronizingly and said, "You're welcome." Looking up at Michael, she inclined her head. "I suppose we have you to thank for John's new lease on life."

Surprised at being addressed, Michael blinked, then shook his head. "Your nephew deserves the credit, mum," he said quietly, earning him a measuring look from Seward. "He's the one doing all the work."

The woman frowned slightly. "Hm. Yes, well, humility is a very becoming trait in a young man. But of course John and I know the real truth, don't we?"

Seward took a sip of his wine. "There are many truths, Aunt Rebecca. We cannot possibly hope to know them all."

Her frown deepened for a moment before clearing. "Yes, I suppose that's true," she said finally, though Michael could tell she hadn't understood a word Seward had said. The conversation faded for a while as they finished their meals.

"As delightful as it is to have you here," Seward said after a few minutes, "you haven't yet mentioned how long you'll be gracing us with your presence."

Seward's aunt looked vastly uncomfortable before gathering herself as for a leap off a cliff. "Well, I had hoped to stay on through tomorrow"—the rest was said in a rush—"and then take you back with me to the city for a visit."

Seward shook his head. "Oh, Auntie, you're so predictable."

Mrs. Anderson's expression grew hard. "Surely you're not going to insist on living as a hermit for the rest of your life. You have obligations—"

"Obligations to whom?" Seward said, voice soft and dangerous. "Obligations to a house that's no longer mine? To a man who disowned me?"

Hell, thought Michael. There was no way he could make an escape now without appearing conspicuous. He wished fervently for the floor to open up and swallow him.

The woman regarded Seward speculatively, as though she were a general searching for weaknesses in the enemy lines. "Myra's been asking after you," she said, her tone wheedling. "You haven't been in touch with her since you've returned."

"Myra is only keeping up appearances," Seward said shortly. "We reached a very clear understanding before I left. If she hasn't hunted up fresh game for herself by now, she's a fool."

His aunt continued undaunted. "Everyone has been very concerned about you. Now that I've told them you're on the mend, they're—"

"Less inclined to think me a raving lunatic taking potshots at visitors?" Seward finished for her.

The woman's pale, cool eyes glittered, all pretense of jocularity vanishing in an instant. "One might hope that you would at least think of your mother—"

"I have told you before"—Seward's tone was knife-sharp—"to never speak of my mother in front of me."

"George used to complain about your unreasonable devotion to her," she sneered. "I believe he once characterized it as pathological."

Michael tensed, waiting for the explosion, but Seward only sat back in his chair and laughed. "That's hardly a surprise," he said, voice so low that Michael could barely hear him. "To Doctor Seward, my very existence was pathological."

Before his aunt could do anything but gape at this, Seward had risen smoothly from his seat. Draining the last of his wine, he bowed slightly to his aunt and said, "Please forgive me, but I find myself suddenly exhausted by the day's events. It's a hazard of my condition. Feel free to stay and allow Mister McCready to serve you dessert and coffee. I understand Mary has prepared her specialty—floating island." And with a final smirk at Michael, he turned and left them alone.

Michael moved forward and silently picked up Seward's plate and glass, then escaped into the kitchen with them. By the time he returned, Mrs. Anderson was nowhere to be seen.

"More floating island for me," Michael said softly, smirking a little himself as he cleared away the rest of the dishes.

LATE that night, after another vivid dream left him restless and shaken, Michael descended the stairs and let himself out into the clear, warm night. As he rounded the corner, the scent of pungent cigarette smoke assaulted his nostrils. Following his nose, he walked to the terrace, where a dim shape leaned over the railing.

It took him a minute for his eyes to adjust, the moon being only half-full, but by the time he reached the stairs, he could see Seward quite clearly. He had his hand cupped protectively over the glowing end of his cigarette, a habit from the front he obviously hadn't lost.

Michael turned and leaned back against the railing, arms folded. "I see you had a secret hoard."

Seward blew smoke into the air. "No lectures," he warned.

Michael raised his hands. "I was only wondering if you might be able to spare one."

Seward turned to look at him for a long moment, then reached into his jacket pocket and extracted a silver case. He handed it to Michael, who removed one and tapped it on the smooth metal before handing it back. Michael felt the warm brush of Seward's fingers against his own, and his breath hitched at the unexpected heat that arrowed straight into his bones at the contact.

Seward gave no overt indication that he'd experienced the same strange effect, but he did make three fumbling attempts to light Michael's cigarette before succeeding. Not long after the first rush of smoke hit his lungs, Michael found his equilibrium returning.

And then he started coughing.

"God, these are awful," he wheezed.

Seward chuckled dryly and released another stream of smoke. "You haven't smoked in a while?"

"I'm trying to quit," Michael managed, dropping the cigarette and grinding it under his heel.

"So am I. Therapist's orders."

Michael raised an eyebrow at him. "Too bad you're remarkably bad at following orders."

Seward stared at him, then started laughing. It was the first genuine laugh Michael had heard from him. "Point taken."

They stood together in almost amiable silence for a while before Michael heard himself say, "Perhaps you should go to New York."

He could feel Seward's eyes on him and waved a hand. "Not for your aunt's benefit, but for your own. Stay in a hotel. See a show. Eat in a fancy restaurant." He looked out across the garden. "Paint."

He heard Seward puff on the cigarette a couple more times before stubbing it out on the railing. "I'm hardly fit to be wandering around Manhattan yet."

"Well, then, in a few weeks," Michael said, not sure why he was pressing the point but unable to stop the words. "See how you feel, at least. I was planning to go back for a weekend. I could drive you."

"Aha, now we get to it. You only want my car." There was no heat in Seward's words, only faint amusement, and Michael found himself smiling.

"You know us Irish, always looking for a free ride."

Seward surprised him when he softly murmured, "No, I don't know. All the Irishmen I knew were fine men. Many of them died beside me." He took a deep breath, let it out. "A few of them died because of me."

Michael said nothing, his hands gripping the railing. Seward's confession of guilt reminded him of his own failure to save men whose lives he'd considered his responsibility, but his tally sheet ran into the hundreds.

"What's in New York?" Seward asked.

"My sister," Michael said. "Friends." *Maybe a fuck,* he thought. He needed one if he was starting to respond to Seward, of all people.

"I didn't know you had a sister."

"You know very little about me," Michael replied, his tone unexpectedly harsh.

"True," Seward murmured after a moment, reaching for another cigarette. "But the little I do know is astonishingly familiar."

Michael turned toward Seward, startled. In the silver moonlight, his green eyes were ghostly and pale, and Michael suppressed a shiver.

"I should…," he said, pointing in the direction of the stairs. "I have an early morning in the garden tomorrow. I have to… mow the lawn."

"Good night," Seward said, sticking the cigarette in his mouth and flicking the Ronson lighter into life on the first try.

Michael launched himself down the stone steps. A couple of minutes later, lying flushed and inexplicably breathless in his bed, he could still see the image of those haunting eyes staring back at him, slicing into his soul with the precision of a gifted surgeon's scalpel.

10

AFTER that, Michael and Seward's working relationship entered a new stage, though Michael was at a loss as to how to characterize it. To say it was combative was wrong, because they worked more harmoniously than they ever had. To say it was friendly, however, was equally incorrect, because there was a new element to their relationship that made friendship impossible, one that Michael did his best to deny—to no avail. That element was an infuriating, electric awareness that hummed constantly under the surface of his skin, making it next to impossible for him to perform his job as a therapist. One moment he would be the efficient, competent rubber, his hands confident on Seward's body, and in the next he would be the awkward boy he had once been, confused and astonished by his own desire.

Unfortunately, his desire was apparently becoming a mischievous bitch in her maturity, because in spite of all reason, Michael found himself increasingly attracted to Seward. The man was maddening and mercurial and haughty and patrician, he told himself, the antithesis of every man he'd ever wanted, but that did not prevent him from staring confounded at the curve of Seward's neck as he bent to inspect Sarah's painting, or listening to the soothing depths of his voice as he spoke with Abbott on the terrace. And then one night, he awoke from an extraordinarily vivid dream involving Seward's hands on various parts of him, hands that were not like an artist's at all but broad and square and strong—

Christ, Michael thought, lying in the dark spent and gasping after waking certain those big hands were wrapped around his cock, *I need to stop this.*

He had no idea whether Seward reciprocated his desire, and he could not decide whether knowing the answer would be a blessing or a curse. Adding to his confusion was the fact that for every time he was sure Seward felt the same tug of connection, there was another incident that proved Seward was not the least bit inclined toward him. Michael knew the rules of attraction in New York, Paris, and London, but a Hudson River country estate was alien territory, a landscape without maps or signposts.

He knew this much: anything more complex than their relationship as it existed now would be disastrous for both of them. No matter what Seward might think of his position in society, the truth remained that he had one, and it was so far from Michael's own position that one of them might as well have been living on the moon. While he was not afraid of imprisonment, he was concerned that Margaret remain ignorant of the truth about him, and Paddy had guaranteed to keep his mouth shut only as long as he kept this job. To plunge into an affair with the nephew of the woman who had hired him was not conducive to continued employment.

The medical argument, while the weakest of the bunch, was nevertheless a sound one as well. Michael was in a position of confidence, of trust, and to compromise that position was unethical. On the other hand, Seward was hardly an invalid but rather an exceedingly irritating man who had never truly behaved as his patient. Similarly, Michael had little inclination to view himself as a therapist any longer.

All of this led to a state of near-constant frustration that his late-night sessions with his right hand seemed only to fuel. The sole mercy was that he was due for his next weekend off soon, and he was determined to take it this time and head back to New York. His uncle be damned, he was going to fuck himself bowlegged for two days. Perhaps then he could return and finish his task with some sense of decorum and self-control.

For it was also evident that Seward was nearing the end of his rehabilitation. While he would continue to require an exercise regimen, the most intensive work was nearly over. Too, Seward's independence had been growing by leaps and bounds over the past week, to the point where he sometimes exercised without any help, a fact which both concerned and impressed Michael. It was as though the same fierce determination that Seward had invested in resisting all attempts to change him was now being employed in his own self-improvement. Unfortunately, as Michael had learned a few hours earlier, this newfound spirit could have disastrous consequences.

"Take off your shirt."

Seward looked up at him as he entered from the garden, startled. "What, no courtship first?"

Michael ground his teeth together. "Don't be funny. You were wandering the grounds for three hours, and your entire body's going to be a knot within thirty minutes if we don't get you loosened up quickly. Strip and lie facedown on the mat."

Seward regarded him for another moment, his gaze more speculative than irritated, then lifted his shirt over his head. As he raised his arms, his face tensed for a moment.

Michael folded his arms. "Sore?"

"Not… particularly," Seward said, bending over and stripping off his shorts with a distinct wince.

"Mmm-hmmm." Seward shot him a glare but walked over to the mat and lay down on the towels provided. Michael dropped to his knees beside Seward's torso, draped one of the towels over his buttocks, and swiftly began a series of hackings, the edges of his hands relentless on the twitching muscles of Seward's back.

Seward's scars were finally beginning to show some real improvement after Michael's diligent work bringing blood to those areas and breaking down the scar tissue with careful fingers. Of course, his skin would never be unmarred, but the improvement was noticeable. Seward was no longer as uncomfortable in his own body as he had once been, it seemed, putting himself on display without hesitation.

Debating with himself for a moment—he usually massaged Seward in the privacy of his bedroom, but it was late and the Abbotts were doubtless in bed—Michael pulled back the towel and began kneading Seward's buttocks. Seward's body jerked under his hands, and he twisted back to look at Michael.

"What are you—"

"It's fine. They're asleep," Michael murmured, graduating to clappings that progressed down his thighs.

Seward grunted and rested his head on his arms once more before subsiding into silence. Michael continued his ministrations, kneading and clapping the muscle groups in his legs, watching for signs of strain. He found them occasionally in the odd twitch or jerk, but he was surprised that Seward was able to control his reaction to that extent.

Perhaps he shouldn't have been. After all, Seward was the master of control, a man who was adept at denying his own pain. Michael envied him that, and his jealousy eroded his own crumbling control.

"Turn over," Michael said softly.

Seward hesitated for a moment, then rolled, eyes staring up at the ceiling. Michael's mouth curved at the corner. Taking the towel, he folded it over Seward's genitals, then began the vigorous massage again, working his way up from the legs. The muscles he felt there were not atrophied, withered remnants but healthy tissue, growing, stretching, no longer weak or incapable. He could feel their power lurking under the surface of Seward's pale, smooth skin, and felt a wave of pride he hadn't experienced in ages.

Another unfamiliar feeling—this one more like possession—assaulted him in the next moment, and he found himself spreading his palms over Seward's chest, kneading with hungry fingers. Before he could warn himself that he was losing his objectivity, it was gone, vanished in the few short seconds measured by the ragged rise and fall of Seward's ribcage. His gaze locked with Seward's, and Michael's heart stopped at what he saw there—a similar confused mixture of denial and desire, the pupils dilating in spite of Seward's ambiguous feelings.

He felt Seward's hands cover his own, though whether his intent was to stop Michael or to encourage him, Michael wasn't sure. Time seemed to slow to a molasses pace as Michael's fingers burrowed into the muscle until he could feel the pounding of Seward's blood against his skin.

Stop, Michael thought, *stop, you fool,* but it was no use; his hands traveled to Seward's shoulders as he lowered his head, drawn to Seward by an invisible force. The soft, startled puff of Seward's breath against his lips brought him back to himself, sending him reeling back as effectively as a roundhouse punch from a Five Points tough.

The moment his hands left Seward's body, they both made a sound lodged midway between relief and anguish. Seward levered himself up on his elbows, then sat up, tying the towel around his waist as he did so. Michael shut his eyes. If he saw evidence of Seward's arousal, what remained of his tattered self-control would be lost in an instant. By the time he opened them again, Seward had lurched painfully to his feet and was halfway to the door. The unassailable certainty that Seward desired him as much as he wanted Seward only brought him more confusion, more frustration, and a bone-deep yearning that left him shaken.

Somehow Michael summoned the voice to croak, "Tomorrow is Labor Day."

Seward stopped but didn't turn. "Yes, I know." His voice was flat, giving no indication of his state of mind.

"We're—that is, Sarah, Mary, Abbott, and I—are going to Hudson for the day. We—ah, Sarah—has been hoping you'd come."

Seward turned slowly, his gaze shadowed. "I… I don't think that would be a good idea." He sounded hesitant and uncharacteristically young, and Michael stared up at him, startled.

"It would mean a great deal to her," Michael said evenly, and waited.

Seward blew out a breath. "You're a bastard, McCready." Then he turned away again and limped out the door.

Michael held out his hands and stared at them. They seemed unfamiliar, as though they belonged to a stranger.

"Point taken," he said softly, to no one in particular.

"THEY'RE selling ice cream over there!" Sarah exclaimed, pointing eagerly. "May I have one, please?"

"For heaven's sake, child, it's eleven o'clock in the morning!" Mary exclaimed, her outraged tone belied by her twinkling eyes.

Sarah looked up at her, gaze pleading. "After lunch? Please?"

"We'll see," Mary said firmly. She pointed at a spot beneath a maple tree on the small rise overlooking the waterfront promenade. "Spread the blanket there."

Sarah's face fell before Michael caught her eye and winked. Smiling faintly, the girl dropped to her knees and smoothed the edges of the blanket. Mary placed the basket she'd carried from the car on one corner, then moved to take her husband's arm as Michael helped him. "You're—oh, my, please be careful—" she fussed.

Abbott grumbled, "I can do this by myself, woman," but allowed himself to be maneuvered. When he was settled, he took a deep breath and looked out over the promenade. "Well. It's a fine day for it, anyway."

It was a fine day for a small-town celebration of Labor Day, or so Michael supposed, not having had much experience with either small towns or celebrations. In the Bowery, the holiday was little more than another excuse to drink to excess, closed taverns being no barrier to a high time. His last Labor Day had been spent on the ward in England. Predictably, none of the men had been in a festive mood.

Enthusiasm was not in short supply on this day in Hudson, however. The new electric street lamps along the promenade were festooned with brightly colored bunting, doubtless hung by the members of one of the trade unions. There was a thirty-piece band tuning up on the platform near the water, and the park was rapidly filling up with people from two to seventy-two, all of them outfitted in their Sunday best. Michael discovered the vitality and joy of an entire town on holiday was infectious and soon found himself smiling and nodding at passersby who tipped their hats to them.

"Sarah, go help Mister Seward," Mary murmured, casting a glance over the hill. Following the direction of her gaze, Michael spotted Seward about two hundred yards away, making his slow progress across the lawn. He had not followed them once Michael parked the car, choosing instead to seek his own route. Michael caught a glimpse of him heading off toward the commercial street, which he thought curious since less than a handful of shops and restaurants in the town were open today.

"I'll help him," Michael offered. "You run along and see if you can find any of your school friends." Needing no further encouragement, Sarah smiled and took off running, her skirts billowing about her legs.

"You're spoiling that child," Mary murmured, though there was no censure in her tone.

"It's a fine day for it," Michael quipped, leaning in to give Mary a peck on the cheek that left her flustered and blushing. He jogged in Seward's direction, meeting him before he had made much progress, then fell into step beside him.

"I don't need a babysitter," Seward groused after a few moments of silence. "I'm merely taking my time."

"Mm-hmm," Michael said. "Where did you go shopping?"

"What?" Seward asked, taken aback.

Michael hooked a thumb over his shoulder. "I saw you heading toward Warren Street earlier. If you were looking to shop, I could have driven you."

Seward shook his head. "I wasn't shopping." The tone of his voice told Michael in no uncertain terms that the discussion was over. Shrugging, Michael subsided back into silence.

Presently Sarah came flying up to them with a handbill clutched in her small fists. "A man gave this to me," she said to them, thrusting the paper at Seward.

Seward unfolded the paper and swiftly scanned the contents, then passed it to Michael. It was an invitation for children to participate in various contests that had been planned for the day, including a shooting gallery and a three-legged race. The prizes were listed at the bottom, but it was an instruction at the top that caught Michael's eye:

Fathers are asked to participate with their sons and daughters.

"I asked him if an uncle would be all right," Sarah said quietly, her gaze on her shoes. "He said that would be fine." She glanced up at Seward before looking away again. "We could pretend. He doesn't have to know you're not really my uncle."

Michael and Seward exchanged mute glances. Michael reviewed

the paper quickly, studying the list of contests. Some of them would be too strenuous for Seward, but he could manage a few without exhausting himself.

"Sarah," Michael heard Seward begin, "I don't know—"

"How about two uncles?" Michael interrupted, squatting down in front of Sarah while the blood pounded in his ears. He felt oddly lightheaded, divorced from his own body, as though someone else were extending the offer to the girl. "Would you mind if we both helped you? I'm a terror at three-legged races. We're sure to win that one."

Sarah's eyes lit up. "Both of you?"

Michael grinned. "Both of us." At her pleased smile, he swung her up into his arms and stood, perching her on his hip. When he looked over at Seward, he was confronted by the other man's raised eyebrow.

Michael clapped him on the shoulder with his free hand, drawing him along with them. "Come on, uncle," he said merrily, ignoring the pointed glare he received.

BY FOUR o'clock that afternoon, Seward lay sprawled on the blanket, one arm shielding his eyes. "I hate you," he groaned.

Michael lifted the arm and peered down into Seward's scowling face. "Now, is that any way to talk? Look how happy she is." He pointed over to where Sarah was showing off her prize for third place to her schoolmates, a two-foot-long wooden ship complete with rigging and sails.

"They expected a boy to win that, obviously."

Michael shrugged. "She seems pleased enough with it. She's not the sort to play with dolls anyway," he added, remembering the neat rows of tin soldiers in the attic. He studied Seward more closely. "Are you truly hurt?"

Seward sighed and pushed himself up on his elbows. "No," he grunted. "Only a little sore."

"I'll rub you down when we get home," Michael said, and only when Seward's eyes widened did he realize how intimate the words sounded, especially after yesterday's impromptu massage.

Seward cleared his throat and looked away, breaking the awkward moment. "I'm sure a hot bath will be sufficient."

Michael reached for a cookie from the basket and took a bite. "Perhaps you're right." He lay back on the blanket, keeping a respectable distance from Seward.

Seward occupied himself with studying the crowd. "I haven't been to one of these since I was a boy."

A smile tugged at Michael's lips. "You were once a boy? Astonishing."

Seward flicked an irritated eyebrow at him, but there was a glint in his eye. "Oh, shut up," he groused.

Michael found he couldn't resist needling him a little. "Were you a good boy or a mischievous one?"

Seward looked at him, then nodded in the direction of the bandstand, where a concert had finished a few minutes ago. "I had my moments. I once tried to set the bandstand on fire."

Michael released a startled laugh. "Did you object to the musical selections?"

The corner of Seward's mouth curved. "Alas, there was no one playing at the time. I wasn't that mischievous, I suppose. What about you?"

"Well, I wasn't an arsonist, but only because I wouldn't have known what that word meant." He looked at his hands. "I did just about everything else, though."

"I think we're allowed some youthful mistakes."

Michael looked up and was immediately trapped by Seward's unflinching gaze. It was the first moment of true sympathy they'd managed to achieve, and yet Michael felt tempted to ruin it. *Would you be so understanding,* he thought, *if you knew my entire life had been a series of mistakes?*

The words hovered on the tip of his tongue, but before he could say them, Mary walked up with Abbott, sending both men scrambling to their feet. "What a lovely concert," she breathed. "The music was stirring. It made me think a little of...." She trailed off, her gaze lighting on something only she could see. "It made me think of happier times." Abbott said nothing, merely sat on the blanket and rested his forearms on his bent knees. Michael thought he had never seen him look quite so old.

It was to this melancholy mood that Sarah returned shortly after, and it was only when Michael looked up at her that he realized she was crying.

"Goodness, sweetheart, what's the matter?" Mary asked, concerned.

Michael tugged Sarah into his arms, and after a moment she sat in his lap, though she remained silent, clutching the boat in her hands.

"Won't you tell us what's the matter?" he asked, smoothing back a lock of her hair. "Was one of your friends unkind to you?"

She shook her head.

"Did you fall down?" Michael said.

Another shake of her head.

"Then why are you sad, sweetling?" Mary asked.

Sarah sniffled, and Seward reached into his trousers pocket and pulled out a handkerchief. She took it and wiped at her nose. "I don't want to be happy."

"Why not?" Michael asked gently.

Sarah's eyes brimmed again. "Because I shouldn't be happy. It's not right."

Michael frowned. Momentarily at a loss for words, he stroked her back while Seward squatted down beside her.

"I felt the same way myself once," he said softly. Michael stared at him, shocked, as Seward continued, his gaze fixed on her the entire time.

"My mother died when I was thirteen, and for a very long time afterward I felt that it was wrong to be happy, since she was not with me."

"Did you miss her?" Sarah asked in a small voice.

"Oh yes, very much," Seward murmured. "There were nights when I was certain I could not live without her."

"What about your father?"

Seward hesitated, as though he was searching for the proper words. "I was angry at my father," he finally said, simply.

"Why?"

"Well," Seward said, "he was a brilliant and very successful doctor, and so he was often too busy to spend much time with my mother and me. And my mother—she tried to recapture his attention by pretending she was sick. Perhaps you once pretended to be sick when you didn't want to go to school so that your mother would fuss over you and be especially nice to you?" Sarah nodded reluctantly. "Of course you have; we all have. Well, it was a little like that, except that of course as a doctor my father could tell she was lying, and eventually he stopped listening to her complaints. And when she truly got sick, he didn't believe her until her condition was very serious. She went into the hospital your grandfather visited, but she never came out."

Sarah looked at him with round eyes. "I was really sick, too, and I didn't get to say goodbye to her. Did you get to say goodbye to your mother?"

Seward shook his head. "No. My father wouldn't let me. I slept on the steps of the hospital for three days waiting for him to change his mind, but he didn't."

Michael's heart stopped, then lurched into motion again. *Dear God.*

Sarah frowned. "Why wouldn't he let you see her?"

Seward scratched his chin. "You know, I never quite figured that out. Some doctors thought—still think, I imagine—that it did not do to upset the patients in any way, and that anyone who might cry and fuss over them should be kept out of hospitals."

"That just sounds mean," Sarah said firmly.

Seward smiled fondly and smoothed his hand over the girl's head. "Thank you. I think so, too."

Sarah patted Seward's arm consolingly. "Is that why the hospital makes you sad?"

"Yes, that's why," Seward answered. He glanced at Michael, then turned back to Sarah. "But my point is that we must remember that the people we loved also loved us very much. What do you think they would say if they were to see us right now and see that we are sad when we should be happy? Would they want us to never laugh again because we feel badly that they are not with us?"

"No," Sarah said. "My m-mother used to laugh all the time."

"Well, then," Seward said, smiling, "I'm sure she would like nothing better than to see you smiling." He touched her cheek gently, then pointed up toward Warren Street. "Now, there is a very nice restaurant over there that has ice cream and cake for dessert. Shall we all go there together for supper?"

"Oh, yes!" Sarah said, clapping her hands and jumping up. "I haven't ever eaten in a restaurant before."

"Well, my fine lady, we must correct that," Mary said, extending her hand for Sarah to take. As Michael rose to his feet, he saw Seward and Mary exchange glances over Sarah's head, saw Mary nod at him and smile her thanks, her eyes bright.

As the Abbotts made their slow progress toward the car, Seward folded the blanket carefully while Michael packed up the scattered remains of their lunch. They did not speak, though Michael had to bite his tongue to keep from asking any of the thousand questions that were crowding together inside his skull. It was as though half the missing pieces of Seward's mysterious puzzle had dropped into his lap, and he was desperate for an opportunity to sort them out, to form from them a picture he could recognize.

And what will you do if you like what you see? a small voice in his head demanded.

Shrugging it off, he hefted the basket, then began the walk to the car, Seward a silent presence at his side.

THE restaurant meal was excellent. Michael ate a steak that was far better than any he'd ever eaten, tender and dripping blood, while the others dined on similarly lavish fare. Sarah asked for and received her ice cream—the waiter took a fancy to her and presented her with a chocolate sundae that was nearly the size of her head, resplendent with whipped cream, slivered almonds, and cherries.

By the time they had finished, it was near time for the fireworks ceremony, and while every one of the adults was tired, no one wanted to disappoint Sarah. They resolved to find a spot on the Promenade that would be close to the car and found it at the far end of the park.

Busy helping Abbott to a nearby bench, Michael did not see the heavyset man approaching until it was too late. He barreled into Seward, knocking him to the ground.

"Hey!" Michael shouted, rounding on the man. "What the devil do you think you're doing?"

The burly fellow wobbled slightly as he faced Michael, and Michael sighed. This, at least, was more familiar to him than sack races and band concerts in the park. "I have no quarrel with you, friend," the fat man said, raising his hands.

Michael stabbed a finger at Seward, who was slowly picking himself up. "If you have a quarrel with him, you've got one with me," he growled. "Now why don't you take yourself home and sleep it off?"

"Sleep it off," the man said, nodding in an exaggerated fashion. "That's a good idea, sleep it off. Why didn't I think of that?"

"Mr. Reilly." Michael had never heard that pleading tone in Seward's voice before this. He would not have believed Seward capable of begging. "Please, I—"

"You shut up!" Reilly snarled, turning to glare at Seward with his fists clenched. "I don't want to hear anything you have to say."

To Michael's dismay another man, this one more fit and a good deal younger, ran up at that moment to join the fray. "Dan, there you are," he breathed. He looked Seward up and down and nodded. "John. I didn't expect to see you here."

"I didn't expect to be here." Seward hesitated, then extended his hand. The young man took it and shook it briefly. In the few seconds before the next explosion, Michael realized that he recognized both men. The younger was the fishmonger at the grocery, and the elder was the proprietor of the feed and grain store from which he'd bought his seeds. More than that: Reilly, Michael could see now, looked a great deal like the young blond man in Seward's paintings. Could they be father and son?

Before he could speculate further on this, however, Reilly decided to lunge at Seward again. The younger man held on to him, and he missed his target. "Don't even think about it," Michael advised lowly.

"He killed my boy!" Reilly shouted, straining forward futilely. Behind him, Michael could hear Seward draw a sharp breath.

"Dan, I've told you a hundred times that Patrick's death was not his fault," the young man said. "We were ordered to hold our positions, and retreating wouldn't have done us any good. They were shelling the support trenches as much as the forward ones."

"You didn't see it happen," Reilly snapped, anguished.

"I was there before the smoke cleared," the younger man gritted. "I helped to dig them out."

Michael glanced at Seward, whose eyes were now fixed and unseeing, as though he had been transported back to another time. Suddenly every one of Seward's injuries—and his reaction to the dirt that day in the garden—made sense.

Christ, he'd been buried alive. During artillery barrages—hell, even in severe rainstorms—the trenches had been prone to collapse, and men could easily be crushed under tons of thick, suffocating mud. That Seward had made it out alive was nothing short of miraculous.

"Come on, Dan," the young man said again, nodding his head at the Abbotts. "This is not the place to be discussing this." He tugged at Reilly, who shrugged him off once more and faced Seward. When the older man spoke this time, though, his voice was low, almost a whisper.

"Why couldn't it have been you instead of him?" he breathed. "Why couldn't you have been the one to die?"

"If it's any comfort," Seward answered brokenly, "I wish to God I had." And before Reilly or anyone else could respond, he was striding off across the park as quickly as his legs could carry him.

Michael turned to Reilly. "Get him out of here before I do," he snarled. The young man nodded, finally getting a firm hold on Reilly's bulk and dragging him off.

When they were a good distance away, Michael turned to the Abbotts. "Did you know about this?"

Mary exchanged glances with Abbott, then nodded. "Johnny has never spoken of it, but we heard enough when we were in town."

Abbott glared at Reilly's retreating back. "That old drunk is no good at keeping his mouth shut."

Mary squeezed his arm. "He lost his son."

"And so did we," Abbott said fiercely. "Any man who's lost a child and can still wish for anyone else's to come to harm is no longer a man." He peered into the darkness. "Did you see which way Johnny went?"

"I did," Michael said grimly. "Will you be all right here?"

"We'll be fine," Mary assured him. "Go after him. Please."

Michael required no more encouragement. He immediately took off across the park after Seward. Catching up to him proved more difficult than he'd imagined, since there was a sizeable crowd assembled to see the fireworks. He threaded his way through the knots of families and excited children, finally closing the distance between them just as the first firework burst over their heads.

Resisting the urge to fling himself to the ground, Michael couldn't help flinching violently at the sound and light; just ahead of him, he saw Seward do the same, stumbling as he did so. Michael reached out and wrapped a strong hand around his forearm, steadying him as the second explosion made them both jump.

"Let's get the hell out of this," Michael breathed, and Seward nodded. Following his lead, he allowed Seward to guide them to a small boathouse a few dozen feet away.

The interior was nearly dark, the only light coming from the high windows as the show continued outside. Michael could make out a few canoes, a couple of them occupied by spooning couples who glared at them as they walked past. They found a relatively private corner and sank down against the wall, shoulders touching. Michael could feel Seward twitch at every fresh explosion, though he wasn't sure how much of the reaction was also his own.

"How long were you at the front?" Seward asked quietly.

"Off and on, about two and a half years." At Seward's surprised stare, he remembered that most Americans would not have experienced much more than a year in the trenches. "I was in Ireland in '14. I volunteered as an ambulance driver with the Red Cross as soon as the war broke out."

Seward flinched at another burst. "I would have gone mad."

Michael shrugged. As horrific as it had been, it wasn't nearly as terrible as the life of a soldier. And the clean, quiet ward back in England had been a thousand times worse.

Curiosity getting the better of him, he asked, "Why did you join up?"

Seward tipped his head back against the wall. Eyes staring upward, he murmured, "When I was growing up, I wanted very little to do with the boys who—shared my background. I never felt that I had much in common with them."

"Why not?"

Seward shrugged. "They wanted to grow up and become their fathers." Hands molding to his bent knees, he added, "I ended up making friends with the young fellows from the village. And when Wilson declared war, they all wanted to go over. Thought it would be a damned adventure, even though by then everyone should have known better."

"You didn't have to go with them."

Seward shook his head. "No. Not until Patrick told me he was joining up."

Michael could fill in the gap easily enough; he'd seen the paintings in the attic. Pitching his voice for their ears only, he murmured, "Did you ever tell him you were in love with him?"

Seward flinched as if another firework had gone off directly in front of him. Michael held his breath, waiting. This was the first time either of them had spoken of it directly, and it seemed strangely illicit to him, here in the middle of this small-town celebration, surrounded by canoodling couples. For a moment, he worried that he'd misread the signs, and he had been sure of the signs ever since he'd been sixteen years old.

"No," Seward said finally. "He was only interested in women."

Michael nodded sympathetically, unsure of what to say. It was useless—not to mention cruel—to point out that in his doubtless much broader experience, very few men were interested exclusively in women, especially when the right inducements were offered. In his view, Seward's loss was magnified by the fact that he had never confessed his feelings to his friend, but the idea of his giving opinions on love was as ridiculous as the town drunk lecturing on the virtues of temperance.

If Michael had been in Seward's place, he would have pushed the pretty blond boy up against the nearest wall and sucked him off so thoroughly he would have never looked at a woman again. But then, putting forth that amount of effort seemed odd to him. He'd never been in a position where one man's regard mattered more than another's.

After a few moments, Michael felt Seward shift against him. Glancing over, he saw the glint of metal in Seward's hand as he tipped a small flask to his lips.

"No," Michael snapped, wresting the flask from Seward's hand before he could resist and flinging it away. He heard it clatter hollowly on the floor, followed by a feminine yelp of surprise as a pair of lovers was startled by the sound.

"God damn it," Seward growled, rounding on him, but before he could get another word out, Michael grabbed for his hand in the dark.

"This," he said fiercely, fingers squeezing, "just this. Hold on."

Another flash of light, another *bang* that rattled the windows in their panes, and Seward's eyes glittered with reflected fire. "And what the hell do I do when you're not there to prop me up?" he demanded bitterly.

"Stand on your own," Michael told him flatly.

Seward snorted. "If you haven't noticed, I'm not terribly

successful at that."

Michael looked down at the fingers that were gripping his tightly enough to cut off the circulation. "You're using your right hand."

Seward stared at his own hand. His grip eased, but Michael continued to hold on, the elation of the moment taking him back to a time when he used to touch to give comfort as well as pleasure. It was addictive, seductive, dangerous.

Seward's gaze rose slowly to his, green eyes illuminated by another flash from outside. This time neither of them reacted to the explosion.

"You didn't kill him," Michael whispered into the ensuing silence.

Seward's eyes widened. "I can't—"

"It wasn't your fault," Michael insisted.

"You don't know a damned thing about it," Seward breathed.

"I know you blame yourself for his death as much as his father does."

"Four," Seward gritted. "There were four of them who died on that day. And there were others before that."

Michael shook his head slowly, deliberately. "It doesn't matter. You were as trapped in that hell as the rest of them."

"I could have retreated. I could have—"

"And they might have shelled that trench, too, or it might have happened the next day, or the next week. And they would have court-martialed you and put another officer in charge who likely would have managed to get even more of them killed."

"Please," Seward said, though Michael could tell it only by the shape of his mouth, because in that instant the sky split open, caught fire, and poured in through the windows. In the conflagration of light and sound, Seward's pale, silenced face resembled the frozen mask of a corpse.

Everything spun away until the few square inches where their fingers twined together were all that Michael could feel, all that he could reliably call his own. The accompanying realization staggered him: he'd spent the last few months running as swiftly as he could from reminders of the war, and to find a sense of belonging in the very thing he'd sought to escape was simultaneously terrifying and reassuring. Instinctively seeking a more secure connection, he wrapped his free arm around Seward's shoulders and hauled him in close as the last firework fell to its death and the blackness enveloped them.

Seward resisted for a moment, then suddenly pressed his face to the juncture of Michael's neck and shoulder, breath gusting unevenly in the heated space between them. Michael felt the body he held shudder beneath his arm, felt the warm tickle of tears against his skin, soaking into his shirt. Seward squeezed his hand convulsively, his grip strong and fierce. Eyes pricking, Michael buried his own face in Seward's soft hair, while around them the boys and girls sighed into one another's mouths, making promises to eternal love in the dark.

11

"DARLING, this proves how much I care for you," Millie sighed as Michael enfolded her in a crushing hug. "Only you could get me out of bed at this unholy hour."

Michael grinned and slid into the booth across from her. "It's half past ten."

"Exactly," Millie—or rather, Henry—said, pointing a strangely unpainted finger at him. Michael had seen Millie only once before without her makeup and wig, and it was somewhat disconcerting to see her as a slight, balding man in his late forties. The Child's restaurant here in the Village was tolerant of the fairy crowd after midnight, but in the unforgiving light of day, they were expected to don less flamboyant garb.

As if sensing his thoughts, Henry raised a plucked eyebrow. "If you want me to be beautiful, you must come down and visit me in my natural habitat," he said tartly. One of the girls sauntered over carrying thick ceramic cups filled with black coffee. Henry blew her a kiss. "You're an angel," he enthused. She didn't bat an eye, but then she'd been working there for as long as Michael could recall.

"God, I remember you here as a boy," Henry sighed. "Three o'clock in the morning when your shift ended, you'd order a stack of flapjacks and bury your nose in a book until the sun came up."

Michael smiled in spite of himself at the memory. "You used to test me. Your Latin pronunciations were horrible, by the way. Everyone laughed at me my first semester at Trinity."

"Oh, shut up," Henry shot back, feigning annoyance. Michael grinned at him, and they both chuckled; then without warning, Michael's throat tightened.

"I've missed you, Millie," he rasped. "You're the only one who—"

Henry looked stricken. Reaching across the table, he took Michael's hands in his own and said earnestly, "You too, love. You, too." In a hushed voice, he demanded, "What was the real reason you left town? Did you have trouble with the law? You know I could have fixed that for you."

"I would have had, if I'd stayed," Michael murmured, looking at his hands. "But that wasn't the reason I left."

"Darling, please tell me," Henry implored. "You know you can trust me."

Michael stared at his hands, the invitation to share his secret finally too tempting to resist. "One of the cops you pay off is my cousin. I ran into him a few months ago when I was finishing my shift, and he went straight to Uncle Paddy and told him. Paddy, in turn, threatened to have me arrested. I told him to go to hell. Then he threatened to tell my sister."

"Oh my God," Henry breathed. "But don't you think she would… understand? You're so close. I can't believe you haven't told her before this."

Michael sighed. "I never wanted to take the chance," he said, taking a sip of his coffee. "And since she had her first child, she's become a much more devout Catholic than she ever was. The churches in the Bowery love to rail against the sin they see around them: burlesque shows, whorehouses, fairy dives."

"Have you been back to see her before this?"

"No," Michael said, the guilt welling up in him. "The job took more out of me than I expected. I've been writing her and sending her money, though." He did not add that Margaret's letters had petered out about three weeks ago, and his anxiety at her silence was growing. He tried to tell himself that Paddy would have contacted him if something had happened to her, and she had to be busy with the new baby, but he was no longer reassured by these rationalizations.

"How are you enjoying the fresh country air, then?" Henry asked archly.

Michael snorted at hearing Millie's inner bitch emerging from the man sitting before him. "It's not as bad as I thought it would be."

Henry's eyebrows climbed toward his receding hairline, and Michael felt his cheeks heat. "And what does that mean?" Henry inquired, and Michael remembered belatedly that the older man had always been too damned perceptive.

"It means—I don't know what it means," Michael sighed. "It's... complicated. Confusing."

He remembered the feeling of Seward's skin under his hands from the night before, his body trembling against Michael's own. It had been awkward, returning to the house that night; the Abbotts had all pitched headlong into bed right away, and Seward had nearly been too exhausted to climb the stairs even with Michael's help. He'd had to haul him bodily up each step, and they'd both been panting and cursing when they reached the top.

"I'm sorry," Michael had said when he'd deposited Seward on his bed.

Seward's eyes had been confused and strangely hurt. Michael had swiftly amended, "For tiring you out today."

Seward's face had cleared a little. "It wasn't your fault. I wanted to help Sarah." His gaze had lifted to Michael's face. "I enjoyed it."

And suddenly it had seemed that they were talking about another subject entirely, and Michael had felt a momentary blaze of panic sweep over his skin. "Yes, it was a fine day," he'd said, too brightly. Seward had frowned slightly before the mask that had once been a permanent fixture had descended over his features.

"A fine day," he'd echoed hollowly. "Good night, McCready."

Michael hadn't slept since, leaving before dawn to walk to the train station in Stuyvesant, with only a brief note to the Abbotts explaining his plan to return late Sunday night.

"What's confusing about gardening?" Henry was asking, his face open and curious.

Michael took a deep breath and let it out in a rush. "Nothing. Nothing at all."

THE stout Italian landlady who oversaw Margaret's building welcomed him like an old friend and regaled him with the latest neighborhood gossip all the way up the three flights of stairs as they climbed. It turned out that he'd missed his sister by only a few minutes; she'd left on some errands just before Michael had arrived. "She gone to Lasky's round the corner and the fish market with my Anna. Not long, you wait."

Mrs. Dinardo turned the key in the lock and let Michael into the small apartment. "You don't look so good," she told him, not unkindly. "You lie down until she comes home, hah?" Smiling and thanking her, Michael saw her to the door, then collapsed onto the bed in the corner. He'd just doze for a few minutes, he thought.

He awoke from a sound sleep to the sensation that he was being watched. Opening his eyes, he nearly jumped out of his skin when he found himself nose to nose with Edith. Her pale blue eyes were huge in her face, and once Michael overcame his shock, he grinned widely.

"Goodness, miss," he said, sitting up and swinging his legs over the edge of the bed, "now who would you be?"

"It's Edith, Uncle Michael!" the girl exclaimed, prodding his legs as though he were still asleep. "Don't you know me?"

He scratched his chin thoughtfully. "I have a niece named Edith, but I'm sure you're not her. She's a very young girl, you see, and you are far too grown up to be my little Edith."

Edith covered her mouth with her hands and giggled. "Uncle Michael, it's me, it's me! I got old!"

"Why, how old are you now?" Michael asked, though he knew perfectly well.

Beaming, Edith held up four fingers.

"Is that so?" Michael said, grabbing her around the waist and swinging her up into his arms as he stood. "Well then, I suppose I'll have to believe you, won't I?"

Edith flung her arms around his neck and squeezed him, and he hugged her back as tightly as he dared.

Hearing a small noise, he looked up to see Margaret watching him from the doorway, a bag of groceries on one hip and the baby on the other. Her expression startled him, because it was cold and distant and made her look nothing like the Margaret he knew and loved.

And then his heart stopped altogether as he realized what must have happened. *Or rather, who,* he thought, the rage beginning to coil inside him like a great, venomous snake.

"Anna," Margaret said, turning to the girl standing behind her, "could you take Donald downstairs for a few minutes? This won't take long." After passing the baby to Anna, she smiled at Edith. "Sweetheart, go with Anna, please." Her smile disappeared, and Michael felt chilled to the bone. "Michael can't stay."

But Edith only clung more tightly to Michael's neck. "Edith, m'dearie, we must do what your mother says," Michael told her softly.

"You just got here," the child whined, looking up at him. "Don't go yet."

Michael gave her a final squeeze before tugging her arms free and lowering her to the ground. "Don't worry," he said, throat constricted. "I'll see you again soon."

Edith stared up at him, gaze wary, and Michael felt his heart constrict. Without another word, the child walked to the door and placed her hand in Anna's, who led her away. Margaret closed the door behind them, then turned back to Michael.

"Well, at least now I know why I haven't received any letters from you in nearly a month," he said shortly. "I'm going to kill that bastard Paddy."

Margaret shook her head. "Uncle Paddy didn't tell me; Aunt Kathleen did. Paddy told her one night when he was drunk—"

"When is he not drunk?" Michael snapped.

"—and she felt it was her Christian duty to tell me."

"God." Michael scrubbed at his face with his hands. As much as he wanted to hate the sanctimonious old cow, he couldn't bring himself to it. She'd never known anything but misery in her life. It wasn't surprising that she'd take it upon herself to spread it around when given the opportunity.

"Is it true?" Margaret demanded, taking a step toward him as if she might embrace him, then hesitating. Michael's heart lurched painfully. "Michael, is it true?"

"Tell me exactly what she said to you," Michael bit out.

Margaret wrung her hands, her face anguished. "She said you— that you're a—" She looked at the floor. "I—I can't say it."

Michael's mouth twisted. "The latest medical term is 'invert'. It's much more modern than some of the words you're no doubt thinking of using."

Margaret's gaze rose to his, shock and revulsion tangled together. "Why?"

It was so far from what Michael had been expecting her to say that he actually laughed in surprise. "Why am I queer? You might as well ask why the world is round."

"You could still renounce your sins," she said imploringly. "You could come with me to Mass. You could—"

"Could what?" Michael spat. "Beg God to make me a real man? To help me find a good woman the way Paul did?"

Margaret turned away. "Don't," she said lowly.

That was the final straw. Michael's fury burst forth like water from a crumbling dam. "Have you heard from him, Margaret? Has he written, cabled, sent you a damned nickel in all this time?"

She kept her eyes averted. "You know he hasn't."

"No, he hasn't, and he isn't going to. When he found out he'd given you another child he ran with his tail between his legs, because he couldn't stand up with you like a man. I've been helping to do that bastard's duty for him for the better part of a year, and you're standing there telling me I'm the sinner?"

"I don't know what you are!" Margaret cried, tears welling in her eyes. "I don't know *who* you are. It's—it's as though a stranger were standing before me."

Michael felt as though his heart were being torn from his chest. "I'm your brother," he said roughly, cursing the tremor in his voice. "I'm Edith's and Donald's uncle. I'm the man who will always love you and look after you. I'm your family."

Margaret stared at him, the tears now spilling down her cheeks. "No," she said finally, chin rising in that determined way he knew so well. He'd always been so proud of her spirit, but it had never before been used against him. "You're not my brother any longer. Not until you—you agree to change."

Michael shook his head sadly. "It's not something that can be changed like a suit of clothes. It's in me. It's part of me, just as surely as my love for you is part of me."

"Oh, God!" Margaret sobbed, tears streaming down her face, mask finally crumbling. "And don't you think I'm doing this out of love for you? It's killing me to think you won't find a place in heaven—"

"Don't talk to me about heaven," Michael said, as close to pleading as he could ever remember. "I need you in this life, not the next. Do you hear me? I need you."

Margaret hesitated for an endless moment before shaking her head slowly. "I'm sorry," she murmured. "Someday you'll understand, and come back to me."

The world blurred. Michael's hands clenched into fists, then swiftly relaxed when he saw the fear flash in her eyes. Jesus Christ, she actually believed he might—

His gorge rose in his throat. He had to get out of there, now. "I'll keep sending you money—" Margaret opened her mouth to protest, and Michael held up a hand to forestall her, "—no. If you give a damn for your children, you won't refuse it. When you find yourself a more suitable provider, get word to me and I'll stop."

He dashed down the stairs, her voice following him as he ran, crying his name over and over. When he finally reached the street with its blessed cacophony of car horns and elevated trains, he leaned against the grimy brick façade until the trembling stopped.

And now, he thought, pushing off from the building and heading uptown, *time to take a few more steps along the road to hell.*

"FUCK, fuck, fuck, fuck, fuck," chanted the man under him. "Harder, fuck, harder, oh, fuck me."

With a growl of frustration, Michael hiked the long legs up onto his shoulders and redoubled his efforts, plowing into the tight ass over and over again.

"Oh, yes, God, fuck, that's it, that's it, that's it—"

I wish you'd shut the hell up, Michael thought uncharitably, his erection flagging at the young man's constant litany. Shoving at him roughly, Michael picked up his pace and achieved a wholly unsatisfying completion in a handful of vicious thrusts. Pulling out of the still-twitching ass, he wrapped his hand around the other man's cock and brought him swiftly to shrill-voiced ecstasy.

Oblivious to Michael's difficulty, the other man sprawled bonelessly on the sheets, smirking up at him. Looking down, Michael realized with a start that the boyish face, freckled skin, and golden-haired thighs that had so attracted him a couple of months ago seemed insipid and unexciting to him now. Instead, his mind's eye was full of dark-haired, tanned skin and haunted green eyes set in a long, patrician face, and against all reason his limp cock stirred.

"God, you're a marvelous carnivore," the young man purred, cupping his hand over Michael's groin. "You fuck with all the determination of your species."

Sighing, Michael flopped onto the mattress beside him, one arm covering his eyes. "That sounds like a line from one of your plays," he muttered.

"It does, doesn't it?" the other man said, sounding pleased. Michael might have known he'd take that as a compliment. "Perhaps I'll find a way to work it in somehow. Properly sanitized, of course. Mustn't upset the theater-going public with foul language." He pried Michael's arm away from his face and smiled down at him indulgently.

Elliott Castleton, Michael thought suddenly. He knew he'd recall it eventually if he distracted himself with other... activities.

"What are you thinking?"

That I couldn't remember your name until a few seconds ago, Michael thought. Aloud, he said, "Have you ever been in love?"

Castleton stuck out his lower lip in a parody of consideration. "Oh, dozens of times," he answered breezily. "What about you?"

Michael snorted and shut his eyes. "Let's just say I'm not so— generous—in my affections," he murmured.

Castleton's eyebrows slowly drew together. "You—ah—you're not saying you've fallen in love with... ah, me?"

Michael cracked open an eye and peered at him balefully, and after a moment Elliott caught on. "Oh, well," he said, flapping a hand, "not that I wouldn't have been flattered, but it does make things... simpler, after all."

"Yes," Michael said, the weight of everything he'd lost this afternoon coming crashing down around his ears, "it definitely is simpler to not give a damn."

Castleton cocked his head. "Then what was the point of talking about it?" he asked.

Michael sighed. "I don't know," he murmured, scrubbing at his face briefly with both hands. "I'm sorry to have brought it up." And he was. God, it was like the blind leading the blind.

Castleton shrugged, then ran light fingers up Michael's arm. "You still haven't told me your plans. Will you be staying in New York?"

"I don't know that either," Michael said, then immediately added, "No. No, I don't believe I will." There was no need for him to stay in his current job now that Paddy had no leverage on him; the threat of jail had never worried him. But he couldn't bear the thought of staying in the same city with Margaret and not being able to see her or the children. And so the obvious decision seemed to be to seek out a fresh experience in an entirely new city: Chicago, New Orleans, San Francisco—anywhere. He was a free man; he could do as he wished. In a world hell-bent on forgetting war, a world turning headlong toward the pursuit of pleasure, a marvelous carnivore could do very well for himself.

The thought of it left him hollow and cold.

"When do you plan to leave?"

Michael pushed away the image of Sarah, her expression disillusioned and yet resigned. "Quite soon, if I can manage it."

"That's unfortunate," Castleton pouted. "A friend of mine is hosting an art show next week. I would have liked to have shown you off a little."

Michael smiled in spite of himself. "Ex-lover?"

Castleton raised an eyebrow. "How did you guess?"

But Michael had already latched on to the important information. "An art show, you say? Your friend owns a gallery?"

Castleton made a derisive noise. "He's a dilettante who dabbles in the arts."

Michael bit his lip to hold back the obvious retort about pots and kettles. "But he puts together art shows?"

Castleton blinked, finally picking up on Michael's uncharacteristic enthusiasm. "Yes. Why?"

"Because I might have a painter he should meet. Will you tell me how to get in touch with him?"

Castleton yawned and stretched. "For you, my darling, I will arrange it personally. Let me know what you need done and he'll do it." At Michael's surprised look, Castleton smiled evilly. "Let's just say he owes me a favor and leave it at that."

"I'll give you the details of his address," Michael said, the plan forming as he spoke. "Give me a couple of weeks to be on my way and then get in touch with him. Make up a story as to how you found out about him; it doesn't matter. Just leave my name out of it."

Castleton's smile turned wry. "Well, well," he said breathily, "someone's excited. I wonder why?"

Michael's heart slammed against his ribs. "Don't fuck with me," he growled. "Just tell me if you can do it."

Castleton blinked at him, all traces of humor disappearing, then calmly said, "I told you I would arrange whatever you wanted."

Michael reined in his stampeding emotions, took a deep breath and let it out. "Yes. You did. I'm sorry."

Castleton frowned at him in curiosity rather than disapproval. "You're a strange bird, aren't you?"

Michael reached up and fisted his hand in the blond hair. Castleton jerked in his grasp, eyes widening in surprise. "Thought I was a carnivore," he growled, pulling him down.

"Oh, God," Castleton breathed, eyelids drooping again as Michael maneuvered him where he wished, and then he mercifully said no more for a good while. Castleton truly did have a talented mouth when he employed it in pursuits that did not involve talking, and that excused a good deal in Michael's mind. Unfortunately, his mind was also given to wandering tonight, and when next he looked down the length of his body, it was to a vision of Seward's mouth engulfing him, welcoming him home over and over again. He screwed his eyes shut to dispel the seductive image, but it remained to torment him. Seward, he imagined, would not be nearly as experienced as Castleton, but he would be rough where Castleton was smooth and unyielding and stubborn where Castleton was pliant and agreeable, and his hair would be soft and his hands would be wide and endearingly unsure—

Michael arched his back and came without warning, groaning as though he were dying. He heard Castleton cough and felt him withdraw abruptly, and murmured a halfhearted apology before flipping him over onto his stomach and proceeding to make it up to him. Within a few minutes Castleton was begging to come as Michael slid his tongue around his hole. When Michael penetrated him with three greased fingers, he screamed his approval and came all over his expensive sheets.

Seward, Michael imagined, would be nearly silent. Michael would try every trick he knew to break through that well-bred veneer, and he would count every small sound as a victory—

Christ, he thought, withdrawing his now-trembling hands from Castleton's spent body, *what am I going to do now?*

Castleton, as always, was centered on his own pleasure. "Michael, I do believe you broke me in the best possible way," he sighed happily.

"Glad I could oblige," Michael murmured, gratefully allowing physical exhaustion to silence his questions for a few hours.

$$12$$

DESPITE his determination to quit his job and bid farewell to Paddy's enslavement as soon as possible, Michael was not eager to broach the subject of his departure with Abbott. The old man seemed to have suffered no ill effects from his strenuous day last week, and he was looking happier than Michael had ever seen him. In fact, all the members of the household—with the notable exception of himself— seemed rejuvenated after their outing, and he was loath to do anything to upset that new balance.

On the other hand, he couldn't continue this way for much longer. Every day he stayed brought him a little closer to imagining a situation that was so patently absurd he should have laughed aloud at the thought. But each time he caught Seward watching him with that fathomless green gaze, with an unsettling mixture of hope and anticipation, he was drawn another few inches toward a dream that would never have a basis in reality. Did he truly think that the lord of the manor would sweep him off his feet and make an honest man of him? Even more ridiculously, did he believe that he knew a damned thing about happy endings?

No. Better to leave as soon as he could and strike out on his own for new territory that was free of associations and memories. He only needed to watch for the right opportunity.

On the Saturday after his disastrous trip to New York, the weather was so hot that he was drenched in sweat by the time he was halfway through the mowing, and Seward was close to heat stroke after two laps of the house. After being thoroughly scolded by Mary, they found themselves packing Sarah and a generous picnic lunch into the car, with strict instructions to enjoy the rest of the day.

They ended up on a stretch of the Hudson just outside of Stuyvesant, on land owned by one of the many branches of the Seward family. Luckily, these Sewards were on an extended tour of Europe, so after a brief exchange of greetings with the caretaker, there was no further need to socialize.

Sarah had brought her model ship, and Seward helped her affix a length of rope to it so that she could sail it on the river without worrying about losing it to the current. The faint breeze puffed out the sails as she sat on the bank admiring its form and speed and conjuring all sorts of grand adventures for her make-believe crew. Michael and Seward flanked her, their feet dangling in the cool water, as she wove her tales around them all, and for the first time Michael found himself humbled by the limitless expanse of a child's fanciful imagination. His youthful dreams had always been of the much more mundane kind, relating to a full belly and a vague, half-formed desire for a freedom he hadn't yet begun to understand.

After lunch they all changed into their swimming gear—Michael in a suit borrowed from one of the trunks in the attic—and splashed about in the shallow cove near the boathouse. He noted with some dismay that Seward was looking tanned and fit, his build now leaning toward athletically slim rather than gaunt. Long muscles Michael had coaxed back to life played under his golden skin as he chased a giggling Sarah around in circles.

As for Michael, he stayed near the shore, watching them warily as they swam and dived in increasingly deeper water. He'd never learned to swim himself. Paddy and his aunt had never encouraged him to visit the public baths as a child, and when he grew older he'd discovered other pursuits to occupy his time.

"Can you hold your breath underwater?" Sarah asked Michael, her small face dotted with sparkling droplets. "I can!"

"Oh, wait—" Michael began, but before he could finish, she had disappeared entirely without a trace. He strode toward her, feet slipping on the slick rocks as he tried to reach her.

"She'll be all right," Seward told him. "She's a champion swimmer, Mary tells me."

"Well, I'm not," Michael gritted, watching the surface of the water with increasing anxiety, "and if she gets into trouble, I won't be able to help her."

He felt a hand touch his arm and jumped; he hadn't realized Seward was so close. Turning, he caught Seward's gently amused expression.

"The water is four feet deep," Seward murmured, hand warm on Michael's bicep. "She'll be fine. And if there's any trouble, I can manage it."

Michael's jaw clenched. "I know I'm being foolish," he snapped.

The hand on his arm tightened, and Michael looked up to meet Seward's unexpectedly open gaze. "You're not being anything of the kind," he said with surprising vehemence. "Don't ever apologize for giving a damn."

Michael's mouth thinned. "It's been a while," he murmured. "I'm not sure I remember how."

"You do," Seward told him firmly. "I know that you do, because you've helped me to remember."

Michael found himself trapped by that gaze, drawn inexorably closer by its warmth. He tried to speak, but his voice had deserted him.

And then Seward's free hand was wrapping around the back of Michael's neck as he leaned in, and Michael could only stare at him, fascinated by the water clinging to his long eyelashes and glistening on his upper lip. He wondered suddenly whether Seward's mouth would be cool from the river—

The sound of a loud splash a couple of dozen feet away threw Michael out of his reverie, and the two of them broke apart as though they'd been caught groping in the bushes in Central Park.

"How long was that? How long did I hold my breath?" Sarah squealed, popping up out of the water.

"Oh, that was—" Seward cleared his throat before continuing, "—that was easily forty-five seconds. Very impressive."

"I'm going to try again!" Sarah exclaimed, and dove under once more.

Michael stared at the place she'd been for a few moments, feeling his pulse pounding in his throat. He looked up just as Seward sank a hand in his hair and crushed their mouths together.

Michael fought for all of half a second before his own hands were cupping Seward's face and he was returning the kiss, licking and biting in his eagerness, the desire he'd spent weeks suppressing flooding to the surface of his skin and drowning him.

"Christ," Michael swore when they broke away and pressed their cheeks together, panting for breath, "this is—"

"We have less than twenty seconds before she pops up again," Seward growled in his ear, the vibration making Michael shudder. "Let me enjoy it." His arm slid around Michael's shoulders, surprising strength meeting Michael's own and mastering it briefly as he claimed one last, bruising kiss.

Right on cue, Sarah emerged triumphantly from the river fifteen seconds later to the applause and cheers of both men. She giggled and bowed to them, then initiated a splashing water fight that soon had them all drenched and laughing.

It was only hours later, when he was driving back with Seward cradling an exhausted but happy Sarah in the backseat of the car, that Michael wondered when the hell his entire life had turned itself inside-out.

THE next few days were a tangle of emotion and mental confusion as knotted and impossible to clear from Michael's mind as barbed wire entanglement in No Man's Land. Luckily, since Seward was becoming more and more independent and the garden was now requiring correspondingly greater time for maintenance, the times in which he was alone with Seward were few and far between. Sarah was their companion during their afternoon sessions in the gymnasium, and Michael shifted his massages to an earlier time when the Abbotts were more likely to be prowling the upstairs halls engaged in one of their many duties. If Seward noticed the change in schedule, he said nothing, and so the incident between them at the river was not repeated.

And then Seward decided to push himself beyond his limits once more, undertaking a hike through the woods that lasted two hours beyond his estimate. The Abbotts were watching the setting sun with apprehension and Michael was considering the best route to take for a search when Seward emerged from the forest, exhausted, arms and legs bloodied by a score of mosquito bites and encounters with hostile flora.

Mary handed Michael the bottle of calamine lotion and sent him off with orders to tend to Seward.

"I don't need to be reminded of my job," Michael snapped. Mary frowned at him but said nothing. When her too-knowing gaze turned speculative, Michael turned and fled.

He trudged up the stairs, thinking he would find Seward barely out of his shirt by now, but he'd apparently underestimated Seward's speed, because when Michael walked in, he was stark naked and inspecting himself in the full-length mirror. He looked up and met Michael's gaze in the glass when he entered.

With a great effort of will, Michael kept his eyes straight and level. "Why do you do this to yourself?" he ground out, fists clenching in frustration. "You're progressing well, but you're not fully recovered, not by a long shot. You're going to suffer a setback if you keep going to extremes like this."

Seward dabbed at a bite on his forearm with a damp handkerchief. "I know it."

"Then why?" Michael demanded.

Seward shrugged. "I suppose the best explanation is that, like Sarah, I don't believe I deserve to be happy."

Michael crossed his arms. "Sarah deserves to be happy."

"Well, of course she does," Seward said matter-of-factly, cleaning another bite.

"And so do you," Michael persisted gruffly.

Seward looked up and met his gaze again. A small smile tugged at the corners of his mouth. "That's open to debate," he said softly. A pause, then: "What about you? Do you deserve to be happy?"

Michael looked away. "There wasn't a lot of it to be had where I grew up. As far as I'm concerned, it's not a commodity that lasts more than a few days, or hours."

To his shock, Seward chuckled dryly. "Ah, it must be a poignant thing to be a simple workingman, a member of the rough and tumble proletariat, gathering your fleeting pleasures hither and yon."

"Fuck off," Michael growled lowly. Unperturbed, Seward turned and walked toward him. His steps, Michael noted dimly, were sure and even. When he was close enough, Seward reached up and rested his hands on Michael's shoulders.

"*Carpe diem*, is that your philosophy?" Seward murmured. Every word was a soft puff of breath against Michael's face, and Michael shivered in spite of himself. "Do you believe that nothing is eternal, that everything is transitory, meaningless?" His fingers slid across the cool cotton of Michael's shirt, caressed his neck, sank into his hair, held fast. "Is that what this is?"

"There is no—this," Michael whispered, summoning every shred of will to sever the connection between them, to step back and back again until Seward's hands fell to his sides. The bereft look on Seward's face made him scramble for an explanation that wouldn't be interpreted as a rejection. "I—"

Seward shook his head once to silence him, and that perfect mask Michael had seen the first day they'd met dropped into place, hiding Seward's every emotion from his prying gaze. "No, it's fine. I understand completely," he said hollowly, turning back around.

"You don't understand a damned thing," Michael snarled, taking two steps forward and feeling his feet march straight off the precipice and into thin air.

"Then for God's sake, explain it to me," Seward begged, the mask crumbling as suddenly as it had appeared, the mirror revealing the reflection of a man completely adrift. "Because I don't want this any more than you do, but I can't seem to stop—"

Michael's gaze dropped to roam shamelessly over the terrain of Seward's body, so familiar and yet unexplored in so many ways. He had never touched for his own benefit, only for Seward's, but now his palms were itching to roam over that flesh, to glide and press and feel it living under them, as though it existed only for this, only for him—

Seward hissed air between his teeth, and Michael looked up to see that his eyes had closed. "The way you look at me," he breathed. Christ, Seward's cock was half-hard already and Michael hadn't even touched him. The thought that he could do this much to him with only a look made his own body respond.

"I'm sorry," Michael said automatically, for many different reasons, not the least of which was that there was no future in it for either of them.

"I don't want you to apologize," Seward murmured, words fervent as a prayer. "Though I can't even imagine why you would want...." He trailed off.

"What?"

"This," Seward said, turning to face him, his hands spreading to encompass the scars and half-formed muscles, the persistent slight droop of his right shoulder. He obviously was blind to the beauty that was revealed by the proof of his survival, the rise of his renewed manhood.

Michael shook his head slowly and moved to close the remaining distance between them, cursing both of them silently in his head but unable to stand against the force of their combined need a moment longer. Seward met him halfway there, groaning helplessly into Michael's mouth, his hands sliding down Michael's shoulders and back.

"Can you imagine it now?" Michael demanded hoarsely, mouth hot against Seward's neck. "I can. I have been for weeks."

"God," Seward breathed, tugging him up for another kiss. His clumsy fingers fumbled over the buttons on Michael's shirt, nearly popping them off in his haste. His rough enthusiasm excited Michael beyond reason. He glided his hands down over the surprisingly firm curve of Seward's ass and felt Seward jerk in his arms.

"Did I hurt you?" Michael asked, releasing him immediately.

Eyes squeezed shut, Seward shook his head. "No, no," he

whispered, "please, don't stop...."

With a growl, Michael gripped his ass and hauled him close, swallowing the moan that escaped his lips as Seward's firm cock was pressed against the rough wool of Michael's trousers. Michael's own erection was already aching. He couldn't remember ever being so thoroughly aroused by a few simple kisses and touches. Seward was tugging his shirt down his arms now, and Michael let go of Seward's body for a moment to help. Seward's fingers tickled his belly as he grasped the hem of the undershirt, then shoved it upward.

Michael emerged from the shirt to find Seward staring at him hungrily. "You're so—" he murmured, then let his fingertips complete the thought, speaking with caresses rather than words. His hands sang praises to Michael's body, and Michael looked up to see his own eyes staring back at him desperately, uncomprehendingly.

He wanted to protest, because he wasn't worthy of that level of reverence. In its own way, his body had been as ill-used as Seward's. Worse, because he'd participated in his own ruination, fed his decline with countless cheap, hasty fucks in back alleys and bathhouses, anonymous encounters with men days from dying, drowning in mud. His skin was too sullied to inspire worship, too flawed for such devoted pilgrimages.

In the end, he said nothing, partly because he knew it would do no good and partly because he wanted to be new again, if only in this man's eyes, if only for this night.

Seward pushed at him gently, steering him toward the bed, and Michael let himself be guided, let himself tumble onto the mattress as Seward straddled him and began attacking the buttons of his trousers. Michael caught one of Seward's hands and pressed the flattened palm to his engorged cock. Seward shut his eyes and shuddered, then dove down for another kiss.

Wrapping his arms around the slim back, Michael rolled them over, reversing their positions, then finished the work Seward had started. Finally naked, he stretched himself out over top of Seward, bracing his hands on the mattress as he ground their hips together.

"Oh, Christ—" Seward swore, throwing his head back, neck muscles straining. Michael licked those sinewy cords, unable to resist.

Seward made another low noise at that, and all of Michael's assumptions about a taciturn bedmate went flying out the window. Seward's noises, however, were nothing like Castleton's whines and demands; instead of being thrown out like disposable, worthless trifles, each one was a finely wrought treasure, the product of fire and need. Michael craved those sounds and did his damnedest to force them from Seward's kiss-bruised lips as he worked his way down that lean body.

By the time he was darting his tongue into Seward's navel, Seward was practically keening with desire, the muscles of his belly taut, his cock radiating heat and musk. Deciding to be merciful, Michael wrapped one hand around the base of him to steady him, then lowered his mouth to the leaking tip. Seward froze and fell silent at the touch. Michael raised his eyes and saw him looking down the length of his body, his mouth open as he panted raggedly.

Smiling, Michael lifted his head and arrowed his tongue, letting Seward see every movement as he swirled it around the head. The green eyes drank him in, reflecting some emotion Michael didn't recognize. Closing his own eyes, he bent again to his task, cheeks hollowing as he began to suck.

At some point, he felt the soft touch of a hand on his face and waited for the inevitable guidance that men seemed compelled to give. But the fingers merely stroked his cheek with the gentlest pressure, as if in gratitude. Michael heard himself groan low in his throat at that unexpected tenderness in the midst of carnality, and within seconds Seward emitted a sharp gasp, and his body shifted, heralding a withdrawal. Michael only redoubled his efforts, and as he reached up, his fingers tightening around Seward's, he felt the first warm jet of fluid coat his tongue.

When it was over, Michael opened his eyes and beheld Seward lying spent and dazed, one arm flung above his head, the other hand still entwined with Michael's. His hair was disheveled, his cheeks were flushed a deep scarlet, and his chest was sheened with sweat, and Michael felt a tug of possession deep within him more powerful than he'd ever known.

As if he'd spoken his fondest wish aloud, Seward stared at him, eyes wide, then mutely rolled onto his belly.

Michael was somewhat slower on the uptake, since the sight of Seward offering his body for Michael's pleasure was enough to momentarily incapacitate his powers of reason. When he could think again, he reached out with one finger and trailed it down the length of Seward's crease.

Seward shivered and jerked under him.

"You want this?" Michael demanded.

Seward nodded.

Another caress, another flinch. "Doesn't seem like it."

Seward twisted his head to glare at Michael out of the corner of his eye. "Would you just do it?" he snapped, and that was so much like the Seward he knew that he had to bite back a chuckle.

"Well, since you ask so sweetly," Michael purred. He snatched a jar of Vaseline off the nightstand and opened it, then coated two fingers with the stuff. Moving between his legs, he nudged the insides of Seward's thighs roughly with his knees. Seward gasped but complied with the unspoken request, his legs widening even further.

Murmuring soft words of encouragement, Michael slid his fingers in slowly, pausing whenever he encountered resistance, allowing Seward's body to adjust to the intrusion. Seward made no move to either assist or hinder him, instead remaining as still as a corpse.

Determined to provoke a reaction, Michael pressed forward until he found the small rise that denoted his pleasure center, then brushed it with the gentlest of touches.

Seward buried his face in the pillow and groaned.

Bending his head, Michael bit Seward's ass lightly. "What was that?" he asked, drawing his fingers back for a fresh assault.

"Oh, Christ, that's—" A sharper cry this time. "God. I didn't know it could—" He trailed off abruptly, hands fisting in the sheets at his sides.

Michael felt anger flare in him on Seward's behalf. Obviously his previous lovers had been incompetent or selfish, to have failed to give him this. "That's only the beginning," he promised, setting up a slow, easy rhythm designed to drive Seward mad.

It had the desired effect; within minutes Seward was all but sobbing his pleasure. However, he was still tense and unmoving, and so Michael decided to try another tack. Withdrawing, he gripped Seward's hips, urging him up. After a tense moment, Seward shoved himself to his knees, his whole body trembling.

Michael rewarded him with a lingering caress down his spine with his dry hand while the other gathered more lubricant and gently rubbed around his entrance. He kept up this teasing treatment until Seward finally moved, rocking back in an attempt to force Michael's fingers back inside. Smiling, he rewarded Seward with a brief touch to his cock, which was already rising again.

"What do you want?" Michael asked. Seward groaned again but said nothing. Michael returned his fingers to Seward's hole. "Do you want this?"

Seward whimpered and angled his hips upward, seeking, pleading. Michael leaned down over his back and bit his earlobe, letting his own cock rest in the cleft of Seward's ass.

"Or would you rather have this?" he murmured, rotating his hips. Seward was now shaking so hard Michael feared he would collapse under him. He was gasping as though his lungs could not draw enough air, his eyes squeezed shut. When he spoke, the sound was so low that Michael had to strain to hear.

"You," Seward whispered, "you, I want you...." The last word trailed off into a moan, and Seward pushed back against him, the sudden sharp pressure nearly toppling Michael over the edge of ecstasy. With a muffled curse, he leaned back, slathered the slick stuff onto his cock, and then slid into Seward as swiftly as he dared, watching as Seward took him in inch by glorious inch.

When he was fully seated, he paused for a moment. Seward made a soft, choked sound and tried to move, but Michael's hands dug into his hips, preventing him. "Wait," he growled. "Give me a moment, or this will be over very quickly."

"Oh, God," Seward breathed, shuddering. "It's so good I don't know if I can—"

"Shhh," Michael soothed, closing his eyes against the delicious sight of that long, lean back, "soon. Soon." Gathering the tattered remains of his control, he began to move in tiny increments, drawing out with excruciating slowness until only the tip of him remained inside the tight heat.

Seward growled low in his throat, practically strangling on his frustration.

"Do you like this?" Michael murmured hoarsely. Seward whimpered and tried to push back against his cock, but Michael only withdrew further in response. "Tell me."

"Yes," Seward whispered, "yes, I like it. I love…." He trailed off, head hanging down, exposing his vulnerable nape. "I love it."

"Then take it," Michael ordered, releasing Seward's hips and allowing him to move as he wished. With a grateful sob, Seward braced his arms above his head and shoved his body back onto Michael's cock, impaling himself.

"Christ," Michael gasped, hips pistoning helplessly as he finally succumbed to his own overwhelming need. Bracing himself with a hand on Seward's shoulder, he moved with him, in him, thrusting deeply, seeking that place of ultimate pleasure. His other hand sought and found Seward's cock, forming a tight tunnel for him to use as he moved.

Seward stiffened and shouted, and then he was pouring himself into Michael's hand as he came. Michael rode out the rhythmic pulls of Seward's orgasm, then redoubled his efforts, fairly pounding into him in his desperation to reach his goal. He fucked into him until he swore he could feel Seward's stuttering heartbeat all around him; then, with a feeling akin to triumph, he rose up and spent himself with one final, forceful thrust.

He withdrew from Seward with infinite care, but there was still a grunt of discomfort when they separated. To his surprise, Seward immediately pulled him into an embrace, and they lay together, sated and panting, recovering by slow degrees.

"Did I hurt you?" Michael asked, his hand stroking down Seward's back.

Seward shook his head. "I'm fine." He turned his head to smile at

Michael. "I must say I believe that to be my favorite form of massage yet."

Michael moved his hand a little lower, finding one of the many shrapnel scars that adorned Seward's back, scars he could map by touch alone. He traced it with a fingertip, and Seward shivered. "Prostate massage is actually described in the textbooks," Michael drawled, "but I think my technique would be considered a little unorthodox."

"Well, I happen to be very fond of your technique," Seward murmured, his expression filled with such open affection that Michael had to look away. Seeming to sense his unease, or perhaps experiencing some of his own, Seward cleared his throat and said, "I suppose I shouldn't have admitted that. Now you'll work me twice as hard."

Smiling wickedly, Michael leaned in and bit Seward's chin. "I'm inclined to be merciful given the proper incentive," he murmured, hooking an arm around Seward's neck and pulling him down into a rougher, more insistent kiss that soon had them both breathless and eager for more.

"What do you want?" Seward demanded, hands roaming over his chest, his shoulders, his face, as though he were trying to memorize the surface of his skin.

"I don't know," Michael admitted, so addled that the words came without conscious thought. "I haven't wanted anything in a very long time."

Seward's hands stilled, and Michael sucked in a breath at his own carelessness. And then those hands cupped his face gently, with a care usually bestowed upon the most fragile and valuable objects, and Michael's heart slammed against his ribs.

"Then you have some catching up to do," Seward told him softly, his green gaze holding Michael's captive. Easing him over onto his back, he bent to Michael's chest and kissed his breastbone. "Let me know when I stumble across something that appeals to you."

As Seward's mouth slid down his body, Michael gasped and gripped the mattress. "You'll—oh—you'll be the first to hear," he promised.

$$13$$

"WHAT'S the matter?"

Blinking, Michael looked up from the bed he was weeding and met Sarah's concerned gaze. "Nothing, m'dearie," he said. "Why do you ask?"

Sarah frowned at him. "You were just standing there staring off into space."

Michael shook himself and affected a yawn. "Didn't sleep very well last night. I'm a little tired."

Sarah eyed him again, and he struggled to hold her gaze. "I remember hearing you climbing the stairs to the attic around dawn," she said.

"Yes, I, ah," Michael began stupidly, "I couldn't sleep, so I walked around for a long time—on the grounds."

She frowned. "Are you feeling all right?"

"Never felt better in my life."

Sarah nodded, apparently satisfied, and they worked in silence for a time until she asked abruptly, "Are you and Uncle John fighting?"

Michael nearly dropped his hoe. "Why do you ask that?"

"You wouldn't look at one another at breakfast."

"Oh, well, that's nothing," Michael said hastily, mind scrambling for an explanation that wasn't *We were afraid that if we looked at one another, we'd start grinning like idiots*, "you see, we—"

"Uncle John!" Sarah exclaimed, interrupting him. Michael spun to see Seward approaching them across the lawn, his steps sure, his gaze determined. Much to his chagrin, Michael felt his body react to the sight and made a grand show of inspecting the flowerbed for any stray weeds, allowing him a few moments to regain his composure.

"What beautiful work you have done, Sarah darling," he heard Seward say.

"Uncle Michael helped," Sarah added, smiling up at Seward as she hugged him about the waist. Michael was stunned to hear Sarah call him "uncle" the way she now did Seward. It would never have occurred to him that she would think of them both in the same way, with a kindred affection.

He then made the mistake of meeting Seward's gaze, and when he did he found that he was trapped between the fire and the warmth in it. "Well, Uncle Michael does beautiful work as well," he said softly. One corner of his mouth quirked, as though sensing Michael's discomfort. Michael's brows knitted together as he countered with his best glare. The bastard was toying with him and enjoying every moment of it.

And if Michael cared to admit it, he was enjoying it far too much himself.

Finally, Seward broke his hold over Michael, shifting his gaze back to Sarah. "Would you be upset if I left you without a helper for the next couple of days?" he asked, playing absently with one of her pigtails.

Sarah shook her head. "Are you going away?"

"Not for long. My doctor called; he wants to see me in the city. I thought Michael might be kind enough to drive me." At this he looked a question at Michael, whose first reaction was consternation. This was the first he'd heard of a call from Parrish, or indeed of any need for a trip, and to be honest, there was little Michael wanted less at the moment than to return to Manhattan. He was trying his damnedest to keep all consideration of his future from his mind, especially after last night, and revisiting the city was the surest way to bring those unpleasant thoughts to the fore once again. But Seward was, if not his boss, then his patient, and he could not refuse Parrish's orders regarding his treatment. After a slight, stunned delay, he nodded imperceptibly and watched Seward's expression clear, dissolving into something oddly like relief.

"Very well, then," Seward said heartily, clapping his hands. "Why don't you throw a few things in a bag, and I will help the lady until you're ready?"

Michael nodded again and headed up toward the house, only stopping for one final look as he reached the kitchen door. The sight that he beheld was startling: Seward was on his knees beside Sarah, his hands buried in the earth as he wrestled with a particularly difficult weed. Michael froze, waiting for an adverse reaction like the one of a few weeks past, but there was none that he could see, and when he realized he'd been staring at the man like a fool for God knew how long, he spun on his heel and sprinted for the kitchen door.

"TURN left here."

Michael braked the car and turned to regard Seward. "New York is to the right."

Seward's gaze was infuriatingly serene and impenetrable. "Yes, I know."

Michael stared at him. "I take it Parrish didn't call, then."

Seward lifted his chin. "No," he said cheerfully, obviously unwilling to give out any useful information. Gritting his teeth, Michael shoved in the clutch and shifted the old clunker into gear. The car lurched into the turn, tires skidding on the loose dirt.

"Aren't you curious to know where we're going?" Seward asked after a couple of minutes.

"No," Michael said tartly, hands gripping the wheel. He had no idea why he was so thoroughly enraged, only that he was livid with anger, his heart threatening to pound its way out of his chest, his thoughts murderous. Though he knew intellectually that Seward was not the manipulative type, the small deception hit him much harder than it would have had Seward been just another fuck. If twenty-four hours ago he had known that the man had the power to transform him into an unreasoning lunatic, he never would have—

Well, all right, that was a lie, but nevertheless, it was frustrating to be so ruled by the tides of emotion after long months floating along on the calm seas of indifference.

"You're not the least bit curious?" Seward persisted, snapping the last thread of Michael's patience.

"I go where I'm told," he snarled. "After all, I'm only the hired help."

"Oh, for heaven's sake," Seward huffed, "it was meant to be a surprise. A pleasant surprise. You have heard of those, haven't you?"

Michael darted a glance at Seward, whose features were refreshingly stormy. As if in response to the blackening of Seward's mood, Michael found his own anger dissipating. "Vaguely," he drawled. "For most of my life, I was too poor to afford surprises. But I have been saving up for one, as I hear they're simply marvelous."

"Oh, shut up," Seward muttered, without real heat.

"All right, so I'm curious," Michael admitted after a few more minutes of silence.

Seward's answering smile was truly wicked. "Good," he said firmly.

It took well over two hours for them to reach their destination. Not being familiar with the byways of upstate New York, Michael soon lost track once they left the main road to Albany, turning when Seward told him to turn and keeping his mouth shut. The further they drove into the wilderness, the more Michael's curiosity grew, until it was a persistent itch under his skin. Since the journey also took them further into the mountains, however, his interest was mixed with concern. It was by no means certain that the car's engine could take the strain of bearing itself, its passengers, their bags, and Mary's three overflowing baskets of food up the increasingly steep inclines. Michael had to stop twice along the way to fill the radiator with fresh, cool water from a nearby stream.

Mercifully, before the car could expire altogether, Seward instructed him to take a road that was little more than a cart path. After following it a couple of hundred yards through dense forest, they suddenly arrived at a small but well-made cabin perched on the edge of a cliff. The engine sighed gratefully as Michael shut it off, and he climbed out, his steps carrying him to the edge of the overlook.

The view left him breathless. A long, narrow lake lay stretched out far beneath him, guarded by steep slopes carpeted with green. He was so amazed that he failed to notice Seward's approach until he was standing right beside him.

"Well, do you like your surprise?" Seward asked, and for the first time Michael realized there was a hint of trepidation in Seward's manner, as though he were uncertain of the answer he would receive. Without allowing himself to think, Michael reached out blindly, slinging an arm around Seward's shoulders and drawing him closer to his side.

"I like it," Michael murmured, turning his head to nuzzle Seward's soft hair, smiling when Seward's tense shoulder relaxed under his hand. "How did you manage it in—" He took a split second to count. "—five hours?"

"It belongs to an old family friend who rarely uses it. He'd told me I could come up whenever I wanted. He was quite surprised when I called him out of the blue this morning, but he was perfectly happy to let me have it for a few days. It was my father's favorite hunting cabin, and he imagined I would have the same interest in the place."

Michael snorted. "I can't imagine you enjoying hunting."

Seward chuckled. "You're right, I detest it. The one time my father dragged me up here, he was terribly disappointed in me. I spent the whole week painting the view."

Michael felt Seward shudder as his lips brushed Seward's earlobe. "Why didn't you bring your painting supplies this time?"

"I did bring my sketchbook, but I believe I have better things to do," Seward murmured.

"And what would those be?" Michael teased, nipping at the soft flesh under Seward's mouth. "Hike to the summit of the mountain? Tame the bears? Get fat on Mary's fine cooking?"

Seward made a frustrated sound that went straight to Michael's groin, and then he was turning toward Michael, one hand gripping the back of Michael's neck to hold him still for a rough, possessive kiss. Michael groaned and slid his own hands to Seward's hips, jerking him forward until their bodies were flush against one another, not a breath between them.

"Any neighbors nearby?" Michael whispered when they finally broke for air.

Seward shook his head. "Not another cabin for miles."

Grinning in response, Michael's fingers began working at Seward's belt.

"What are you—" Seward choked on his words as Michael slid to his knees in front of him, eagerly tugging at his trousers to free his cock. Seward's cock was astonishingly pretty in daylight, long and flushed and already fully erect. Michael's mouth watered in anticipation as he leaned forward and swallowed it down without preamble.

"Oh, sweet Christ," Seward groaned, one hand flying to Michael's head, the other flailing out as he tried to maintain his balance. Michael bracketed Seward's hips with his hands, helping to steady them both as he sucked greedily. While it certainly wasn't the first time he had done this outdoors, it was the first time he had done it in such a setting. The cramped shadows behind the bushes in Central Park late at night, where a thousand others had gone on their knees before him, could hardly compare. Here there was no one to judge, no one to point and scream for a copper, only the soft afternoon breeze and the song of the sparrows and Seward's gasped, breathless entreaties as Michael took what he needed and gave what he could no longer deny he must.

"I WAS wondering if you might like to pose for me."

Startled by the statement, Michael turned away from his contemplation of the scenery to study Seward. After a dinner of thick ham sandwiches, Mary's coleslaw, and beer, they'd spread a blanket over the grass overlooking the cliff to watch the sunset, which Seward had assured him was spectacular. At Michael's insistence, Seward had retrieved his sketchbook and had immediately set to work on capturing it. "Switching to nudes, are you?"

Seward smirked. "While the rest of you is certainly inspiring, I was thinking of a portrait to start." As if mapping out his brush's course, one of Seward's hands reached out and stroked gently over Michael's forehead, cheeks, nose, and chin before coming to rest on his lips.

Michael felt his heart stutter in answer. "I'm not worth the paint," he murmured.

Seward frowned, then slid his hand into Michael's hair. "Would you like a professional opinion on that?" he growled, leaning in to kiss Michael thoroughly.

Michael returned the kiss with equal fervor, his own hands busy mapping Seward's skin. For the hundredth time, he marveled in the strength that met his own and battled it for supremacy. Seward, he realized abruptly, was ready to seek his own independence. Provided he kept up with the exercise regimen they'd developed, there was no need for Michael to continue working as his therapist.

No need, he repeated silently. *No need for any of this, but God, I still want it.* Shoving the thought aside, he broke away to ask, "Are you a professional, then?"

Seward delivered one final kiss to Michael's lips before pulling back. "I sold all of three paintings before the war," he said.

"That means yes."

"I suppose," Seward sighed. "Before I left, it was all that I wanted to do. I even moved to the city to become a starving artist, and I almost succeeded—at the starving."

Michael glided his fingers over Seward's cheek. "Is that why you and your father had a falling out?"

Seward chuckled hollowly. "No. My father and I had a falling out because he found a series of ridiculously sentimental love letters I'd written to Patrick." At Michael's look of surprise, he added, "Never posted, of course. I didn't have the courage for that. He disowned me, I moved to Hell's Kitchen, war was declared, and the next thing I knew I was on a troop ship bound for England." He smiled wryly. "The spring of 1917 was very eventful for me."

"And now?" Michael asked. "Is it still what you want?"

Seward appeared to consider it. "I don't know. When I came back, there seemed to be no beauty left in the world. I painted what I remembered of the war instead."

"The trenches are best forgotten," Michael murmured, looking away.

There was a pause. Michael could feel the weight of John's penetrating gaze. "I don't think I'll ever be able to forget," he said quietly. "I don't know if I want to. Too many things I loved are buried there." Another pause, and this time Michael felt the touch of Seward's fingertips on his chest, over his heart. "But there are other things I want to paint now."

Michael felt the warmth of the words spread over his skin, into his pores. It was arousing and soothing all at once. Having never experienced those sensations together, he had always believed them incompatible. To find so much of what he craved here, in this impossible situation, frightened the life out of him.

"Do you think you might like to show your paintings?" he asked abruptly, wanting to banish the feeling.

Seward's expression grew puzzled. "I'm a long way from an exhibition," he said carefully. "At any rate, I have no connections in the art world at the moment."

"What if you knew someone who did?"

Seward frowned. "Is this a hypothetical question?" Michael nodded. "Then the answer would still be no. I'm not ready."

You hoped you could hand him this last gift and leave with a clear conscience, Michael's inner demon cackled, *but he's not going to make it easy for you.*

"Would you mind telling me what's going on in your head?" Seward asked softly.

"Yes," Michael murmured, some part of him hoping to raise Seward's hackles, create some distance between them.

Seward barked a laugh. "Well, you're honest, at least," he said, annoyingly unperturbed. "I never asked you about your trip to New York. Did you see your sister?"

Michael's jaw clenched. "No," he lied. "I tried to see her, but she was… away."

"Next time, then," Seward persisted. He leaned in and kissed Michael softly, and Michael's eyes squeezed shut. "And perhaps I could come with you."

That was as much as Michael could stand. Wanting nothing more than to stop thinking, he took Seward's mouth, thrusting his tongue into its depth with unmistakable intent. "You can come right now," he growled, sitting up and attacking Seward's shirt buttons.

"Michael, what the hell are you—" Seward began, irritation finally evident in his voice. Michael ignored him, continuing with his task until Seward's hands bracketed his face and forced him to meet his gaze.

"Slowly," he murmured, thumbs stroking over Michael's cheekbones. "We have time. Please."

It was that gentle "please" that was Michael's undoing. With a soft noise, he allowed Seward to lean in and kiss him as he wished, with deliberation and focus and a passion so deep that Michael was shaking by the time Seward drew back and began to undress him. Each patch of skin bared was a revelation, the setting sun bathing it in warm, silken light that made it seem to glow from within, made it seem a crime not to pause to touch and kiss every inch of it. When they were finally naked, they maintained the same gradual pace, caresses avoiding the obvious terrain, instead striking out into the uncharted regions of hipbone and inner elbow and small of the back. They remained strangely silent throughout, as though a word or sigh would break the spell that had been cast.

They moved together, as if reading one another's minds, and Michael found his arousal building more gradually than it ever had, its progress more astonishing than anything he had ever experienced in another man's arms. As soon as he thought it, his gut knotted unpleasantly, reality coming crashing in again around his ears. God, he was in imminent danger of losing his way, of surrendering every fortification he'd worked so hard to construct, and if he lost this battle, he would lose the war.

Summoning every bit of his tattered resolve, he closed a hand around Seward's shoulder and pressed down gently but insistently. Seward resisted for a moment, looking up at him with a question in his eyes. Michael had no idea what answer he found, but in any case he followed the direction, rolling over on the blanket so that he was lying prone facing the setting sun.

Taking a deep breath, Michael sat up and positioned himself between Seward's legs, then nudged them further apart. Seward shivered, then seemed to forcibly relax, resting his head on his folded arms.

Slowly, Michael reminded himself, fanning his fingers over the globes of Seward's ass and sliding his thumbs down the crease, then spreading him gently and breathing hotly over his center.

Seward jerked under his hands. "You—y-you," he spluttered, and then Michael's tongue followed his breath and Seward produced a soft, surprised noise.

"Yes?" Michael asked archly.

Seward's answer was to grip a fistful of the blanket in each hand.

"Don't let go," Michael whispered into Seward's skin as he parted him once more. It was a sure bet that no one else had ever done this to Seward, and even odds that he hadn't even known men did this to one another, and the thought that Michael was in some respects exploring virgin territory excited him far more than he was willing to admit. Forgetting the injunction to proceed slowly, he breached Seward's body and was rewarded with a gasping, hitching moan. After that, it was all madness and musk and heat, Michael lapping, darting, advancing, and retreating until Seward's pride was gone and he was reduced to pleading for release in a harsh, broken voice.

With a force of will, Michael pulled away, tearing a sharp cry of loss from Seward's throat. Michael slapped his ass. "Up," he grunted, and nearly laughed aloud as Seward scrambled to obey. Guiding him to his knees, Michael spit liberally into his hand and coated his cock, then used the other hand on Seward's hip to direct him to sit back.

At the first blunt pressure, Seward twitched, then settled back into Michael's lap with a ragged, relieved sigh. Michael pressed his forehead to Seward's shoulder as Seward's tight heat enveloped him.

Christ, it had been less than a day, and he craved it as though he had been without it for months.

When Seward's ass was flush against his groin, Michael bit his earlobe and growled, "Do it." He licked the spot he'd bitten. "Fuck yourself on me."

Seward shuddered again. "God, you're vulgar."

Michael chuckled lowly. "And you love it." He wrapped an arm around Seward's chest to steady him, then withdrew slightly, teasingly. "Take it."

Seward shook his head. "I'm not—strong enough."

Michael pressed in to the hilt. "You are. You don't need me."

Unexpectedly, Seward chuckled at that. "What's so funny?" Michael demanded.

"I'd say you're—fairly essential—for this activity," Seward retorted between gasps. "Nevertheless, I don't think—"

"That's right." Michael slid his free hand down Seward's belly to his cock, where he trailed his fingers up the length. "Don't think." Seward bucked in his hold, giving the lie to his supposed frailty. "Just do it. Now. Look at that damned sunset and think of soaring out to meet it. Think of running without worrying if your leg will betray you. Think of painting the most beautiful picture you can imagine."

Seward groaned, then reached up to grip Michael's arm as he began to move. His motions were tentative at first, increasing in range and intensity as he gained confidence. As a reward, Michael kissed his neck and whispered praise and encouragement in his ear until the intimate clasp of Seward's body stole his breath and his words, until he was as undone as Seward, his chest heaving against Seward's sweat-slick back.

"Oh, God, touch me," Seward panted, and Michael was compelled to obey, wrapping his free hand around Seward's cock and circling his thumb over the slit until Seward groaned and spurted into Michael's hand, spilling his seed onto the earth as the sun dipped below the leaf-soft mountain peaks. As for Michael, he felt the first tug of Seward's body and followed it like a siren's lure, dashing himself to pieces on the rocks below.

IN ALL, Michael spent twelve days in the curious dreamland that he inhabited with Seward, three of them at the cabin in the woods he was certain had been enchanted. He had no notion that it would last that long and every expectation that they would suffer a rude awakening at any moment. He considered doing the job himself on a number of occasions, but when it came down to it, he lost his nerve every time. While he did not wish to admit it to himself, he was swiftly losing his preference for harsh reality. Dreams, he was learning, were much more pleasant, as long as one conveniently forgot they were utterly impossible.

As for their daily therapy routine, little actually changed. Michael still pushed Seward, Seward still complained of being pushed, and they argued over nearly everything. But at night, when the house was quiet, Michael would come to Seward's bed and they would stay there for as long as they could. Seward might be all bluster and sharp angles in the daylight, but in the wee hours of the morning, he had considerably fewer defenses, and in his presence, Michael abandoned a few of his own.

He did his best to avoid thinking of the vague plans he'd articulated to Castleton. The prospect of a rootless life spent in the pursuit of mindless, anonymous pleasure would have seemed as good as any other a few months ago, but now it merely seemed desperate and pathetic. It shocked him when he could no longer summon the same contempt for those who led a more stable, meaningful existence, but he could not deny that late at night, when Seward was a warm, living weight in his arms, he caught himself wandering through fantasies of a home that he could never have. For it was ridiculous to think that this could last, that he and Seward could simply live happily ever after. A fairy tale, in more ways than one, he thought viciously.

"Michael!" Mary's clear, strong voice carried across the lawn, interrupting his musings. Sighing, he obeyed her summons, practically jogging to the kitchen. When he arrived, her expression was troubled, and for a moment his heart leaped crazily. "What is it? Is Abbott all right?"

She nodded. "He's fine. There are two… gentlemen here to see Johnny. They say you asked them to come."

Michael stared at her, momentarily at a loss. After his conversation with Seward that evening at the cabin, he'd planned to go into town and send a wire to Castleton withdrawing his request but had never gotten around to it. In his defense, he'd never expected Castleton to send his friend so soon, and certainly not unannounced. "Has Seward seen them yet?"

"He's in the parlor with them now," she said.

"Wonderful," Michael muttered, stripping off his gloves and heading for the door to the hall. The parlor was the place where Seward had been storing his latest paintings.

As he approached the room, he pricked up his ears, listening for any conversation, any signs of how Seward might be reacting to his uninvited guests, but heard none until he was nearly at the door. The voice that emerged wasn't one he'd been expecting. It was Castleton's, and the words it uttered made his stomach lurch.

"Yes, Michael is an extraordinary creature. So good with his hands. It's no surprise you want to keep him all to yourself, but you know those Irish. They're a nomadic people at—"

Fists clenched, Michael stepped into the room. Three faces turned toward him, one fat and placid, one darkly amused, and one furious.

"Oh, my," Castleton breathed, "how your ears must be burning."

THE fat one was Winston van Eyck, the rich art patron that Castleton had promised to contact, and he, at least, seemed oblivious to the storm raging around him. After enthusing over the quality and boldness of Seward's work, he proceeded to suggest a tour of the gardens so that they could "iron out the details of a show." After shooting Michael a pointed look, Seward followed van Eyck out, leaving Michael alone with Castleton.

"Fancy meeting you here," Castleton drawled, smiling crookedly.

Michael rounded on him. "What the hell are you trying to do?"

Castleton had the effrontery to look innocent. "Why, I'm trying to introduce your friend to the New York art world, as per your request," he said simply. "He should be perfect for it. He's got the brooding lord of the manor act down pat." Leaning in, he added conspiratorially, "Honestly, I didn't know you went weak in the knees for the tragic figure. Really, it lends you hidden depths that I find terribly attractive."

"Did you forget," Michael ground out, trying to hold himself back from punching Castleton on his perfect nose, "that you weren't supposed to be here for at least another week?"

"I had no choice. Winston's sailing for England tomorrow, and this was a last-minute whim of his."

"There's this invention known as the telephone," Michael snapped. "I hear it's been around for about forty years."

Castleton smirked. "You didn't leave me your number, darling."

Michael surged forward, startling Castleton and forcing him back a step. "I told you once before not to fuck with me," he growled.

Blanching, Castleton held up his hands in surrender. "I thought you'd be long gone by now!" he squealed. "How was I to know you'd still be here playing house?"

Michael glared at him for two thudding heartbeats, then turned away, suddenly disgusted with himself. That was exactly what he'd been doing, mooning like a love-struck schoolgirl. What the hell had he been thinking?

Perhaps it was better this way. Perhaps it was better that Seward found out now rather than later.

"How much did you tell him?" he asked hollowly.

"Not much more than what you overheard," Castleton said, squirming. "But Winston might have told him you were the best rubber in any bathhouse in Manhattan."

Michael closed his eyes. Shit. "He didn't look familiar."

"Well," Castleton soothed, patting his shoulder, "you meet so many people."

MICHAEL found a gardening task in the front yard that required his immediate attention, so that when van Eyck and Castleton left, he would know it immediately. They emerged barely a half hour later, both with grim looks on their faces. Michael took a deep breath, peeled off his gloves again, and went inside.

Predictably, he found Seward in the library, pouring himself a drink from some bottle he'd managed to keep hidden. Standing in the doorway, Michael paused, uncertain. "I'm sorry," he said softly.

Seward did not look at him. "For what?" His voice was chillingly calm. Michael tried to answer in the same fashion.

"For not telling you I'd talked to Castleton about your painting, about asking someone he knew in the art world to evaluate your work."

Seward took a sip of his drink. "Not for exposing me to humiliation in front of your lovers?"

Michael frowned. "First of all, neither of those men is my lover. Second, there was no humiliation—"

"I'm not a charity case," Seward said shortly, slamming the glass down.

"What did you tell van Eyck?"

"I told him I wasn't interested, of course." His gaze lifted to Michael. "Do you suppose I'm totally without pride?"

Michael shook his head slowly. This conversation was deteriorating even more rapidly than he'd imagined. "Van Eyck said you were talented because you are talented," he said, as evenly as he could. "I didn't fuck him to get him to come up here, if that's what you're thinking."

Seward's eyes blazed with anger and hurt. "But you did, didn't you? At some time or another?"

Michael hesitated; the truth came harder than he'd expected it would. "I don't remember. I fucked so many men the first six months after I came home, I wouldn't recognize half of them if they were standing right in front of me."

Seward stared at him, horrified. "And what did you suppose these last few days would be? A parting gift? A little occupational therapy for the poor cripple?"

"You're not a poor cripple," Michael rasped. "You never were. And for the last few days, the farthest thing from my mind was leaving."

"Do you expect me to believe that?" Seward snapped. "Did you and Castleton laugh about me while you shared his bed?"

Michael's fists clenched. So help him, if he ever laid eyes on that little bastard again, he'd rip him limb from limb. "I *fucked* Castleton when I got back to New York, because I needed a *fuck*," he gritted. "I didn't *share* anything with him."

"And now you've—fucked me, and you're free to move on," Seward said hollowly.

"That's not what happened," Michael protested but cut himself off when he realized he had no words to explain it. He'd never done anything but fuck, and Seward had never done anything but love. Had they been living in some no-man's-land, some middle ground that belonged to neither of them?

Or had it belonged to both of them?

"Then what did happen?" Seward demanded, rising to his feet. "What did you imagine would become of… this?"

Michael shook his head, all of his doubts and fears suddenly returning, overwhelming him. Wearily, he murmured, "Nothing. I imagined nothing."

"I'll ask you one more time," Seward said slowly. "What do you want?"

Michael took a deep breath. *Even if I wanted you,* he thought, *it wouldn't change anything. This had to end eventually.* Aloud, he said, "When I came home from the war, I only wanted one thing: to forget."

"And you still want to forget."

Michael nodded. "Yes."

Seward began unbuttoning his shirt, stripping it from his shoulders as Michael watched. When he lifted his undershirt up and off, revealing his landscape of scars, Michael understood.

"If that's still all you want, then there's nothing for you here," Seward whispered.

14

THE early November wind was unusually bitter, bringing the promise of a harsh winter. Ignoring a cheerfully decorated shop window filled with toys, Michael hunched his shoulders inside his too-thin coat and hurried along the sidewalk until he reached his destination. Pulling open the door, he welcomed the assault of hot, humid air and the chance to escape from reminders of the upcoming holiday.

In the end, his half-formed plans to start over again had come to nothing, for he realized that a change of location would not change his situation or his outlook. Millie had welcomed him back with open arms, and he had clung to her like a drowning man to a bit of flotsam. Eventually he knew he'd go under, but for the time being he could see no other way to survive.

He debated about saying hello to Millie, then vetoed it. He'd overslept after staying out too late the night before, and she would not be pleased with him. Feeling like a burglar, he crept past her open office door on his way to the massage room.

"Michael, darling, don't run away," Millie sang, and Michael winced. Sighing, he straightened his shoulders and turned back the way he had come.

She invited him in with a solemn air that immediately raised his hackles. He'd been late for a shift only a couple of times before, and he was never less in the mood for a lecture. Folding his arms, he drew himself up and glared down at her.

Millie, predictably, was completely unperturbed. "Oh, my, now I know what they mean by the Black Irish," she breathed, pretending to fan herself. "You're positively melting my corset with that fearsome glower."

Sagging, Michael threw himself into a chair. "All right," he said heavily, "you win."

"I didn't realize it was a competition," Millie said gently. "You're in a foul mood tonight, aren't you? But then, you've been in a foul mood for—" She laid a finger against her lips, pretending to think about it. "—hm. How long have we known one another?"

"Very funny."

Her eyes sparkled. "Well, I thought so." Sobering, she indicated a stack of books on the table beside her. "Relax, my sweet. I only wanted to give you these."

Michael stared at them dumbly for a moment, then leaned in and studied the spines. "These are medical textbooks."

"Yes, I know. I was cleaning out a closet in the back the other day and found them. You must have forgotten them before you left for school."

Michael picked up the first one and opened it to the frontispiece. "This book," he said carefully, "was published last year. I sailed for Ireland in '13."

Millie craned her neck to peer at the page. "Oh, well, you know how these books are. It must be a misprint."

"Millie…," Michael warned.

"Just take them," she said softly. "Please."

"I can't," Michael returned, just as softly, even as he found his gaze roaming over the spines. She had obviously had some help in picking them out; he recognized most of the authors as the foremost authorities in modern physical therapy, but some of the titles were so recently published as to be unknown to him.

Millie leaned back and gazed at him for a long time before speaking. "When I met you, I knew you deserved so much more than the life you were living."

Michael stiffened. He didn't like to remember those times, and

Millie knew it. "I was barely sixteen and paying my room and board by sucking cock in rat-infested alleys," he said, as calmly as he could. "I can't think of anyone who deserved that fate."

Millie glared at him, and he fell silent. "I also knew that you deserved more than the life I could give you," she added. "But I gave you all I could."

"You gave me more than I can ever hope to repay," Michael said fiercely. "Don't ever think otherwise."

Millie waved away his passionate words with a hand. "Darling, I gave you a fancier venue, that's all. But in the end, you were still selling your body and your very talented hands. And for that I apologize; it was the best life I could provide."

"You encouraged me to learn, to study," he said helplessly. "You sent me to school."

"And what has that ever brought you but misery and regrets?" Millie countered with surprising vehemence. "You're never going back, are you?"

Michael opened his mouth, then closed it again. He didn't want to tell her that he'd been dreaming nearly every night of dying, though not in war as he'd imagined a thousand times before, but of old age, gasping his last breath in a freezing and threadbare furnished room, with nothing and no one to warm him. Nor could he tell her that he was beginning to doubt that any amount of time and distance would insulate him from this raw, unfamiliar ache of loss, this bizarre conviction that he no longer belonged in the life he'd lived for so long. The last thing he should be doing was giving either of them false hope, and yet he heard himself saying, "I'll take the books home with me after my shift," surprising them both.

Millie nodded. Michael tried to ignore the way she blinked furiously before speaking, or that her voice was still rough when she did. "Oh, I almost forgot," she said, mercifully changing the subject. "There was someone in here earlier looking for you."

Michael sighed. He had developed enough of a reputation that he was acquiring new customers through word of mouth. Some salesman from Newark would whisper about him on a train, and the next week his friend would be lying on Michael's table with a hard-on and a complaint about his terrible lumbago. "Did you set him up with an appointment?"

Millie shook her head and flung one powdered arm over the back of the divan. "He didn't want one. He only wanted to talk to you. Apparently he's been trolling every bathhouse in the city looking for you. He looked nearly worn to the bone, too. He walked with a limp."

Michael ignored the sudden leap in his pulse. "What was his name?"

Millie's gaze dropped to her nails. "I don't remember if he told me, to be honest. Since you finally told me about that trouble with the bull, I haven't been terribly inclined to give out your personal details to men I don't know. When I wouldn't confirm you worked here, he shut his pretty little mouth and left."

Michael ignored the irrational surge of disappointment. "Yes, of course. Thanks for that."

Millie eyed him. "Do you know who he was?"

Michael considered lying to her but discarded it when he saw the concern in her eyes. "I think so, yes."

"Friend or adversary?" she asked softly.

Michael's hands gripped his knees. "I don't know."

"Well, darling," Millie said kindly, "you must admit you've always been notoriously bad at telling the difference."

HE IS in the baths again, but unlike in his other nightmares, his body is still young, his skin supple, his hands strong. He is working on a man whose back is muscled, unmarred, perfect, and Michael feels himself growing hard as he kneads the firm flesh. When Michael nudges him to turn over, the man rolls obediently—and Michael stares in horror at the blood-streaked face, half of it ripped away, the left eye socket empty and bottomless.

"Why did you leave us?" the man rasps, and his voice is Seward's. Michael cannot breathe. He stumbles and whirls around, trying to escape, but the floor has changed to thick, cold mud, sucking at his shoes, holding him fast. It closes around his ankles, his knees, his waist; he tries to fight it but finds his body refuses to obey him. As it rises past his chin, he cries out for help, but it is too late, too late—

Michael woke sweating and shivering. He wiped at his eyes to clear his vision, and his fingers came away damp with tears. Sitting up, he swung his legs over the bed, his bare feet hitting the chilled wooden floor of his room. Like an old man, he shuffled to the window and peered out into the night. Huge, fat snowflakes were falling, whipped up by an early winter storm that blanketed the city in white, temporarily obliterating the ever-present layer of filth and making everything new.

He was not aware of how long he stood at the window watching the snow fall over the nearly deserted street, but his back protested when he finally straightened. About to turn away and make a futile attempt to get some more sleep, he paused when he saw a milk wagon approach and pull up outside his building, its lone quarter horse plodding through the drifts that had begun to form.

And then from around the corner came a skidding, careening motorcar, the driver obviously either drunk or stupid. Taking the turn too quickly, it spun out of control and slammed into both horse and wagon. Michael could hear the dull thud of the collision and the scream of the animal as the wagon teetered and fell onto its side, toppling the injured horse as well.

Without thinking, Michael snatched up his trousers and his coat, stumbled into them quickly, shoved his stockingless feet into his boots, then tore a blanket from the bed as he ran out the door. He practically flew down the three flights to the ground and waded through the snow and over to the wagon. The horse was still screaming, and he tried to block out the all-too-familiar sound as he clambered over the wagon searching for the milkman.

"Jesus Chris'!" The voice did not come from inside the wagon but from behind him, and the slur told him all he needed to know. "I didn't see'm, I swear—"

Michael pointed behind him without looking at the man. "Go to the police box on the corner and call for help, if you're able." The unearthly glow of the streetlamps in the storm made it easy to see the milkman. Unfortunately, he'd had a large crate of milk beside him, and it had fallen onto him as the wagon toppled. Gingerly, Michael lowered himself into the cab and crouched down, feeling for a pulse. He found it after a moment, faint and fast but definitely there.

The milkman groaned and stirred weakly. "Don't move," Michael ordered. "I have to get this crate off you." Bracing himself on either side of the man's body, he lifted the heavy crate off and away, then hefted it into the back of the wagon. He then crouched down again and reached up under the man's trouser leg to pinch the skin. "Can you feel that?"

"Touching—my leg," the milkman gasped, and Michael felt his heart leap in triumph. Likely it wasn't a back injury, then, but moving him without assistance was impossible, since it would require hoisting him up through the side of the cabin, now the top of a five-foot pit, or through the back, which was presently littered with smashed crates and milk bottles. Standing up, Michael grabbed the blanket he'd left outside, then shook it out and draped it over the man. "Help will soon be here," he said softly, smoothing back the man's hair. "We'll get you to a hospital."

"Horse," the milkman said weakly, trying to move. Michael stilled him with a firm hand on his shoulder. The animal's cries had died down, but he was fairly sure it had broken at least one leg in the fall, if the injuries it sustained from the crash weren't fatal.

"We'll do what we can," he said reassuringly. "For now, try to rest."

When Michael lifted himself out of the cabin again, he saw the driver stumbling toward him. "I called the p'lice!" he bellowed proudly, as though he'd just discovered the cure for polio. "They're comin'."

"Good. Now shut the hell up before I give in to my desire to put a fist through your face," Michael snarled. The man's wide-open mouth clapped shut with an audible noise, and he backed away until he tripped and fell on his arse in the middle of the street. Michael suppressed a wish that he be run over.

Within ten minutes a pair of police cars arrived, and with the assistance of one of the younger men, Michael lifted the injured man out of the cart. He was thankful the milkman was unconscious by then, because that way he didn't see the sorry state of his horse, which indeed had severely broken its right hind leg.

"His pulse is faint and slightly arrhythmic, and there are possible internal injuries," he instructed the young man. "Make sure you tell the doctors that when you get to the hospital."

One of the older officers eyed him. "You a doctor?"

"No," Michael answered.

"Maybe you better come with us just the same," he said. "I don't know nothin' about that stuff, and neither does Ted."

"Hey, Sarge, what about the horse?" one of the other cops asked.

The older man shook his head. "Put it out of its misery." The other cop drew his gun almost eagerly, and Michael felt his stomach churn.

"For God's sake, wait until we're out of the area," Michael spat, and around him the policemen froze. "I didn't tell him about the horse."

The sergeant nodded at the other officer, who holstered his weapon, then motioned Michael toward the car. "You sure you're not a doctor?" he asked conversationally. "Because you're bossy enough to be one."

The ride to the hospital felt like another dream. Michael sat in the cavernous backseat of the police sedan, the milkman's head cradled in his lap. When they arrived, he gave his report to the duty doctor, who looked at him oddly but listened nonetheless. After the milkman had been wheeled into an examining room, the sergeant walked up to him and patted him on the shoulder.

"Thanks, bud. C'mon, we'll drive you home."

Michael did not answer at first, busy taking in the scene around him as he took a few moments to calm down from the events of the night. The reception area here bore more of a resemblance to that of one of the base hospitals in France than to the one in sleepy Hudson.

Here there was movement and urgency and purpose. It was clear that the milkman's was not the only accident of the night, and the nurses were bustling back and forth, the heels of their shoes tapping out a fast-paced tempo on the polished floor. As Michael watched, one of them knelt down before a small child sniffling in her mother's arms, touching her hair briefly before escorting mother and child to another examining room.

"Hey, you okay?"

Michael shook himself from his stupor. "I'm fine. And thank you, but I don't believe I'll be needing a drive home." Walking away from the bewildered cop, Michael started down a hall. The increased activity in the reception area meant that no one had the time or the inclination to stop him. He wandered for some time, up stairs and down corridors, forcing himself to look into wards and to listen to the nighttime sounds of loneliness and distress. There were considerably fewer cries than there had been in the hospitals he'd known, but even the softest moan was enough to set his teeth on edge. By the time ten minutes had passed, he was shaking and nauseous, but still he pressed on.

He would have known the amputee ward without the sign; it was isolated from the rest of the wards, as though there were a need to protect the other patients from the most obvious evidence of war's horror. As he stood in the doorway, gazing out over the neat rows of beds faintly lit by dimmed Mazda lamps, he saw one man stir in his sleep, obviously caught in the throes of a nightmare. Every fiber of his being screamed at him to turn, to run; instead, he forced his feet to move, forced himself to pull up a chair and sit beside him. When Michael brushed the back of the man's hand with his fingers, he started awake with a sharp gasp.

"It's over," Michael reassured him. "You're safe."

The man stared at him uncomprehendingly for a moment—God, he was young, so young—then slowly shook his head. "It'll never be over."

"You're right," Michael agreed. "But it is for tonight. And perhaps that's all we can hope for." He gripped the young man's hand in his, squeezing it briefly before letting go.

"No." The young man's voice halted Michael's attempt to rise.

"Could you—" He looked about him and licked his lips before continuing. "—could you stay until I fall asleep?"

"I'd be happy to stay," Michael said, taking the young man's hand in his once more and sitting with him for long minutes. When his breathing evened out and his grip relaxed, Michael watched over him for a while longer, guarding him against the return of the nightmares.

He rose to his feet on legs turned to water and turned toward the door, only to see a woman's figure silhouetted in the doorway. With a sigh, he trudged toward her, anticipating the stern lecture that would follow.

The first words out of her mouth were not the ones he'd been expecting, nor was the vaguely familiar voice. "You're a sight for sore eyes," she said, her accent crisply English, and Michael, who had never believed Fate was anything but a malicious bitch, began to wonder if she could also be blessed with a kinder, more compassionate side.

"Elizabeth," he breathed, leaning against the door frame, suddenly feeling weaker than a baby as the fact of what he'd just done caught up with him. "It's good to see you."

"I saw you wander past my station like a man in a trance and followed you," she said, reaching out to grip his arm as though she feared he would collapse at any moment. "What the devil are you doing here?"

"I, ah," Michael said, and this time he ignored the tears as they began to trickle slowly down his cheeks, "I believe I'm looking for a job."

MRS. DINARDO shook her head. "No, she no here. She move last month."

Michael glared at her over the stack of Christmas presents he'd brought for Edith and Donald. "Then where did she go?"

The plump woman shrugged casually, then betrayed herself with a sidelong glance up the tenement stairway. "She no tell me. Please, you go now, hah?"

Michael closed his eyes briefly. "I know my sister hasn't moved, Mrs. Dinardo. I watched her walk into this building yesterday afternoon." He had wanted to see her, wanted to know how she was getting along. She had been returning from the market, a paper bag clutched in one arm, the baby in the other. Edith marched proudly along ahead of them, hugging a smaller bag.

She's growing up, Michael had thought, a lump forming in his throat.

Mrs. Dinardo slumped visibly when confronted by her own deception. She shook her head again, but sadly this time. "She tell me to lie to you," she said heavily. "This I do, many times; many woman hide from a man. But you no look so terrible."

Michael sighed. "Thank you for that. I won't cause you trouble. I only want to give her these. Will you give them to her for me?"

"I no think she take them."

Michael transferred them into her waiting arms. "Then give them to your own children, or someone else's. It doesn't matter to me." He reached into his vest pocket and passed her the envelope he'd filled at the bank. God only knew if she'd refused the money he'd sent her last month. "This, too."

"I am sorry." Michael turned back to look at her. "I tell her nothing is more important than *la famiglia,* but…."

Michael forced a small smile. "Thank you for that, too. Merry Christmas, ma'am."

"*Buono natale,*" she answered softly.

Michael let himself out. The snow of last month was long gone, but the chill in the air had persisted, and Michael hitched his coat collar up around his neck as he descended the steps. When he crossed the street, he turned and looked up at the tenement, gaze scanning the windows on the top floor. He caught the movement, the brief flash of a face, then a pale hand as it drew the faded curtain closed.

I'm not giving you up. I'll never give you up, Michael thought fiercely, his fists clenching. *You're worth more than all the gold in the world.*

A WEEK before Christmas, Michael was making his last rounds of the ward when Elizabeth informed him he had a visitor. He followed her to the gymnasium, only to find one of the last people he'd expected to see.

"Doctor Parrish," Michael said, stepping forward with his hand extended.

The little man met him halfway, a wide smile on his face. "It's good to see you, my boy," he said warmly. "The compliments of the season to you."

"You too, sir." Michael tried not to let the tension show in his face, but Parrish obviously sensed his mood, for he held up a hand.

"While I'm sure you know I'm pleased to see you back working in medicine, I'm not here to press you. I know you'll come to me when you're ready to take the next step."

Michael felt himself relax. "I appreciate that." The fact that Michael felt no urge to amend Parrish's "when" to "if" showed how far he had come in the past month.

Parrish smiled again and patted Michael's arm. "I can't stay long. I'm here to fulfill a promise I made." With that, he reached into his coat and drew out an envelope, which he held out to Michael.

Michael stared at it. The envelope bore his name, written in strong black capitals with a grease pencil.

Parrish's voice was kind. "Go on and take it; it won't bite you." Michael obeyed, trying to ignore the way his fingers suddenly itched.

"Who gave this to you?" he asked, though he suspected he already knew the answer.

"Open it and find out."

Bracing himself, Michael tore open the envelope and extracted the note, written in the same decisive hand. Even though he fancied himself half-prepared for whatever was inside, the words still struck him like a roundhouse punch to the gut.

Sarah has been asking after you for months. She now insists that seeing you again is the only Christmas present she wishes to receive this year. She and I will be in town this Thursday the 21st after eight at the address below. I would like to be able to keep my word.

The scrawled note ended with an address on the Upper West Side in lieu of a signature. Michael folded the note and stuffed it in his pants pocket, hoping Parrish would not notice his hands were shaking, though he imagined it was a futile wish.

"How is he?" he asked, forcing his gaze to meet Parrish's.

Parrish softened. "His progress is slower, but he's still improving. His temperament, however...." He rolled his eyes, and Michael couldn't help but chuckle.

"Yes, I know all about his temperament," Michael murmured, and damned if he didn't hear a wistful tone creep into his voice. He felt his cheeks heat under Parrish's gray-eyed scrutiny and looked away.

"He'll be pleased to see you, my boy." Michael jerked his head up, startled. "I hope you'll go."

Michael nodded, unwilling to refute Parrish's assumption. He would go, but it would be for Sarah, no other reason. He had as much desire to see Seward as Seward doubtless did him.

"Good," Parrish said, smiling up at him. "Oh, and"—Parrish reached into his pocket and produced a second envelope—"Merry Christmas, son."

Michael frowned in consternation. "Doctor, you didn't have to—"

"Oh, but I did. It's a letter of acceptance to the New York Medical College, with credit for your first year at Trinity. Provided you start your studies within the next two years, mind you. If you take longer than that, they'll insist you write entrance examinations and start again from the beginning."

Michael stared at him, slack-mouthed. "Didn't you say something about not pressing?" he asked weakly.

The old man smiled wickedly at him. Jabbing a finger at the ceiling, he said, "Don't forget, I have my immortal soul to think of." And with a final wink, he left Michael alone with his roiling, unsettled thoughts.

MICHAEL arrived on the appointed day a half hour early, wanting to get the lay of the land before meeting Seward again. He was not surprised when the address turned out to be a posh three-story brownstone. From what he could glean through the windows, there didn't seem to be a great deal of activity going on; in five minutes, he saw no one enter or leave the house. He was about to walk on and return later when the front door flew open and a head poked out.

"Well, don't just stand there, come up!" it said imperiously. "You're late enough as it is."

Frowning, Michael began to climb the stairs. He pulled out his pocket watch and checked the time, then held it to his ear. Still ticking.

When he reached the top and the bright lights over the entrance, he could finally make out the other man's features.

"Oh, it's you!" van Eyck exclaimed, drawing back slightly to peer at him. "I'm sorry, I thought you were one of the hired help."

"Don't worry," Michael drawled. "You're not the first to make that mistake."

"I suppose you're here to see the show," van Eyck said, rubbing at his triple chin.

"I'm early," Michael interrupted. "I was planning to go for a short walk—"

"No, for heaven's sake, no, it's freezing out there!" van Eyck bubbled, stepping aside to allow him to enter. "You come right in and make yourself at home—oh, where to put you—ah, would he be angry, do you think, if you saw them before he got here? He can be so temperamental—but then, I imagine you're quite familiar with…." He shrugged, then turned his head and yelled, "Randolph!"

Michael was still trying to sort out the question in that mishmash when a tall man in a gray suit, presumably Randolph, appeared. "Yes, sir."

"This is Mr. McCready. He's here for the show. Please take him to the conservatory."

"Certainly, sir." Randolph's gaze swept over Michael, categorizing and filing him under *not worth the bother*. "If the gentleman will follow me."

Gritting his teeth—he had no choice but to go along unless he wanted to forgo seeing Sarah—Michael followed. The servant led him down a long hall and into a room made entirely of glass that seemed to take up the width of the house. The bright moonlight shone down upon the room, bare except for a collection of paintings perched on easels. The small electric lights that were hung above them were the only artificial illumination.

Michael did his best to avoid seeming impressed, but it was difficult. The effect was exactly the one he imagined van Eyck was hoping to achieve: dramatic yet simple, focusing one's attention completely on the art.

It was then that he took a closer look at the nearest painting, and his heart lodged in his throat.

"Sir? Sir?"

Michael blinked, realizing Randolph had probably been trying to get his attention for some time. "Yes."

"May I take your coat?"

Michael shook his head. "No. I don't intend to stay long." Judging by the sour face the servant made, he could tell this was the wrong answer, but he couldn't be bothered to care.

"Then perhaps the package?"

What—oh. He'd almost forgotten the small parcel tucked under his arm, a Christmas present of artist's supplies for Sarah. "No. No thank you."

Randolph nodded stiffly. "Then may I leave you to your perusal of the artwork?"

"I wish you would," Michael muttered, taking a halting step

forward, then another. He didn't notice when Randolph left, because his world had suddenly narrowed to the two-by-three-foot stretch of canvas in front of him.

It was Seward's art, without a doubt. He'd seen this particular painting not long before he left. It was an abstract, like many of his more recent works, and full of a rage Michael could understand too well. He stared at it for an indeterminate stretch of time, then moved on as if in a daze to the next, and the next. Though none were quite as angry as the first, each one was bursting with emotion, practically bleeding it onto the expensive marble floor.

There were a few representational pieces scattered here and there, including the portrait of Abbott he'd seen in the attic, a stunningly accurate rendition of the sunset from the cliff near the cabin, and a new portrait of Sarah sprawled in a pile of dead leaves, her arms spread wide and her mouth open. The flame-colored leaves licked at the edges of her body, scorching her skirts, burning her splayed fingers. She seemed at once to be a modern martyr laughing at her immolation and a young girl reveling in the joy of living, and Michael was shaken and moved by Seward's vision of her.

By the time he reached the last painting, he was trembling with the weight of the memories pressing upon him. It was as though Seward had taken his anguish, fury, and frustration at the futility of the war and exorcised it with each savage brush stroke. The emotions that Michael had sought to bury beneath indifference and a dogged pursuit of meaningless pleasure were here on display, naked and unashamed, a gruesome reminder for a world poised on the brink of amnesia.

Lest we forget, Michael thought, his heart struggling to beat under the crushing pressure of all that he had seen, all that he had done and failed to do. Slowly, he shuffled toward the last canvas, one that stood apart from the others, bathed in its own solitary light.

The last painting was of him.

Unlike the portraits of the young Reilly, however, this rendering captured every flaw in his face as faithfully as a photograph. More faithfully, in fact, because to Michael it seemed as though every minute of his history had been distilled and transformed and made somehow strangely beautiful, as though the moments of his life were worth recording for future generations. As though everything that Michael had survived, everything he had become, was cherished. And all at once, the weight that burdened him was lifted away, because for the first time in his life, Michael realized that there was someone else who understood him, who wanted to know him, if he chose to allow it.

If I choose. The thought was both terrifying and liberating, in a way nothing had ever been.

"What do you think?"

Michael turned slowly, as if in a dream, and faced him. He looked healthy, if a little tired; there was no sign of the old limp as he approached. "I think you're a very great artist," Michael said quietly, his hands clenching at his sides, aching to reach out.

Seward nodded toward the portrait. "Not very flattering, I know," he murmured. "I was working from memory."

It's beautiful, Michael wanted to say. *You've made me beautiful.* Aloud, he asked, "Where's Sarah?"

"With Mary in the kitchen, being plied with hot chocolate. I asked her if I could speak to you first. She gave me five minutes, no more." Seward shifted on his feet, and Michael looked him up and down, searching for signs that he might be in pain.

"Don't worry," Seward said without rancor. "I've been keeping up with my exercises."

Michael shook his head. "I'm sorry. I don't have any right."

Seward smiled faintly. "You have the right, if you'd care to claim it." As Michael digested this extraordinary statement, Seward added, "I had a hell of a time finding you; it took me well over a month. Castleton seemed to think you'd left town."

"Castleton doesn't know anything about me."

"Yes, I gathered that eventually," Seward said wryly. "I tried Parrish first, but he told me you had vanished from his sight as well."

"I went back to the baths," Michael said harshly.

Seward didn't so much as flinch. "Yes, I know that, too," he said, matter-of-factly. "I looked for you in every one I could find, but I had no luck."

"I was back at the Saint Alex. Millie doesn't like strangers."

Seward actually chuckled at that. "Yes, I remember Millie. I think she believed I was a policeman at first, though she questioned me as if I were a murder suspect."

Michael frowned. Millie hadn't mentioned that part of the conversation. "Why did you allow her to?"

"I think I was too stunned to do anything else. I have to admit I wasn't at my best when I came to see her, but in no time at all she had me quite turned around."

"She's exceedingly good at that," Michael muttered.

Seward took a step forward. "She was also good at piquing my curiosity. You see, I was left with a certain… impression of you, and it wasn't compatible with a person who could have such a fierce ally. I could almost believe Sarah could be deceived, and as for myself… well, that's neither here nor there. However, Millie didn't seem to be one to waste her faith on an unworthy object. Also, I began to wonder from whom she thought she was defending you, and so I asked her."

"Asked her what?"

Seward took another step forward. "Asked her what I was to you," he murmured, gaze unwavering and hypnotic. "Asked her if you'd ever spoken of me once in three months."

Michael tried to look away but was caught, held, trapped. "What did she tell you?" he whispered.

Seward reached up with a trembling hand and cupped Michael's jaw tenderly. "She told me I'd have to ask you myself but that I'd have to wait until you came to me. And I did my best to follow her advice, but Sarah forced my hand. She's become quite the tyrant since you left, and it's all your fault."

"My fault?" Michael asked, arching a brow. "She learned tyranny at your knee, not mine."

"Michael," Seward growled, "I only have two minutes left before she pops up again."

Michael closed his eyes and shook his head.

"Look at me," Seward snapped, "and for once tell me the goddamned truth."

Michael's eyes flew open while his gut churned and his palms sweated and he could feel every one of Seward's fingers against his skin. "No," he rasped. "No, I've never spoken of you. Not even to Millie." Seward took a stumbling step backward, his hand falling away. Michael took a deep breath and added, "But I've thought about you every day. Every day."

Seward's hands clenched into fists, as though he were restraining himself from leaping at Michael. "Why didn't you come back?"

"Because it wouldn't have changed anything. This is as impossible now as it was then. You're not going to set up housekeeping with me at the country estate. You'd be out on your arse faster than—"

And then Seward started to chuckle, and Michael trailed off, staring at him as though he'd gone mad. "Why is that so damned funny?" he demanded.

When Seward could draw breath again, he answered, "Because I'm moving out in the new year. I bought the Abbotts a house in Hudson and set them up with a pension from my mother's inheritance, and Sarah has a small trust, and with the little that's left, I have just enough to rent a flat in the Village. It's got three rooms and a bath and a huge wall of windows to let in the sun, and it's absolutely freezing in the wintertime but I don't give a damn, because it's mine." He closed the distance between them then, taking Michael's hands in his and squeezing them. "It could be ours if you'd say the word."

Michael sucked in a breath at the emotion revealed in those green eyes. "John," he murmured, watching the fire in Seward's gaze flare brightly at the sound of his name, "this can't be what you want. I can't be—what you want."

"Why not?" John asked, leaning in to nuzzle Michael's temple, brush his lips over Michael's cheek and jaw.

"Because it doesn't make any damned sense!" Michael cried, exasperated but somehow unable to pull away.

John pressed his mouth to Michael's jugular, and Michael shuddered at the brief swipe of John's tongue. "I believe we're now down to under a minute. Do you suppose we could speed up the process?"

Michael shook his head, fear warring with hope. "I know that it's common for patients to develop... inappropriate feelings for their therapists...."

He was abruptly cut off by the sound of John's laughter. "For God's sake," Seward wheezed, "I believe that you and I were the worst therapist and patient in the history of medicine. Do you imagine I fell in love with you for your soothing bedside manner?"

"You—"

John threw up his hands in frustration. "I'm in love with you, you blasted idiot."

"Oh," Michael said softly, his mouth insisting on breaking into a foolish grin. Of their own accord, his hands came to rest on John's hips. "I suppose I could have gathered that from the painting," he murmured.

"Good. I'd hate for my art to be inaccessible to the proletariat."

"Shut up," Michael growled, leaning in to kiss him hungrily. After a moment, Seward groaned into his mouth and opened beneath him while his arms wrapped around Michael's back, holding on, holding on.

"About that flat," John said breathlessly, "would you, will you—"

"Yes," Michael murmured, lips against John's ear, "yes," because no one had asked him before and because now that he had this, he didn't believe he would ever be able to let go of it.

"Uncle Michael!"

Well, perhaps he could be persuaded for a moment. Releasing Seward hastily, he looked up to see Sarah racing toward him, her velvet dress billowing about her ankles. "You came to see our exhibition!"

He exchanged glances with John, who nodded. "Sarah has three of her paintings in the show as well," he said proudly. "I think she will become a very famous artist someday, and I want to be able to say that I helped launch her career."

Michael bent down and handed her the package he'd tucked under his arm. "Hold your Christmas present," he ordered. Sarah giggled and took it from him, thanking him shyly, and Michael grinned and swept her off her feet and into his arms.

"They're in the next room," she said, resting her small hands on his shoulders as though he'd never been away from her. "Would you like to see them?"

"Yes, I'd like that very much," he told her. Squeezing her tightly to him and looking over her shoulder at John, he repeated, "I'd like that very much."

May 1925

MICHAEL schooled his features to reveal nothing as he pressed his palm to the girl's forehead. She was a wisp of a thing, perhaps eight or nine years old, and from the heat that greeted Michael's touch, it was a wonder she hadn't burned away to ash by now.

He looked up at the anxious parents, their gazes fixed on their ailing daughter. "How long has she had the fever?" he asked. They looked back at him, incomprehension in their eyes, and then turned to one another and had a rapid, whispered conversation in what Michael recognized as Italian. After eleven hours working in Saint Vincent's woefully understaffed admissions section, he could barely remember his own language, so the words he summoned were clumsy at best. "*Tempo*—ah, *tempo e caldo*—no, *calda?*" he asked, motioning to the girl.

Another whispered conversation, and then the father held up three fingers.

"*Ore?*" Michael asked, dreading the answer already when the man shook his head.

"*Giorni,*" he said. Michael's expression must have betrayed him—three days of high fever was a great deal more serious than three hours—because the mother's hands flew to her mouth, not quite bottling the sob that escaped.

Michael spun on his heel and addressed the nearest intern. "Prepare an ice bath as soon as possible," he instructed, "and find Sister Loretta if she hasn't gone off shift yet. I need someone who can speak

Italian a damn sight better than I can."

The intern—he was new, and somewhat overwhelmed by all the activity on busy nights—blinked at him for a moment. "Which one should I do first?"

"Which one is more likely to save this girl's life, Stewart?" Michael asked between gritted teeth.

"Oh, right," Stewart said, nodding.

"Stewart?"

"Yes, sir?"

"*Move,*" Michael bit out.

"Right!" Stewart said crisply, sprinting off.

Mustering a reassuring smile, Michael turned back to the anxious couple. Taking one of the mother's hands, he gently wrapped it around the limp hand of her daughter. They nodded at one another in a moment of silent understanding, and then he went in search of Sister Loretta himself.

Six hours later, Michael was finally relieved of his duties by another of the senior residents and, after discussing with him all the particulars of the girl's case, trudged to the doctors' lounge to retrieve his jacket. As he started to push the door open, his ears were immediately assaulted by Stewart's patrician, nasal tones.

"—don't see why these dagos can't learn some English," Stewart was saying, waving a hand at Morgan, another new intern. "I mean, the level of ignorance is appalling. They didn't even have the sense to bring the girl into a hospital when she became ill."

Morgan, his back turned to Michael, murmured something too low for Michael to hear through the crack in the door, after which Stewart said, "Well, at any rate, if she dies it won't be on my conscience. Medical science can only do so much."

Somehow, even exhausted as he was, Michael managed to shove the door with such force that it hit the stop with a loud *bang*, causing both men to start violently. Before he could manage to think better of it, Michael had stalked across the room and was shoving Stewart back against the wall. Stewart gaped at him like a landed trout, his well-fed face purpling.

"Don't mix in," Michael growled at Morgan.

Morgan held up his hands in a placating gesture. "He's all yours," he said, stepping back.

Michael looked Stewart right in his watery blue eyes. "Her name," he said, slowly and deliberately, "is Sofia Andretti. Her father's name is Paolo. Her mother's name is Francesca." He pushed a little harder against Stewart's chest. "Say their names."

"I don't—"

Michael slammed his open palm against the wall beside Stewart's head, making him flinch. "Say them, goddamn you!"

"S-Sofia An—An—"

"Andretti."

"Andretti," Stewart parroted. "P-Paulo. Francesca."

"Very good," Michael said. "Perhaps the next time you are tempted to use a foul epithet, you will take five seconds and learn the *names* of the people you are pledged to help."

Stewart opened his mouth, then wisely clamped it shut again. Michael nodded.

"And as for levels of ignorance," he continued, almost conversationally, "the Andrettis know something you obviously have failed to grasp. They understand that most of the time, the hospital is a place people like them go to die, because when they get there they encounter doctors who look down their noses at them and, after deciding their consciences are *clear*—Stewart winced—"fail to do every last thing they can to save them."

"I didn't mean—" Stewart spluttered. "Of course I would do all I could—"

"Shut up," Michael snapped. "You are right about one thing: medical science can only do so much. The ice bath we gave her tonight will keep her brain from cooking with the fever, but it's not a cure, and if she dies, it won't matter. The only thing that can truly save that girl is her spirit, her will to live. Perhaps a few prayers from her parents will help, who the hell knows. But most of the time, Stewart, we are stumbling around in the dark, and it's sheer bloody luck that we save anyone at all."

As Stewart stared at him, Michael finally removed his hand from his chest and stepped back. "It's not all your fault, I suppose," he sighed, the exhaustion suddenly slamming back into him. "They convince you you're a pack of modern gods, striding around the wards with the secret of life and death in your hands." His gaze flicked over both of them. "You'll find out soon enough you're as human as the rest of us."

And with that, he turned on his heel and left the room as swiftly as he'd come. He was halfway home before he noticed he'd forgotten his damned jacket.

MICHAEL awoke at the sound of the bedroom door creaking on its hinges. He opened his eyes just sufficiently to see John dressed to go out. "John?"

John turned and made a calming gesture with his hand. "I didn't mean to wake you," he whispered. "Go back to sleep."

"Where're y'goin'?" he slurred, still half-unconscious.

John hesitated, then answered, "To the appointment we talked about the other day."

Michael blinked at him. "That's tomorrow."

John's expression turned to that mixture of fondness and exasperation that Michael had grown increasingly familiar with since he'd started his residency at Saint Vincent's. "It's today, Michael my lad," he said, walking over to the bed and sitting on the edge. "You slept through Tuesday."

"Fuck," Michael sighed. "I promised I'd come along, didn't I? I'm sorry."

John shook his head. "Don't be. You looked terrible when you came in early yesterday morning."

"And now?"

John smiled and brushed the hair away from his forehead. "Oh, much better. Back to your usual homely self."

Michael snorted.

"Tell me?" John asked softly, hand still gentle on Michael's face.

Michael took a calming breath through his nose. It didn't help. "A girl we admitted on my last shift," he said. "I believe it's rheumatic fever." Another pause. "She's nine years old."

"God," John breathed. "Will she—"

Michael passed a hand over his face. "I don't know. I have another shift tom—shit, I mean this afternoon—and I'm dreading going back." He didn't tell John that he couldn't stop thinking that she was Edith's age, that for one horrible second, he'd wished she were Edith, because at least then he'd know what had happened to her—

It had been six months now since he'd known Margaret's whereabouts. He'd turned the Bowery upside down, and all he'd heard of his sister was that she'd left New York. There was no way to know for certain if that was true, or where she'd gone if it were. None of which he'd told John, of course. John would only want to spend his money—as though he hadn't spent far too much of it already helping to put Michael through medical school—on a detective who wouldn't be able to learn anything more than Michael already had. Still, the guilt of the lie tasted sour on top of the worry and the fear for Margaret. Half of his rage at Stewart the other day had been anger at himself, punishing himself for his thoughts and his doubts.

"I can stay," John said quietly, startling Michael back to the present with a gentle stroke to his hair.

"No, I'm fine," Michael said, that lie coming easier. "I'd like to get a couple of more hours' rest before my shift."

John watched him for a moment longer, then nodded. "All right. Will you try to come next week?"

"I'll try, though I don't see why you can't tell me what these appointments are. You've been going every Wednesday for two months."

"Perhaps because I'm afraid that if I tell you, you won't agree to come," John murmured.

Michael frowned. "I don't understand."

John blew out a breath. "I'll be late," he said. He made to rise from the bed, but Michael's hand shot out and caught hold of his wrist, stopping him. John looked down at his wrist, then back at Michael.

Michael's hold loosened, and he stroked a thumb across John's pulse point. "Please."

John continued to watch him, gaze searching. "I've been going to see an alienist, Michael," he said finally.

Michael blinked at him, shock rendering him numb. "You've been seeing an alienist," he repeated.

"He's very good," John said, then chuckled without mirth. "And very reasonable."

"You—are you *mad*?" Michael hissed, sitting up.

"Quite probably."

"For Christ's sake, do you have any idea what alienists do to us?" Michael snapped, anger suddenly slamming into him broadsides, nearly blinding him. "They try to *convert* us. They brand us as deviants. They help send us to *jail*."

"This one won't," John returned, maddeningly calm.

"And how the hell do you know that?"

"Because he's *one of us*," John gritted.

Michael swallowed his retort and stared at him.

"Doctor Collins came highly recommended by a friend," John continued. "He served in the war, and he's worked with shell-shock cases. He's already helped me, and I think he might be able to help you."

Michael waved a hand, utterly at a loss. "I didn't realize you were—that it still bothered you."

"It does," John conceded quietly. "And if your tossing and turning in bed is any indication, it does you as well."

Michael couldn't say that most of his dreams lately had been of Margaret and her children, nightmares in which he ran toward them as they screamed for help and never reached them. "I thought you liked my tossing and turning in bed," he said instead, laying a hand on John's thigh.

John looked down at Michael's hand for a moment, then sighed and enfolded it in his. "One easy thing about you," he murmured, "is that I always know when we've arrived at an impasse." Raising the hand to his lips, he kissed it fondly and rose to his feet. "Sleep well."

"You could talk to me," Michael blurted just as John reached the door.

John paused, back still turned. "No, I can't," he said. "Perhaps someday, but for now you're carrying enough burdens. I refuse to be another one."

"You're such a self-sacrificing prick," Michael snarled, the anger flaring in him again, making him want to lash out, to engender a kindred reaction in John.

At that, John did turn, but his expression only held sadness and concern. Michael balled his hands into fists.

"Pot and kettle, Michael my lad," John said softly. "Pot and kettle."

"THANK you for seeing me on short notice, Michael," Doctor Parrish said, taking the hand that Michael extended and shaking it firmly.

"No thanks necessary," Michael told him. The warm spring day was perfect for a walk through Central Park, and privately he was glad Parrish had suggested they meet here. It seemed far too long since he'd simply taken some sun and fresh air.

"Nevertheless, I know you've been busy with your residency. How much longer do you have, by the way?"

"The day after tomorrow will be my last day."

"And graduation?"

Michael snorted. "If I manage to avoid punching any of the new interns in the face—not a sure thing, I might add—I should be graduating next week."

"Splendid, that's splendid," Parrish said, practically rubbing his hands together in glee. "And so I take it you've received no offers of employment yet?"

Michael glanced at Parrish out of the corner of his eye as they walked. He should have sent out letters of introduction to the local hospitals by now, but the paper and envelopes remained in his tiny desk at home, untouched. "No, not yet."

Parrish's eyes twinkled. "Well, then, I have a position you may be interested in. I'm hoping you'll be more than interested, actually, as it's been designed with you in mind."

Michael stared at him, thunderstruck. "I'm sorry?"

"Do you remember the idea I mentioned to you—oh, it must be four years ago now—about an idea I had for a veterans' center downtown? It would focus on physical rehabilitation of the wounded, of course, but would offer other services for all veterans, from literacy training to recreation?"

"Yes, I remember. You described it as a cross between a YMCA and a settlement house."

Parrish laughed. "Well, the idea has evolved considerably since then. Of course, the Veterans' Bureau has its hospitals and occupational therapy, but it offers nothing like what I'm envisioning, nor anything that serves veterans living in lower Manhattan."

Michael's jaw twitched, though he was aware he needn't bother to hide his reaction. Parrish knew there was no love lost between him and the notoriously corrupt organization. "From what I've heard, they're not in the habit of welcoming immigrants or colored men," he observed, "and downtown that's about all you'll find."

"All the more reason to do this thing," Parrish said solemnly. "We both agree that every man who served his country deserves our help.

Luckily, the Bureau has finally decided to see it our way in this case. I've been in talks with General Hines, the new director they brought in after the scandal, and he's done a great deal to reform and expand the organization. Last week we signed the final paperwork, and we'll be starting the renovations to the building we've chosen by the end of the month."

Michael stopped in his tracks and stared at his old mentor. "You could charm the devil out of his hole."

Parrish laughed merrily and clapped him on the shoulder, and they resumed their walk. "Thank you, my boy. Of course, there are some things I'll not be advertising to the Bureau. I've already hired a young colored doctor, a very promising graduate of Howard University, and we have your old friend Elizabeth on board as administrator. I need people I can trust in key positions, people who are not bound to old, outmoded traditions and prejudices."

Michael blinked. "I only saw her yesterday. She didn't breathe a word of this to me."

"I asked her to let me have the pleasure of telling you. It nearly killed her to keep mum."

"I'm sure," Michael drawled. "And so you'd like me to help with the physical therapy?"

"That, and much more. Michael, within a couple of years, I'm hoping to retire—" Michael snorted, and Parrish amended, "—well, all right, perhaps slow down is a better term—and I'll want someone to carry on the good work we've begun. I can think of no better man to do that than you."

Michael reeled in shock. "I can think of a dozen. I'm hardly a green kid, but neither am I anywhere near the most experienced."

"You experienced more in four years of war than most doctors do in four decades of practice," Parrish returned. "But more importantly, you are one of those rare physicians who listens to his heart as much as his head. Your first loyalty is not to science or self-aggrandizement, but to the best interests of the men, and that must be the guiding principle of this place if we are to be going on with it."

Michael ducked his head, feeling an unexpected wave of pride wash over him at Parrish's praise. "Your guiding principles sound positively Bolshevik, if you ask me. Not that I mind, but I thought you were securing yourself a place in heaven. Are you certain God would approve of your colored and Irish doctors and your women wearing the trousers?"

Parrish grinned. "I've always privately suspected that Jesus is in favor of revolutionaries, seeing as how he was a bit of one himself. Does this mean you're saying yes? I must warn you, the pay will be nowhere near what you'll deserve."

Michael opened his mouth but was suddenly assaulted by a wave of what felt disturbingly like panic, and no sound emerged from his throat. What the hell was the matter with him? This was an ideal position, one tailor-made to his skills and abilities. Furthermore, he would be doing important work under a man he loved and respected. Why, then, did the thought of taking this position fill him with unreasoning dread?

"I—do you mind if I take a day or two to think about it?" Michael asked. "It's only that—I wasn't expecting anything like this, and these last weeks of residency have been so hectic—" He clamped his mouth shut around the babbling, sure Parrish would think him mad if he went on any longer.

For a moment, a flicker of what looked like disappointment appeared on Parrish's face before the usual serenity descended again. Michael's gut churned at the knowledge he was causing Parrish more worry in what had to be an extremely stressful time. "Of course, my boy. Take all the time you need."

"You don't need to be so softhearted," Michael muttered. "I know how important this is. I'll let you know as soon as I can."

Parrish's too-knowing gaze searched his face, and it was all Michael could do to keep from squirming under the scrutiny. "I can't help being softhearted toward you, son," Parrish said, reaching up to give Michael a fatherly pat on the arm, "because you're hard enough on yourself for both of us."

"MR. MCCREADY, may I see you for a moment, please?"

Michael stopped in his tracks, knowing full well he couldn't hope to escape old Mulcahy when she used that tone of voice. Plastering on his most blandly innocent expression, he turned and faced her as she regarded him impassively from the door of her office.

Damn. His last shift of residency and he was about to be kicked out on his arse. Shame, that.

"Yes, Mother Superior?" Michael said, attempting a small yet hopefully professional smile.

Unfortunately, this only made her frown. "Come in, please," she invited brusquely, spinning on her heel and retreating inside. Michael took a moment to be impressed once more by her ability to glide as though she were perched on casters; most nuns could only yearn for that level of proficiency, if nuns could yearn for anything.

As soon as Michael had shut the door behind him, she came directly to the point. "I notice that Mister Stewart's work habits and attitude have improved remarkably over the last week. I heard a rumor that you might have had something to do with that."

Michael clasped his hands behind his back. "I'm flattered to think I could have that kind of influence over the next generation of young doctors."

"Hmph," Mulcahy said. "Your facetious streak is one of your least becoming traits, Mr. McCready."

Michael's mouth twitched. "My apologies."

The Mother Superior waved a hand at him. "Yes, well, while I would hazard a guess your action did not arise from the purest of motives, the outcome of it was beneficial, so we'll leave it at that. He reported to me about the Andretti girl earlier and was sure to give you the lion's share of the credit for her recovery."

Michael shook his head. "I prescribed the initial treatment, but he worked diligently on her case after that. He's the one who deserves your praise."

Mulcahy's eyebrows rose slightly. It was the closest thing to outright surprise he had ever seen cross her features. "This mutual admiration is touching, but I will praise who I please, thank you."

"Yes, Mother Superior," Michael said primly.

The Mother Superior looked at him keenly for another moment, then sighed heavily and sat in her chair. Gesturing to him to take a seat, she said, "What are your plans after graduation?"

Michael opened his mouth, then closed it again. He still hadn't called Parrish to give his answer, and the guilt arising from it gnawed at him. "I don't know yet," he answered honestly.

"I thought as much," said the Mother Superior. Michael looked at her, surprise no doubt evident on his face, and she huffed, "Give me some credit for perception. It's clear you've been troubled these last few months. Oh, your work hasn't suffered; far from it. If anything, you've been even more driven and dedicated. But a doctor who has nothing more than his work will eventually stumble and falter."

Michael shifted in his chair. "Thank you for the advice," he said coolly.

Mulcahy continued undaunted. "I realize you're not a practicing Catholic. I've never asked you why; quite frankly, it's none of my affair. However, should you feel I may be able to help you in some way, I want you to know that my door will always be open." She raised a hand. "Please understand that I have no motive other than to keep you in medicine, Mr. McCready. This world needs doctors who strive for excellence as much as it needs men of faith, though if you claim outside these walls that I said so I will of course deny it."

Michael stared at her, nonplussed by her uncharacteristic display of kindness toward him. The Mother Superior was a humane and giving woman to her patients, but to the interns and residents she was an unrelentingly strict and exacting taskmistress. While he had always respected her—for she was also fair, level-headed, and a brilliant nurse—he found that this was the first time he could truly say he liked her.

"Thank you, Mother Superior," he said, rising to his feet. "I may take you up on that one day."

She stood with him, a touch of something approaching regret in her eyes, as though she knew it to be a lie. "May God be with you, Michael," she said, making the sign of the cross, and it was so heartfelt that Michael could only nod and murmur his thanks.

MICHAEL came home from his shift at St. Vincent's to find John gone and a note lying on the table by the door. *Left to run errands and then to my appointment; if you get back in time, I hope to see you there.* The time and the address—a few subway stops away in the West Fifties—were printed at the bottom. Michael checked his watch and saw that he would indeed have time to make this appointment. He supposed he could lie, tell John he'd arrived home too late, but it felt like a coward's choice.

Not that you've been behaving at all like a coward lately, a small, annoying voice reminded him, one that Michael swiftly stomped on as he picked up the envelope he found underneath the note. Turning it over, he was startled to realize it was from his eldest brother. Colm McCready was over fifteen years Michael's senior, and they had had little contact since the death of their mother. However, at forty years of age, Colm had finally married, and his new bride, a widow with three children, had more of a sense of family than all the McCreadys put together. Whether Colm's desire to restore the lines of communication was genuine or motivated by his wife's influence was immaterial to Michael; for his part, he was cordial in response to Colm's overtures, but no more. Now, however, the renewed connection had served him well, because he had written to his brother last month in the desperate hope that Colm might be able to locate Margaret where Michael had failed.

Ripping open the envelope and tearing the corner of the letter inside in his haste, he unfolded it and began to read.

It was good to receive your letter last week, and to hear you are nearly ready to graduate from medical school. I never expected that any of us would

*amount to so much as you have. It is to your credit,
and I am proud of you.*

*You asked about Margaret. I can tell you that she
and the children are well. Six months ago she found
out that Paul had been killed in an accident at the
foundry and she had been left a small settlement
from the union's widows and orphans fund. At that
time Catherine and I convinced her to come to
Boston, and she is living with us now. She is going
to a business school and when she graduates I will
get her a job at the dockyard office.*

*I do not know why you are not as close as you once
were; I have not asked and she has not told me. I
will tell her you were asking after her and it will be
her choice to contact you or not. We have never
been the best of families but I am trying to make it
up now and be a better brother to both of you. If I
am forced to choose, I will have to choose her since
you are making your own way in the world. Try not
to worry; she is in good hands.*

Go with God—

Colm

Michael crumpled the letter in his fist after he finished it, the
words echoing in his head as the rage built in him. The next thing he
knew, he had picked up the table and flung it across the room, where it
smashed against the wall and broke apart. After consigning him and
Margaret to the hell of Paddy's tender care so that he could continue
whoring his way across the South Seas, after all these years of neglect
while she rotted in the Bowery, that Colm had the gall to play the
responsible brother made him furious. At the same time, though,
Michael acknowledged that the lion's share of his anger was reserved
for Margaret, who had so little regard for him that she had subjected
him to half a year's worth of grinding worry for nothing. She knew he
had remained aware of her whereabouts, for she had been receiving the
money he'd sent when he could. How could she simply pack up and

leave without letting him know she was safe?

Guilt followed hard on the heels of the anger, leaving him shaken. How quickly he had lost sight of the most important thing: the fact that Margaret and the children were well. Picking up the letter from the floor, Michael smoothed it out, his hands trembling. In the end, his hurt feelings didn't matter a damn, and the sooner he realized that, the better.

Checking his watch again, he cursed softly. He needed a shower and a change of clothes, and quickly, the prospect of John's carefully concealed disappointment too much for him to bear on top of this news.

IT ONLY took five minutes for Michael to decide he disliked John's alienist intensely.

It had nothing to do with the fact that Doctor "call me Nathaniel" Collins was easily two decades younger than Michael had been expecting, with a full head of wavy blond hair and the long, lithe build of a runner. His toothy smile and his overly familiar manner set Michael on edge from the beginning.

"Michael, you've been quiet," Collins said, bringing Michael back to the conversation. "Would you like to tell us what you're thinking?"

Michael smiled. "I was thinking you looked familiar, Nathaniel."

Collins nodded. "It's entirely possible you've seen me before. I sometimes consult at Saint Vincent's—"

"I was thinking more of the Saint Alex," Michael interrupted, lifting his chin. He could feel John's gaze on him but did not turn his head to meet it.

"The Saint Alex?" Collins asked, a faint frown marring his serene features. "I'm not familiar with that hospital."

"It's not a hospital, it's a men's bath in the Village," John murmured. This time Michael did turn to face him and saw John's jaw was tight, his shoulders tense.

"Oh," Collins said, nodding. "Well, I haven't been to a bath in quite some time, so I doubt I would have seen you there—"

"I wouldn't be so sure," Michael said airily, throwing his arm over the back of the chesterfield. "I started sucking cocks in the baths when I was fifteen."

John blew out a breath. "Michael, do you have to—"

"I thought you said he was one of us," Michael gritted. "Surely he's heard of cocksucking before."

"I have heard of cocksucking," Collins said, unfazed, "even been known to participate in it enthusiastically on occasion."

John snorted in amusement, and Michael's fist clenched where it lay on his thigh.

"Is that what this is, then?" Collins asked, still maddeningly calm. "A test? Because if it is, I understand your wariness completely. Homosexuals usually have much to fear from psychoanalysis."

"I don't fear you, Nathaniel," Michael returned. "But I am curious: how the hell did you manage to become an alienist?"

That startled a laugh out of Collins. "I lied, of course. I completed my studies in Vienna, where they had slightly more—enlightened— views of us. While there, I studied Ulrichs and other homosexual theorists, and I learned that I could be an alienist without judging and criminalizing our behavior. But when I came home to America and sought my license, I hid that part of myself, and I told them what they wanted to hear." He paused, searching Michael's face. "We have to lie—to authorities, employers, family, friends—in order to survive. It's a terrible burden."

"We lie to ourselves most of all," John murmured.

Collins nodded. "There's no doubt it appears easier to many of us to try to deny our natures, to shoehorn ourselves into one life instead of two. Thankfully, you and Michael have already embraced the truth, and one another. That takes enormous courage."

John brushed his fingers over the back of Michael's fist. "I spent many years ashamed of who I was," he said softly, "but I'm not any longer. I have Michael to thank for that."

Michael's head snapped up, and he stared at John, shocked. He'd never heard John say anything of the kind before, and the fact that he was finally making this confession now, in front of a stranger, made Michael furious. What Svengali-like hold did Collins have over John that he was now able to divulge secrets he'd kept from Michael for years?

"Michael? How do you feel about that?" Collins prodded.

Michael jerked his hand away from John's. "I'm not doing this," he ground out. "I'm not carving myself up and spilling my guts on the carpet for your entertainment."

Collins regarded him steadily. "Believe me when I tell you I don't find any of this entertaining. Our lives, the compromises we make, the self-hatred we accumulate inside us until it bursts from every pore and consumes us—they aren't the least bit entertaining." The sincerity in his voice and demeanor was evident to Michael even in his agitated state.

"I can't," Michael rasped, shaking his head. "I'm sorry."

"Michael, please," John began, but Michael was already on his feet and heading for the door.

WHEN John returned to the apartment in the late afternoon, Michael greeted him with a wave of his half-empty glass. "Good'fternoon," he slurred.

"Well, this is a switch," John said tightly, shrugging out of his jacket and hanging it on the peg by the door. Even as well-oiled as he was, Michael didn't fail to notice the slight wince that accompanied the movement.

"Why is your shoulder hurting you?" Michael demanded.

John sighed. "Because I've been walking the streets for the past three hours. My entire body hurts." He pointed at Michael's glass. "Where'd you get that?"

"From Mr. Radwanski, the lovely Polish gentleman on the second floor. He has connections." Michael held up the bottle. "Aged three whole months."

John rolled his eyes. "More like three whole hours, if that. Give it to me before you go blind." He strode forward, his limp more pronounced than Michael had seen in some time, and snatched the bottle from Michael's hand.

Michael made a valiant but ineffectual attempt to recover his liquor. "Hey, that's mine."

"Congratulations," John muttered, setting the bottle down out of Michael's reach. "You're an even more pathetic drunk than I was."

"I strive for ex'lence," Michael retorted. He drained his glass. Christ, but the stuff was vile.

"Michael," John said softly, pulling up a chair and sitting in front of him where he sat sprawled on the chesterfield, "please tell me what's troubling you."

Michael frowned, instructing his lips and tongue to enunciate the words more clearly this time. "Are you fucking him?"

John straightened. "Who?"

"Don't be stupid," Michael snapped.

"Oh, for God's sake, you mean—I'm not going to dignify that with an answer."

"You're not fucking me as much as you used to, so you're probably fucking him," Michael pointed out. The logic was flawless; Michael was quite proud of it.

"I'm not fucking you as much as I used to because you've been spending eighty hours a week at the hospital!" John snapped. "It's not my fault you're too damned exhausted most days."

Michael nodded, vindicated. "You see? Makes perfect sense. You're not getting enough, so you're fucking him. He's got wavy hair."

John stared at him. "I'm going to make you some coffee." He made to rise, but Michael sat up and caught him by the wrist before he could stand.

"Why did you say it in front of him?" Michael demanded.

John shook his head. "What?"

"About not being ashamed anymore."

John's gaze softened, and he twisted his arm in Michael's hold until his own hand was gripping Michael's wrist as well. "In case you haven't noticed, it's not always easy for me to admit my deep, dark secrets."

"And Collins helps you with that."

"He does," John said. "And it's not because he has wavy hair. I've realized it's easier to discuss some things with a person you *don't* care about, because—" he sucked in a breath, "—you don't have to worry they're not going to love you after you tell them."

The words penetrated Michael's alcoholic stupor like a kick to the solar plexus. "Do you honestly think that I would stop—"

"No," John interrupted, squeezing Michael's wrist. "But this isn't about what I *think*, it's about what I *feel,* and sometimes all the reasoning in the world doesn't help."

Michael released him and ran a hand over his face. "Fuck," he breathed, the fight suddenly deserting him, leaving his limbs feeling heavy and lethargic.

John moved to sit beside him. "Does this have something to do with the letter from your brother?"

Michael's head jerked up, and John must have read something in his expression, because his own expression became stricken. "What's happened?"

"Nothing," Michael said dully, "nothing at all." When John stiffened beside him, he drew a breath and added, "I had lost touch with Margaret, but it's all right. She's living with Colm and his wife in Boston now."

John studied him carefully. "When did you lose touch with her?"

"Six months ago."

"Dear God," John breathed. "You must have been sick with worry."

Michael barked a harsh laugh. "I needn't have been. She was fine all along. She just didn't bother to let me know whether she was alive or dead."

"Oh, Michael," John murmured, laying a tentative hand on his arm. "I'm sorry. But why didn't you tell me from the start? I could have hired a detective—"

Michael shoved himself to his feet and was mildly alarmed when the room swayed. "That's exactly why I didn't tell you," he snapped. "You've already spent far too much of your money on me."

John looked up at him, expression unreadable. "I've never been particularly interested in money for its own sake," he said quietly, "so you'll forgive me if I choose to spend it to help the people I love."

"You've been saving for Sarah's college tuition—"

"Which is secure—"

"And for that trip to Paris—"

"Which can wait."

"God damn it!" Michael exploded. "You shouldn't have to wait! You could have gone on that trip three years ago if it weren't for me, and your career would be so much further ahead. You've sacrificed too much, done too much, and it's not—I'm not—" Michael shook his head, his thoughts muddied by the whiskey.

John rose stiffly. "Not what?" he asked softly. "Not worth it?"

Michael stared at him, heart leaping into his throat.

"We're very much alike, you and I," John continued, brushing back a lock of Michael's hair that had fallen in front of his eyes. "It can be a damned nuisance, but sometimes it allows me to know exactly what you're thinking. And I know because I've thought the same thing myself, a hundred times. But it's a lie, one we have to let go of if we're truly to be happy."

Michael stood stock still, as though he were a deer in the forest caught in the hunter's sights. It was madness, he knew, but he couldn't help himself. There was a visceral fear that still arose in him whenever he felt exposed and vulnerable, and while John had done more to ease that fear than anyone, there were times when Michael wanted nothing more than to run from that too-perceptive scrutiny. This was one of them.

John took Michael's face in his hands, forcing him to meet his gaze. "Michael, I'm sorry I haven't told you this as much as I ought to, but listen now: you're worth more to me than anything on this earth, and I—"

Michael jerked away from John's touch as though he'd been burned. "I have to—" he rasped, "I have to—to go." And before John could try to stop him, he tucked his tail between his legs and fled.

THE ensuing week passed in a blur of alcohol and a parade of sickeningly familiar sights and sensations. By the night before his graduation ceremony, Michael had vague memories of bad jazz played at breakneck speed, bathtub gin that tasted like bathwater, and puking up the same gin some time later in a nondescript alleyway that already stank of piss and rotten fish. He made the rounds of the Five Points dives and the Village speakeasies and walked through Central Park in the early-morning darkness, listening to the sounds of men seeking their illicit pleasures in the shadows beyond the reach of the streetlamps. He was propositioned several times by boys looking for a fast dollar, but when he looked in their eyes, they all seemed too hungry, too desperate, and far, far too young. In the end, he turned every one of them down with a polite shake of the head and a regretful smile.

It was inevitable that he ended up at Millie's apartment. At three o'clock in the morning, Michael knew she would be relaxing after her night at the Saint Alex, perhaps adding up her profits or updating her books. Millie was a conventional business owner in many ways, and she always liked to work on her accounts when no one could see her wearing her reading glasses.

Sure enough, Millie was in one of her silk dressing gowns, the rich, deep red of the material lending her a regal air. A raised eyebrow was her only comment upon seeing him before she silently stepped aside to give him room to enter.

"Tea?" she asked. "I've just boiled some water."

Michael nodded. "Please," he managed, trailing behind her into the kitchen.

"I don't suppose I have to tell you that you look like utter shit," she said conversationally as she took the kettle off the stove and poured some water into a bone china teapot. Finely painted swallows chased one another across its surface, doomed never to meet.

"Not really," Michael muttered.

"John called me yesterday, checking to see if your body had turned up. We had a lovely chat."

Michael winced. "Marvelous."

Millie handed him a cup of strong black tea. "Are you going to let him know you're alive, or shall I?"

"I will," Michael said. He took a sip of the tea, relishing the bracing burn as the liquid went down his throat. "Stop nagging."

Millie glared at him, and Michael subsided. "Sorry."

"You deserve to be nagged to within an inch of your life, but I'm not going to do that," Millie told him. Shooing him out of the kitchen, she pointed him toward an overstuffed chair. "Sit."

"What are you going to do to me?" Michael asked warily.

Millie's smile was frankly terrifying. "I'm going to listen to you, darling," she drawled, "while you tell me all about it."

"Oh, Christ," Michael said, flopping into the chair. "I changed my mind. I think I'd prefer the nagging."

BY THE time dawn was rising over the city, Michael had guzzled his way through two pots of tea, his eyes were dry and itching from a lack of sleep and an excess of emotion, and he was beginning to feel like nothing so much as a wrung-out dishrag.

"So, Mother," he rasped, "how many Hail Marys?"

Millie laughed. "I can honestly say that's one costume I've never worn, and I've worn quite a few. If you're looking for absolution, you've come to the wrong place." Millie leaned back in her chair, watching him. "The trouble is, I'm not quite sure what you *are* here for."

Michael sighed. "A boot in the arse?"

"I suppose," Millie mused. "It would seem the best option, since anyone showing sympathy or understanding still makes you run for the hills. I had hoped you'd gotten over that."

"I was working on it," Michael huffed.

Millie cocked her head. "So of course our question is, what's prompted this latest setback? Some things remain constant: your sister is still—pardon my French—a cow, John's still putting up with you. But today you graduate from medical school, and you're about to be handed a dream job—not one that will make you rich, certainly, but one that will grant you financial independence from your moderately successful—and very handsome—boyfriend. Your stubborn Irish pride will finally be satisfied, and you can begin fresh."

"Sounds like I'm getting nearly everything I've ever wanted," Michael muttered.

"Yes, exactly," Millie drawled. "I knew you'd work it out on your own eventually."

Michael frowned at her. "I don't understand."

Millie pinned him with her gaze. "It's very simple, darling. You're a veteran of two wars: the one in Europe and the one that kills queer boys the world over. There are bodies strewn from the Bowery to Belgium, and you don't even have the comfort of a mind-numbing faith to explain why you're not one of them." Leaning forward, Millie flipped open the cigarette box on the table in front of her and took one. On instinct, Michael fumbled for his lighter and lit it for her. He noticed his hands were shaking.

"When I first found you," Millie continued, "you reminded me of myself at that age. Oh, you were quite a bit more rough-and-tumble, of course, but still. It was like looking in a mirror, and it scared the hell out of me, because it reminded me of those days, of how it was."

"You've never told me about that time," Michael murmured.

Millie laughed. "It wasn't much different from what you

experienced, I expect. There were plenty of Italian boys looking for a good time even then, but they were new and exotic, and so goddamned beautiful it made your heart hurt. As long as you were pretty and they were the ones who fucked you, having another man didn't bother them in the slightest. They were young and sex-starved, so they were very enthusiastic about it. Not always terribly concerned with getting you off, but it wasn't usually difficult to work up some enthusiasm of your own when they were that delicious.

"Of course, there were also the sailors and the marines. God, the seafood was abundant; the Great White Fleet indeed. But you had to be careful with them. They weren't all accustomed to the demimonde, especially the young ones who had joined up from some hick town where they'd never even heard of a fairy. They preferred us because they thought they couldn't get the clap from other boys and we gave absolutely top-notch head, but some of them were—uneasy about it, probably because they enjoyed it more than they wanted to admit. We learned from the older queens that as soon as you'd collected your money, you got the hell out of there, because the next thing you knew you'd have a black eye, and *oh*, how that would eat into your profits!" Her laugh was a parody of merriment. Michael's gut churned at the sound.

"And then one of us, a sweet young fairy by the name of—the name of—God, you know, I don't remember—at any rate, she decided that she was in love with one of her regulars, a marine from Ohio or Idaho—one of those O states in the middle somewhere. We tried to tell her not to be stupid, but she was convinced he was in love with her, too—he was always so kind and tender with her afterward, even kissed her. So one day, she told him." Millie's gaze became unfocused, as though she were looking at something far away. "And then he strangled her."

"God, Millie," Michael breathed.

Millie blinked rapidly. "She was a slight little thing—probably took him no time at all. At least I hope not. Apparently she looked a lot like his girlfriend back home in the O state. He couldn't fuck her, of course, so he found the next best thing." She stared at her teacup, held between her hands. "Gwendolyn, that was her name. Gwendolyn. How could I have forgotten?"

Michael opened his mouth to speak, then realized he had nothing at all to say. He shut it again swiftly.

"So you see, darling," Millie was saying, "I'm not unfamiliar with the constant, nagging feeling that you're not good enough, that God or Fate or whoever you want to blame has made a horrible mistake and you should have been among the casualties. And there have been a great many casualties over the years. Too many.

"You might say, then, that I sympathize. But the truth is, as much as I'd like to, I don't."

Michael's head snapped up.

Millie spread her hands. "Michael, I'm fifty-two years old, and I'm starting to show it, no matter how much I trowel on the makeup. Love isn't going to start beating down my door, and even if it did, I'd probably shoot it down before it reached me; I'm suspicious of strangers. But you—" She offered a wan smile. "—you are far too young to be this tragic. Given that I wouldn't recognize it if it came up and punched me in the nose, it's still obvious to me that John loves you, and you love him. If you throw away something that comes to us all too rarely, you don't deserve my sympathy."

Michael closed his eyes and nodded. "I suppose… I suppose you have a point," he managed, voice faltering.

"Glad you see it my way," Millie said, not unkindly. "Now, you must be on your way, because there's someone waiting for you and I need my beauty sleep. Not to mention the fact that if I don't get this makeup off my face in the next five minutes it may just stick there forever."

They rose together, and Millie enfolded him in a hug that had Michael swallowing around the lump in his throat. "Thank you," he said simply.

"Anytime, my darling boy," she murmured. "Anytime."

WHEN Michael opened the door to the apartment, he found another note waiting for him on a new hall table.

*Millie called me. Glad to know you're alive. It
will make it much more satisfying for me to tear
a strip off you when I see you.*

*I had to leave early to meet some friends. Your
suit is pressed and on the bed. I'll see you after
the ceremony. Be prepared for shameless
displays of emotion and sentiment; I've decided
the occasion warrants it.*

I love you.

Michael sucked in a breath and closed his eyes against the sudden sting of tears. When he opened them again, he folded the letter carefully so that he could fit it in the breast pocket of his suit jacket.

IT WASN'T until Michael was holding the diploma in his hands that he allowed himself to think it.

Doctor Michael McCready.

"Jesus Christ," Michael muttered under his breath as he stepped down from the stage, his legs wobbling as he took his place with the other graduates. He had actually done it. He had realized a dream that had once seemed impossible, a dream he'd buried along with the numberless dead, just another casualty of war. He was almost afraid of believing it to be true.

The rest of the ceremony seemed interminable. He spent it restless, practically frantic with the urge to touch John, to embrace him. He had a great deal of apologizing to do, and right now the prospect of groveling at John's feet didn't seem humiliating at all.

Finally, the last graduate had crossed the stage and the last droning speech had been delivered, and Michael all but ran through the crowd to reach the reception area.

"Uncle Michael!" The call cut through the sedate gathering, and then there was a pale yellow missile flying into Michael's arms. He had just enough time to brace himself before it struck and wrapped itself around him.

"Sarah!" he exclaimed, winded by the impact. "What on earth are you doing here?"

"Uncle John invited us," Sarah said, and Michael looked up to see the Abbotts standing behind her, along with John. As his gaze locked with John's, Michael realized he was making no attempt to hide what he was feeling, but the Abbotts almost certainly knew about them already and no one else was paying them any mind. John smiled fondly at him in return, his gaze like a warm caress, and Michael felt the relief pound through his veins.

Sarah drew back, her own smile wide as the Hudson. "Grandpa's been looking forward to it all week. He said he wanted to see a doctor who's not 'an old quack' for a change."

"I can speak quite well for myself, thank you, Sarah," Abbott muttered, taking a step forward and extending his hand to Michael. "Congratulations, son," he said. Michael stared at his hand like an utter fool before he reached forward and shook it firmly. Next came Mary, her warm embrace and whispered congratulations making his eyes sting. Finally, he turned to John, who was looking at him as though he'd thought he might never get another chance.

Stepping forward, Michael hooked a hand around John's neck and tugged him in, and John's arms went around him without hesitation.

"You did it," John murmured in his ear. "I couldn't be prouder."

"We did it," Michael whispered back. "And I love you, too. More than you will ever know." John's arms tightened, then released him.

"Well," John said, voice ragged and eyes suspiciously bright, "what do you think of Sarah's new dress?"

Grateful for the distraction, Michael turned his full attention to Sarah and was astonished at her grown-up appearance. She was even wearing a touch of makeup. "Well now, when did you become such a fashionable young woman?" he asked.

"It's your fault—yours and Uncle John's," Sarah replied. "I bought it with the money you sent. Isn't it beautiful?" She twirled in it, the skirt flaring to reveal her knees as she did.

At Michael's pointed glance, John nodded once in acknowledgment. Michael hadn't heard anything about a dress, but then he hadn't been expecting the Abbotts either. "It's very beautiful," he agreed. "A suitable match for the elegant lady wearing it."

Sarah giggled and said in a stage whisper, "I know Grandma thinks it's quite scandalous, but she didn't object when I picked it out. She says that modern women need modern clothes."

Michael raised an eyebrow at Mary, who pursed her lips. "I may have said something along those lines. I'll have you know I was a girl once too, back in the Dark Ages."

"Some of those young bucks like it a little too much, if you ask me," Abbott said gruffly. "Especially that William of hers."

"He's not mine," Sarah countered darkly. "Not anymore."

John frowned. "Why, what happened? I thought you two were great friends."

"Who the hell is William?" Michael demanded, fighting the growing feeling that he had been missing a great deal lately. John's pitying glance seemed to confirm it.

"He's a blockhead," Sarah said with unusual vehemence. "We were talking about our plans for college, and he was shocked I actually wanted to study the sciences. He thinks that girls are stupid and cannot learn science! I said, well, it seems I've beaten you in quite a few tests over the years, what about that? And he said that's only high school, it's not *real* science. I asked him what about Madame Curie, then? She did *real* science, and he answered that her husband had done everything and that she only helped him! Anyway, he's not worth the bother. I'm done with him forever."

"Never say never," Mary murmured. "He's young. He may grow up yet."

"Well, I can't be waiting around for that unlikely event. I have things to do," Sarah told her primly. Turning back to Michael and John, she said, "I sent letters to over twenty colleges, and I'm waiting to hear back. Do you think I'll have to go to a girl's school, Uncle Michael? They don't usually have much of a science department, and that worries me. Do you suppose you could write a letter of reference for me?"

Michael glanced at John, and the barely repressed mirth in his expression was all it took to send Michael into gusts of laughter. John soon joined him.

"What's so funny?" Sarah squeaked, her glare darting between the two of them.

Michael smiled and shook his head as he put an arm around her shoulders. "I'm sorry, m'dear. It's only that we remember when you hardly said a thing. Now you're overflowing with words, and it's wonderful."

Sarah bit her lip, then ducked her head and smiled. "Oh, I see."

"And I'll be very pleased to write you all the letters you wish."

"Thanks, Uncle Michael," Sarah said, grinning. "I can't wait for next month—you'll be coming up to Hudson to attend my graduation, won't you?"

Michael leaned down to give her a kiss on the cheek, his heart swelling close to bursting. "I think that's only fair, considering you're here to attend mine." Looking at both Mary and Thomas, he added, "And I'm very grateful you did."

MICHAEL and John stumbled back into their apartment late in the evening after seeing the Abbotts to the train station. Michael had been nearly silent on the walk home. What he needed to say to John couldn't be shared with the world, and if he'd started to speak, he was sure it would all come spilling out of him. John seemed to sense this as well and hadn't attempted to engage him in conversation.

"Thank you for tonight," Michael finally said when the door closed. "Dinner was wonderful."

"Well, it wasn't Delmonico's, but the food was still enjoyable."

"I wasn't talking about the food," Michael said, closing the distance between them and tentatively placing his hands on John's hips.

"I was talking about the company. Thank you for inviting them." He paused, searching John's face. "And thank you for being there—today, and every day."

"No need for thanks," John murmured, laying a finger over Michael's lips when he made to speak. "Or apologies. No one knows better than you what a pain in the ass I can be. It was simply your turn."

"Still, I shouldn't have walked out like that."

"No, you shouldn't have." John soothed the words with a caress of Michael's cheek. "But I understand why you did."

"I don't think—" Michael sucked in a breath, let it out. "—I don't think I'll ever be able to give up on her." He chuckled hollowly. "Much as I know it would be easier for everyone."

"Nor should you. I have faith you'll see her again one day. And in the meantime, I wanted to show you you're not without a family."

"I'd lost sight of that," Michael admitted. "And you've reminded me that those who accept me as I am deserve my attention, and my love."

John's other hand joined the first. "On one condition," he murmured, leaning in and brushing his lips against Michael's. "That you let us love you back."

Michael closed his eyes. "I think... I think I might be able to do that. With practice."

"I'll give you all the practice you need," John promised, fitting their mouths together.

"I'll even go with you to the alienist, if that's what you want," Michael added when they parted. "And I will do it gladly this time. I promise."

John leaned his forehead against Michael's. "Michael, as pleased as I am that you're able to confront your fears without sprinting for the door, I'd really like for you to stop talking now and fuck me." His long, deft fingers began working on the knot in Michael's tie. "Do you think you can do that?"

Michael's cock stirred at the sound of the crude word on John's lips. "I believe so," he growled, backing John against the door and propping his hands on either side of John's head, trapping him. John groaned and tilted his head back, and Michael licked a broad stripe up the graceful column of his neck. The pulse beat strongly against his tongue, and Michael pressed harder, savoring the life-giving rhythm.

John raised his head, and Michael reveled in the twin spots of bright color on his cheeks. Tugging the tie free of Michael's collar, he then started on Michael's shirt buttons. Michael reciprocated, and the shedding of clothing soon turned into a race, with both of them panting and breathless at the finish.

Michael kicked away his trousers and pressed the length of his body against John's, shoving him more firmly against the door. Reaching down, he palmed John's cock briefly, then began mouthing his way down John's body. He bit down lightly on a nipple before bathing it with lazy swipes of his tongue.

"Michael," John groaned, "shouldn't we move this away from the front door?"

John sucked on the other nipple. "Why?"

"Because—ah—because—" John's head tipped back against the wood. "I have no idea."

Michael chuckled, straightening again and capturing John's mouth in a bruising kiss. "Come on," he said as he stepped back and took hold of John's hand.

Endearingly dazed by lust, John staggered forward, just managing to avoid tripping over his own feet. He followed Michael into the bedroom, where John turned him around and pushed him back against the bed before dropping to his knees and swallowing John's cock whole.

"Oh, Christ," John whimpered, hips shoving up helplessly as Michael began to suck in earnest. When he felt John getting close, leaking on his tongue, he drew back and replaced his mouth with his hand, slowing the pace. John panted and clenched his fists in the sheets.

"You—seem to be even better at that than the last time," John gasped.

"I'm a doctor," Michael murmured, tightening his grip. "We go through rigorous training to develop our dexterity."

"You've always been—God—quite dexterous," John managed. "A natural talent, I'd say."

Michael's fingertips skated over the dampening head of John's cock. "You're too kind," he said, biting John's earlobe.

"Michael, oh, God, please," John begged when Michael slowed his pace even further. As a reward, Michael leaned down and tongued the sensitive head. John shuddered.

"I've missed watching you come apart," Michael growled, and John groaned, his cock slicking further in Michael's grasp. "Missed you."

"Then for God's sake, don't wait any longer." John gripped his shoulder, urging him to his feet. When Michael obeyed, John stood with him and turned him around, shoving him onto the bed with a surprisingly hard push. Michael bounced once, startled by the sudden turn of events as John climbed up and straddled his hips.

Michael tried to sit up and roll John onto his back, but John resisted, planting a hand in the center of Michael's chest and pushing down firmly.

"No," he panted, his smile a wicked curl, "like this."

Michael's cock strained as John reached for the Vaseline jar on the nightstand and proceeded to dip his own fingers in it. Fuck, watching John prepare them both always aroused him beyond reason. John gasped and undulated against him as he made himself ready, his lip caught between his teeth in a gesture that made him look much younger. He then used more of the slippery stuff to coat Michael's cock. When John lowered himself onto Michael, Michael's hands flew to his hips, to steady himself as much as John.

When he was fully seated, John closed his eyes and took a few moments to calm his breathing. Michael could feel the snug heat surrounding him, keeping him safe, protecting him. In a similar fashion, he had entrusted his heart to John's care, and he was sure he would never have occasion to doubt that decision. That certainty was the greatest gift anyone had ever given him, and he would not risk losing it again, no matter how many fears he had to face.

Michael looked up to find that John's eyes had opened again and that he was studying Michael with a combination of affection, desire, and love. Michael smoothed his palms down John's straining thighs, reveling in his strength.

"Come on, then, love," Michael whispered. "Come on."

Smiling, John leaned down as his hips began to rock in a slow, familiar dance. Michael groaned and arched up, threading his fingers through John's hair and meeting him halfway, in the territory they'd created together.

G N CHEVALIER has lived in Ottawa, Toronto, Québec City, and Montréal but currently resides in Nova Scotia with her partner of many years. A longtime student of history, she is particularly interested in helping to tell the hidden stories that are only now being rediscovered. Some of her hobbies include playing music, video remixing, and photography.

Also from DREAMSPINNER PRESS

http://www.dreamspinnerpress.com

Also from DREAMSPINNER PRESS

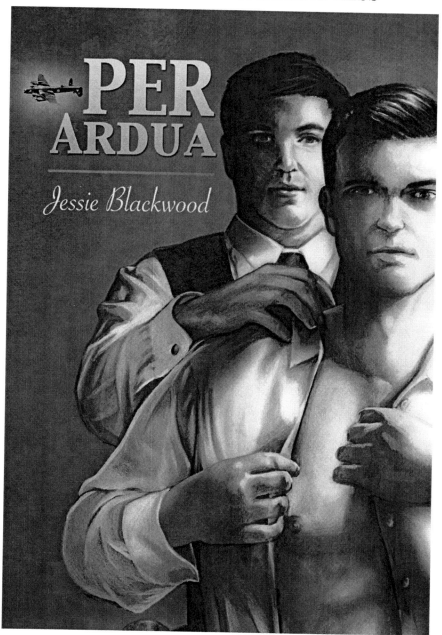

http://www.dreamspinnerpress.com

CPSIA information can be obtained at www.ICGtesting.com
Printed in the USA
BVOW011903180112

280822BV00006B/255/P